Taste of
Passion

DON'T MISS THESE OTHER NOVELS BY BESTSELLING AUTHOR BRENDA JACKSON

THE MADARIS FAMILY NOVELS

Slow Burn
Unfinished Business
The Midnight Hour

PLAYERS SERIES

What a Woman Wants
No More Playas
The Playa's Handbook

STAND-ALONE NOVELS

Her Little Black Book
The Savvy Sistahs
Ties That Bind
A Family Reunion

SHORT STORY COLLECTION

Some Like It Hot

ANTHOLOGIES

Mr. Satisfaction
An All Night Man
Let's Get It On
The Best Man
Welcome to Leo's

Taste of
Passion

BRENDA JACKSON

ST. MARTIN'S GRIFFIN
NEW YORK

Published in the United States by St. Martin's Griffin, an imprint of St. Martin's Publishing Group

TASTE OF PASSION. Copyright © 2009 by Brenda Streater Jackson. All rights reserved. Printed in the United States of America. For information, address St. Martin's Publishing Group, 120 Broadway, New York, NY 10271.

www.stmartins.com

ISBN 978-0-312-94050-8 (mass market paperback)
ISBN 978-1-250-21864-3 (trade paperback)
ISBN 978-1-250-62386-7 (trade paperback)
ISBN 978-1-4299-1760-5 (ebook)

Our books may be purchased in bulk for promotional, educational, or business use. Please contact your local bookseller or the Macmillan Corporate and Premium Sales Department at 1-800-221-7945, extension 5442, or by email at MacmillanSpecialMarkets@macmillan.com.

Second St. Martin's Griffin Edition: 2020

10 9 8 7 6 5 4 3 2 1

Acknowledgments

To the love of my life, Gerald Jackson, Sr.

To all the members of the Brenda Jackson Book Club who joined me at the BJBC Meet-and-Greet in Maryland to attend the Bill Pickett Invitational Rodeo.

To all the guys and gals of the Bill Pickett Invitational Rodeo circuit. You are a wonderful group who brings to life a part of our western history. Thanks for sharing so much information about what you do best!

Let us not love (merely) in theory or in speech but in deed and in truth—in practice and in sincerity.

I John 3:18 AMP

Chapter 1

Mackenzie Standfield took a deep breath when she saw Luke Madaris excuse himself from the group of men that he'd been talking to—other rodeo riders—and head over in her direction. Irritation washed through her, but she forced it away, thinking that it wasn't his fault he was such a good-looking man; one who oozed sex from the Stetson he wore on his head all the way down to the well-worn leather boots on his feet.

He was tall, probably at least six foot three, and from the fitness of his body it was easy to tell that he worked out regularly. He was too toned and had too many muscles not to. The front of his Stetson was worn low and nearly covered his dark piercing eyes, making him look the part of a renegade. A very handsome renegade.

As she watched him approach, she remembered the first time she had seen him. Had it been almost five years already? It was the night of the Brothers' Auction where the proceeds had gone to benefit the Children's Home Society. He had been one of the men auctioned off.

Nothing in her life could have prepared her for the man who had walked onstage after being introduced as championship rodeo rider Lucas Madaris. That night, even while dressed in a black tux and white shirt, he had exuded an air of ruggedness, arrogance, and maybe even something a bit untamed. He had looked across the audience and seemingly his penetrating gaze had latched on to hers.

At the time she couldn't bring herself to believe such a thing was possible. After all, Sisters, the upscale restaurant and nightclub where the benefit was held, had been packed that night with over three hundred people, and she had purposely taken a table in the back so as not to be seen until the appropriate time. She had been there on an assignment for her newly opened law firm's first client, who just happened to be her cousin Ashton Sinclair.

But still, Luke had proven her wrong when his gaze kept returning to hers time and time again. She had been tempted to bid on him and had almost given in to that temptation. The only thing that had kept her from doing so was the reminder that her presence at the auction had a purpose and that purpose was strictly business.

There had also been Lawrence Dixon, the man she had fancied herself in love with six years ago while living in Louisiana. The same man who had betrayed her trust. She had eventually left Louisiana and moved back home to Oklahoma to start her own law practice. And that was a decision she never regretted making.

Which brought her focus back to Luke . . . not that it had ever left him. That night after the auction she had gone out for drinks with him and his two cousins, twins by the name of Blade and Slade, who had also been auction participants. And since she was a relative of their family friend Ashton Sinclair, they considered her a close friend to their family as well. As she'd gotten to know the Madaris family—and there were a lot of them—she had discovered they were good people.

She basically got along with everyone in the family . . . except for Luke. They didn't consider themselves enemies, but for some reason they were always trying to avoid each other. The only reason she was here tonight was because he had personally issued an invitation. At least some may have considered it an invitation, but she had seen it for what it truly was. A dare. He hadn't expected her to show up. And from the expression on his face she wasn't sure whether or not he was glad to see her.

It was a hot June night in Oklahoma. Everyone had come out to see the rodeo riders perform and the arena was filled to capacity. As far as she was concerned all of the riders had nerves of steel and a skill she couldn't help but admire. This wasn't her first rodeo but it was the first she had attended in a long time. She hadn't been to one since she was twelve and now in a few months she would be celebrating her twenty-eighth birthday.

She held her breath and forced a smile when Luke came to a stop in front of her. "Mac," he remarked, calling her by her nickname.

"Luke," was her reply.

"Thanks for coming," he said, taking his thumb to push his hat back on his head. And the grin that touched his face almost made her breathless. It showed dimples that usually were kept well hidden. "I didn't think that you would," he added.

She had figured as much. "I told you that the next time you were in my neck of the woods I'd come."

"Yes, so you did."

She glanced around and saw the group of men he had been talking to earlier were looking at her curiously. Then she saw the women staring, too, with both envy and dislike in their eyes. And she knew why. Not only was Luke Madaris a rodeo superstar, he was also a body magnet. He had the ability to draw women to him in droves. And from what she'd heard, he made no promises and preferred no-strings-attached flings. But to some women that didn't matter.

"Do you like your seat?"

She looked up and met his gaze. His eyes were dark, appeared almost chocolate, and she tried at that moment to forget how she was known to have cravings for chocolate on occasion. "Yes and thanks." He had reserved a seat for her toward the front.

"You were to sit with Blade, but he called earlier today and won't be making it. Something has come up."

"All right. When was the last time you talked to Slade?"

Another smile touched the corners of Luke's lips. "I talked to him earlier today as well. He and Skye were flying out to visit with her aunt in Maine."

"It doesn't seem like they've been married almost a year," she said.

"No, it doesn't but they have. I'm happy for them. They make a great couple."

She was happy for them as well. She liked Skye. Mackenzie had known that of the three cousins who were thick as thieves—Slade, Blade, and Luke—it would be Slade who would settle down first. Blade, she figured, wouldn't be settling down any time soon since he loved his bachelor status too much. Luke wasn't any closer to settling down than Blade, but for a different reason. Unlike Blade, who enjoyed chasing after women, Luke was chasing after his dream of another national championship. Over the years he had received numerous awards and had several titles under his belt, but she knew that what he wanted more than anything was to regain the national title he had lost last year.

"Hey, Luke, it's time to chute up, buddy," one of the men called out.

"Okay, I'm coming," he called back.

"I guess it's time for me to take my seat," Mackenzie said.

"Yes, I guess it is."

"Hey, Luke, you haven't been doing so hot lately, maybe you ought to kiss the lady for good luck," another man called out.

"Go to hell, Bobby Joe," Luke threw over his shoulder. But the look he was giving her made Mackenzie think he was considering the idea. She decided it was definitely time to leave. "Good luck tonight, Luke," she said, and took a step back.

"For some reason I'm not feeling so lucky. Maybe Bobby Joe had the right idea after all," he said, recovering the distance separating them. And before she could utter a single word, he pulled her into his arms and kissed her.

* * *

This was not a good idea, Luke thought, feeling Mackenzie's mouth open beneath his. Then he quickly thought, when her tongue twined with his, that although the idea might not be a good one, her taste was the best he'd ever sampled.

He would be the first to admit he had wondered how she would taste from the first time he had laid eyes on her. He had anticipated and fought this moment ever taking place between them. Yet now, he couldn't resist this sampling even if he wanted to, which was just plain crazy. Luke Madaris never kissed a woman in public. Doing so would be like laying a claim, which was something he just didn't do when it came to women. However, here he was, standing in front of both friends and enemies alike, kissing Mackenzie as if his entire life depended on it.

Why?

Was he trying to convince himself that he could share a kiss with her without any undue hardship? Or that, contrary to what his great-grandmother Felicia Laverne thought, he did not have designs—of any kind—on Mackenzie. Hell, he would be the first to admit that he was attracted to her and had been from the first. But he would also be the first to admit that some things just weren't good for you, and he had decided five years ago that Mackenzie Standfield was not good for him. The last thing he needed in his life was a woman who could make him lose focus. A woman who could make him realize that at thirty-three he couldn't take bruises, scrapes, and broken bones forever, and that at some point in his career as a rodeo star, he needed to think about settling down and starting a family to continue the Madaris legacy.

And the last thing he needed was a woman who could drive him to take her mouth with a hunger he didn't know he had while crushing her to him so tight she could barley breathe.

Like he was doing now.

And damn it, she was so responsive. Who would have

thought that buried beneath all that primness and proper-
ness was a high degree of passion and sass? Enough to
make even the most unwilling man consider how it would
feel to have the liberty of taking that passion and sass over
the edge any time he wanted.

The realization that he was even considering such a
thing had him suddenly ending the kiss. But he felt a sense
of loss the moment their lips separated. Sensations he
wasn't used to feeling crept up his spine and began invading his body, and he had to inwardly admit that the real
thing had been better than the dream he'd had of her.

He watched her shake her head, as if she were trying
to force some sense into herself, saw how the mass of jet-
black hair swinging around her shoulders gave her a blatantly sexy look, especially with her just thoroughly kissed
lips. At that moment he thought what he did whenever he
saw her: Mackenzie was a beautiful woman, the most
beautiful woman he had seen in his entire life, and he was
used to seeing, as well as being around, plenty.

He would never forget how she had come forward that
night at the Brothers Auction. As Ashton Sinclair's attorney, she had followed her cousin's orders to place a bid
on him so that Ashton could end up choosing the woman
he wanted—Nettie Brooms. The moment Mackenzie had
come forward, both men and women alike had been
spellbound, taken by her exotic beauty—a mixture of
African American and Cherokee Indian. Her features
were flawless ... especially the lips he had just tasted.
Now he watched her eyes, darker than any color he'd ever
seen, narrow as they looked at him.

"Why did you do that, Luke?"

He sighed, knowing he could give her a number of reasons. None that he actually liked since they would only
verify that he hadn't been able to resist temptation. So instead he said, "For good luck."

"You took me by surprise."

He started to say, "welcome to the club," and that he
had been taken by surprise himself, but decided against

it. He was a man known to always be in control and could just imagine what Bobby Joe and the others, who had to be standing over there staring, were thinking. Hell, Nadine Turner was probably lurking somewhere in the shadows. He had dated the spoiled and wealthy socialite, who was the daughter of a rancher in Austin, a couple of times last year, and for some reason she'd figured the two of them had become an item—although he had taken the time to tell her up front that they weren't, as well as several times after that when she'd begun making a pest of herself. She saw him as a challenge, was determined to bring him around to her way of thinking, and refused to accept that it wasn't going to happen.

"Don't you like surprises, Mac?" he asked, forcing a smile on his lips. He was tempted to pull her back into his arms and taste her mouth one more time for good measure, but knew that wouldn't be a smart move.

"No, I don't."

Now why wasn't he surprised? The one thing he had discovered about Mac was that she liked being in control. That facet of her personality didn't bother him, since he liked being in control as well. However, what did bother him was that she tended to be way too serious most of the time, was always focused, and didn't seem inclined to have any fun. He took his work as a cowboy seriously but liked letting his hair down too. He was a man of passion and enjoyed messing around with it every once in a while. Evidently she preferred keeping her passion hidden, which was probably the reason she was glaring at him now. He had long ago decided that he and Mackenzie were from different worlds. He was from the hot hemisphere and she was from the cold . . . at least he'd thought so until their kiss. Now he was convinced that no matter how cold she was, with the right man she could definitely thaw out.

"Luke?"

Another thing he had discovered was that he liked hearing how she said his name. She seemed to develop a huskiness in her voice whenever she said it. "Yes?"

She lifted her chin, met his gaze. "Keep your kisses to yourself, or better yet share them with those women who make it their business to fawn over you. I am not one of them."

She definitely wasn't. In the five years they had known each other, he had formed a fairly good picture of the women that came in and out of his life. His list wasn't as enormous as Blade's, but he could boast of having women whenever he chose since they seemed to enjoy throwing themselves at him. Although he wasn't a moody person, he was selective. Not just any woman could share his bed. He avoided those who might be candidates for a serious relationship. He didn't want or need a woman, especially not now. In fact, he couldn't even imagine becoming involved with someone in the near or distant future. His life was built around his rodeo career. He enjoyed what he did and it was what he'd wanted ever since his uncle Jake had given him his first horse at six and had taught him how to rope his first steer at eight. He had won his first steer-roping title at twelve.

"Don't take it so personally, Mac," he heard himself saying, even though that kiss had been the most personal thing he had shared with a woman. Oh, he had kissed women before, but never with the same intensity and lack of control as this.

"I won't."

"Good. Now I guess you'd better go take your seat if you want to see all of the show." He knew he sounded cool and distant, nothing like the fire and heat he was still feeling in his bones. Mac was the last person who needed to know just how he was feeling. Just how much he had needed that kiss from her. And only her.

He forced those tempting thoughts from his mind to keep from pulling her back into his arms and kissing her again. He took a step back and came close to asking her to meet him afterward when he and some of the guys—along with their favorite girls—would be going out to one of the nearby restaurants after tonight's show. But the last thing he needed or wanted was to be in Mackenzie's presence any more than he had to. He had kept his promise to Great-grandma Laverne and had invited her to the rodeo. His great-grandma claimed it would be so ungentlemanly to show up in her hometown and not at least invite her. Okay, he had done it, and as far as he was concerned, that was enough.

"See you around and thanks for the ticket, Luke."

"You're welcome."

Then he watched as she turned to leave, and thought how nice she looked in her jeans and pullover top. And she had a walk that was perfect. She could have been a model easily since she had the looks, height, shape, and size for it. He felt the racing of his pulse and the pounding of the blood in his veins at the same time he heard Bobby Joe call his name. He tried ignoring all three.

"Here, take this."

He glanced up, but only after Mackenzie had disappeared in the crowd, to find his good friend Camden Bannister standing beside him offering a plastic cup with a cold soda.

He took it, grateful, since he definitely needed to cool his overheated body down some. "Thanks," he said, taking a big gulp.

"So, was that her?" Camden asked, raising his brows ever so slightly.

"Her, who?"

"The attorney. The one you talk about sometimes."

Luke frowned. Did he actually talk about her? Damn. Things were worse than he'd thought. "Yeah, that's her."

"She's definitely a looker."

He shot Camden a glare and then quickly decided he couldn't get upset because what Camden had said was true. Mackenzie was a looker. She was also a pretty damn good kisser even when she wasn't trying to be.

"So, will you be joining us after the rodeo or have you made other plans?" Camden asked.

Luke raised a brow as he took another sip of his drink.

When he lowered the cup from his mouth, he said, "Nothing has changed, Cam. I'm joining you and the guys to celebrate our victory."

"You feel that lucky, huh?" Camden asked, grinning.

Luke remembered the good-luck kiss he'd shared with Mackenzie and gave him a smile that touched each corner of his lips. "Yeah, I feel that lucky."

Mackenzie leaned forward in her seat, watching with rapt interest and anticipation as steer ropers and daredevil bull riders took center stage in the arena. The crowd surrounding her was energized and she couldn't help being affected by it. Again she was reminded of the last rodeo that she had attended with her parents, the year before they had gotten killed in that plane crash.

Her mother had been a Cherokee Black Freedman and her father a full-blooded Cherokee. She had been their only child. After their deaths she had remained in the Cherokee Nation in Oklahoma, under the care of her paternal grandfather. After he died she was sent away to Boston to live with one of her mother's distant relatives, Aunt Gloria. At eighteen, she had made the decision to return to the Cherokee Nation. After college she had a job offer from a well-known law firm and had made the move to Shreveport. A few years later, a broken heart had brought her back home to Oklahoma.

Although she tried not to think about it, she couldn't help but remember Luke's impulsive kiss. What had he been thinking? She knew the answer without giving the question much thought. For him it had been all in fun, nothing more than that. She seriously doubted his lips were still tingling, or he was still trying to downplay the adrenaline rush it had caused. Men. Did they ever take anything seriously? She had found out the hard way that they didn't thanks to Lawrence. Those lessons had come hard but would stay with her forever. Trust was something she wouldn't give easily to another man, and her love was something no other male would ever claim. She just didn't need the heartache and pain.

A short while later, after intermission, it was time for the steer ropes. She glanced down at the printed program supplied by the Professional rodeo Cowboy Association. It seemed that Luke was last man up. She couldn't help but read his career highlights and found them impressive. Just this year he had been the all-around and steer-roping winner at the Cheyenne, Wyoming, Frontier Days; had taken first place at the Grand National rodeo in San Francisco; and had set the PRCA team-roping record in Utah.

An hour or so later she stretched out her legs thinking her seat was very comfortable as well as accommodating. She had a front-row seat close to the chute that Luke would be coming out of. It wasn't long before she saw him. She leaned forward and placed her arms across the top rail to get a better look at him. She tried to ignore the flutter in her heart as she watched the chute team assist him as he swung his long legs over his horse's back. Beneath the black Stetson on his head he looked fearless, strong, and invincible. Handsome as sin. And just like that night five years ago, as uncanny as it seemed, his gaze found her in the stands, held a moment before an irresistible smile touched his lips. She couldn't help but smile back, thinking his smile was contagious.

Apparently she wasn't the only female who thought his smile had been just for her. The cheers that came from the women in the crowd indicated he was a cowboy who was appreciated in every sense of the word, and although he might be a heartache just waiting to happen to some, Luke Madaris had still won the hearts of most of the women there that night.

The arena suddenly quieted, and Mackenzie watched as the gate flew up and the steer was released. Seconds later Luke, riding expertly and skillfully, was right on its tail. In less than three heart-stopping seconds, Luke was off his horse with his rope in his hand. Dirt and dust flew everywhere but it was evident who was in control; before anyone could bat an eye, Luke had the steer on the ground and efficiently roped.

When he began walking away the people in the stands broke into cheers, whistles, and applause. Luke hadn't made it back to the chute when the judges posted their scores. There was no doubt he was the winner. The crowd went wild and the announcer's voice beckoned Luke to come back onto the field to take a bow for his cheering fans.

Then suddenly everything got quiet and Mackenzie saw why. Behind Luke a chute gate flew open and out tore the most ferocious-looking bull Mackenzie had ever seen. A scream caught in her throat as she watched everyone go into action to stop the bull, which was headed right in Luke's direction. Clowns tried doing everything they could to distract the bull and some got more than they bargained for, when the animal's horned head sent a number of them flying.

From where Mackenzie sat it wasn't apparent whether Luke had managed to jump out of the way before the bull could charge him. All she saw was that a number of cowboys had finally gotten the bull under control and were returning him to the pen. But Luke was lying flat on the ground, unmoving. Paramedics were rushing out on the field with a stretcher.

While fear of the unknown gripped the suddenly hushed crowd, Mackenzie whispered his name out loud. "Luke." And then she sprang from her seat, threw her legs over the top rail, and was running down from the stands and toward the fallen cowboy.

Chapter 2

"How is he, Camden?"

Mackenzie asked the question as she looked up into the charcoal-gray eyes of the man whom she knew to be a close friend of Luke's. Security and paramedics, assuming she was just one of Luke's adoring fans, had stopped her from getting close, but Camden had grabbed her hand after quickly introducing himself and pulled her through the crowd to see firsthand the extent of Luke's injuries. He'd told anyone who asked that she had a right to be there since she was a very close friend of Luke's.

She could tell from the way some people stared at her, some of the same ones who had probably witnessed the kiss she and Luke had shared earlier, that they assumed she and Luke were an item. She decided not to worry about what anyone thought. Luke was her main concern. She had ridden in Camden's truck while following the ambulance transporting Luke to the nearest hospital.

Mackenzie could tell Camden's smile was forced as he said, "A busted knee and cracked rib, which means he'll be out of competition for a while. I figure for at least six weeks. But at least he's alive. He's damn lucky that Scar Face, who is one mean son of a bitch, didn't rip him in two."

Mackenzie closed her eyes as she relived that moment when she had seen the bull charging at Luke, thinking she hadn't been so frightened in her life.

"Luke wants to see you."

Mackenzie snapped her eyes back open and met Camden's gaze. "Me?"

"Yes. He's back from being X-rayed and the doctor and nurse are in there with him now. They've assigned him to a room and I figure he'll be here for a day or so. And although they've given him something for the pain I can tell he's still hurting like hell."

"And he wants to see me?"

"Yeah."

"You sure?"

Camden chuckled. "Hell, he's been asking for you for a while, even before I told him you were here at the hospital. He knows the entire thing was televised on ESPN and figures his family is probably frantic with worry right about now. It's my guess that he'd like you to contact them and assure them he's doing okay. The last thing he wants is for them to show up here to baby him."

He paused and then added sheepishly. "I could call them myself, but if I were to tell them he's doing fine, they may not believe me since I've kept the truth about his other injuries from them in the past, and they know it."

Mackenzie nodded. "Okay, I can do that. I'll contact his family." She figured she'd call Blade and Slade first, and they would handle things from there.

Moments later, after talking with Blade, she was walking with Camden toward Luke's hospital room. Without bothering to knock, Camden pushed open the door just in time to see a nurse—a very young one at that—about to straddle Luke's body.

"Excuse us," Mackenzie said sharply. The woman jumped, almost falling off the bed in the process. When she looked over at them, her face showed her embarrassment, while one of pure relief was reflected on Luke's. Evidently the brazen woman had been about to take advantage of the fact that he was drugged with painkillers and intended to have her way with him.

As an attorney who had handled a number of paternity cases involving high-profile individuals and celebrities,

Mackenzie knew that some women would seize any opportunity to impregnate themselves by a famous person or a person known to have a nice bank account.

"I—I was about to take his temperature," the nurse said, pulling the hem of her uniform down.

"Yes, I just bet you were," Mackenzie said, coming to stand before the woman and looking her up and down. "Find yourself another patient to take care of. I don't want you to come near Mr. Madaris again," she added in a firm voice.

From the expression that suddenly appeared on the woman's face it was evident she didn't like what Mackenzie had said or the tone of voice she'd used. She flung her hair back from her face and asked haughtily, "And just who are you supposed to be?"

"His fiancée," Camden said before Mackenzie could respond. Although Mackenzie didn't refute what he said, her response would have been totally different. She would have claimed to have been Luke's attorney and nothing more.

"And if I were you I'd do what she said. She's a person who wouldn't hesitate to sue your panties off if you messed with her," Camden added in a sharper tone than the one Mackenzie had used.

Mackenzie decided to give what Camden had said time to sink in before she added, "We walked in on you about to behave in an unprofessional manner with a patient who is not in his right frame of mind due to the medication he's been given. If you need your job, you'll make it your business to see that he's assigned to another nurse."

Evidently the woman knew Mackenzie meant business, and without saying anything else she merely glared at Mackenzie before turning to leave the room.

Camden shook his head. "She's one bold, brassy, and assy woman. I can't believe what she was trying to do."

"Believe it. I've handled enough paternity cases to know it can and does happen to unsuspecting men. They end up fathering babies but can't recall anything about the conception mainly because they were drugged. Date rape can happen both ways. In the end most of the men pay the woman off with a huge sum of money to avoid causing a scandal that can hurt their careers."

"Mac. Cam."

They turned at the sound of Luke's strained voice. His eyes were glazed and he'd barely been able to get out their names. They quickly walked over to the bed and saw he had been strapped down. That angered Mackenzie even more.

"Thanks," Luke whispered in a hoarse voice. "I wasn't interested in her."

"Yeah, tell us anything," Camden said, laughing as he undid the straps. "You were just going to lie there while she had her way with you. Who do you think you're kidding?"

Instead of answering his friend, Luke glanced over at Mackenzie. "Please. Call Blade for me."

Mackenzie came to stand closer to the bed. "I already have. He told me to tell you to just get better and that he and Slade would take care of the rest."

Luke nodded, and Mackenzie realized it was taking a lot out of him to even do that. And then without saying anything else, he dozed off.

It was almost a full hour before Luke awoke and Mackenzie was aware the moment that he did so. She glanced over to find him staring at her. She stood up to approach his bed the exact moment that Camden returned from getting a cup of coffee. It had to be past two in the morning.

"How do you feel?" she asked him in a quiet tone.

"Sore."

He then glanced up at Camden. "Who let that damn bull out?"

Camden shrugged. "The sorry truth is that no one knows. But you best believe Gilmore is going to get to the bottom of it. Somebody's head is going to roll behind this one for being careless."

Mackenzie could tell from Luke's expression that Camden's words had satisfied him somewhat. But still, she figured he had to be pretty upset knowing he would have to skip competing for a while. "Has the doctor said anything about how long you will be here?" she decided to ask him.

He glanced back over at her and a part of her inwardly shivered from the impact of his gaze. She actually felt a tug deep in her stomach. She slowly took a deep breath, wondering what in the world was happening to her. "Yes, and that's what I want to talk to you about," he said in a low tone.

He glanced back over to Camden. "Can you give us a few moments alone?"

Camden's face broke into a grin. "Sure thing. I think I'm going to find that pretty little nurse and see if she'd be interested in me instead, since things didn't work out with you."

Mackenzie raised her brow, hoping the man was merely joking, but since she'd just met him a few hours ago, she couldn't be sure. Evidently, Luke figured out what she was thinking and said, "No, he's not kidding." His grin spread wide—at least as wide as his bruised cheeks would let it. "He's as much of a ladies' man as Blade," he added.

"Oh." She then asked, "So you remember the incident with the nurse?"

He nodded. "Yes, I remember. I wasn't that drugged but I was strapped down and there was nothing I could do to get her off me. Having sex with any woman was the last thing on my mind."

When he momentarily closed his eyes Mackenzie thought that it evidently hadn't been the last thing on that woman's mind. She had looked pretty determined to have her way with him. The more Mackenzie had thought about it, the madder she'd gotten, and after Luke had drifted off to sleep earlier, she had decided to bring the incident to the attention of the hospital authorities after all. She did not want the nurse to get away with what she had done. When Mackenzie met with the floor's nurse supervisor she was told that the nurse in question had surprised them when she had left that night, actually walking out without turning in a resignation. However, Mackenzie managed to get the nurse's name, so she could file a report and have the woman's behavior documented.

Mackenzie let her eyes assess Luke, noting the cut under his right eye as well as the scrape on his shoulder, the portion of him that was not bandaged. "So, what did you want to talk to me about?" she decided to ask before he drifted off to sleep again.

He opened his eyes and met hers and again that tug she felt earlier in the bottom of her stomach returned. "I want to ask a favor of you," he said.

She lifted a brow. "What kind of favor?"

"I talked to the doctor earlier and he said that I'm going to be laid up a while until my rib and knee heal."

She nodded. She'd figured as much. "Did he say for how long?"

"Four to six weeks. My goal is to be ready to participate in the Reno rodeo in September."

She nodded again, thinking that was pushing it pretty close. "Is that the rodeo where you want to try and get your title back as a bull rider?"

"Yes. And I will."

After an irritated snort, she said, "Haven't you had enough of bulls yet, Luke?"

"No."

She didn't say anything for a moment, and then after deciding what he did was his business and not hers, she said, "You still haven't told me what the favor is."

He tried shifting in the bed, and she watched as he gritted his teeth against the pain he evidently felt. She started to reach out and help him but quickly changed her mind. If she touched him in an area that hurt she would be causing more harm than good. Besides, she wasn't sure just exactly what touching him would do to her. Even flat on his back, the sheer power of his presence, his allure, was almost overwhelming. She was woman enough to acknowledge that she was attracted to him and had been from the first. And the kiss they'd shared before the start of the rodeo hadn't helped matters. It certainly hadn't brought him the good luck that he'd assumed it would.

"I need a place to stay," he said, pulling her out of her thoughts. "And I was wondering if I could hang out at your place until I get better."

At first Mackenzie thought he was joking, but when she looked at him and saw him staring at her from beneath dark serious eyebrows, she knew that he wasn't. "You want to stay at my place?" she said, just to make sure she'd heard him correctly.

"Yes, just until I'm back on my feet."

Which was four to six weeks, she thought. She didn't have a huge place and could just imagine him there. She wasn't sure she'd be able to handle it. "What about your place?" she couldn't help but ask. Houston wasn't too far away and she was fully aware that he owned a condo near the business park that Slade and Blade had developed.

"I can't go there." At the lifting of her brows, he clarified. "I don't *want* to go back there; especially not now. My family means well but they will smother me. The last time I got hurt was awful. My great-grandmother moved in to look after me. Can you imagine that?"

Mackenzie fought back the smile that touched her lips. Yes, she could imagine it. Felicia Laverne Madaris, who was close to ninety if she wasn't already there, was one feisty lady who loved her family enormously. "Were things that bad, Luke?" she couldn't help but ask.

"Worse. Mama Laverne meant well and I love her to death but she almost drove me crazy. And my grandmother wasn't too much better. Mama Carrie would drop by at least twice a day to make soup or fluff my pillows, monitor my calls, and—"

"Monitor your calls?"

"Yes. Mama Laverne had convinced her that I would try and leave to rejoin the rodeo group before my release date from the doctor, and she was determined to make sure that I didn't."

Mackenzie's lips quirked at the corners. "Doesn't sound like you had much fun while recovering."

"I didn't. It was pure torture and I doubt very seriously that I'll be able to handle a repeat performance. If Ashton, Nettie, and the kids were in town I could stay with them for a while, but they're in Houston for the summer. My other option is to check into a hotel, but if either Gramma Carrie or Mama Laverne found out I was there alone, they wouldn't hesitate to come out here to take care of me. I need to convince them that I'm being taken care of."

"And you think they'll believe I'm the one taking care of you?" she asked.

"Yes, they would believe it if I were to tell them I moved in with you for a while."

"But they know I have a full-time job," she said.

"Doesn't matter. They'd still assume you're taking care of me."

Mackenzie wondered how they would assume that but figured he knew his family members a lot better than she did. But still, she wasn't sure the two of them living under the same roof was a positive thing, especially with Roger Coroni's case coming up. She would need her full concentration while trying to keep the old man from losing his land; and it was land this big-time developer was determined to take away from him. How on earth was she going to stay focused with Luke around?

"So what about it, Mac?"

She glanced up and found his gaze pinning her, and at that moment she knew the answer. He evidently wasn't feeling the same vibes as she was. "And are you sure that moving in with me for a while is what you really want to do?" she couldn't help but ask.

"Yes, I'm sure," he said, still holding her gaze. She felt her heart skip a beat. "Unless there's a reason you wouldn't want me around," he added.

She could think of a few but they weren't any she wanted to share with him. "No, there's no reason. So the answer is yes, it will be okay for you to stay with me until you get better."

"And Mac agreed to let you stay at her place while you're recuperating?" Blade Madaris asked his cousin to make sure he was hearing right. When it came to the opposite sex he was a very observant man. And the one thing he'd observed that night five years ago, even if Luke hadn't, was that Mac was interested in him. At least there had been a noticeable amount of sexual attraction between them.

He'd also observed it that night on Luke's end, as well, but he knew that unless it dealt with livestock or horses, Luke was slow when figuring out things. So it came as no surprise to Blade that Luke didn't have a clue about the heated chemistry he and Mac were stirring up. And Blade knew it was probably safe to say that he wasn't the only Madaris who'd picked up on it, although Mac and Luke made a point of staying clear of each other at most of the family functions. Whether they knew it or not, that in itself was a dead giveaway. More than once he'd felt the strong vibes radiating between them. Mac was a stunningly beautiful woman, the type that turned heads and could make a man's mouth drop to the floor whenever she walked into a room. She was a woman to draw the attention of any red-blooded man. She had definitely drawn Luke's.

"Yes, and that's where I'm going to need your help," Luke was saying, drawing Blade's attention back to the conversation.

Blade lifted a brow. Carmen was in her bed, already naked and waiting on him. It was a good thing she knew he was a very busy man and that she was a very patient woman. The only reason he had answered his cell phone was because he'd seen the call had been from Luke. Not too many people were privileged to interrupt his personal and private time with a woman. "What kind of help do you need from me?" he asked his cousin.

"I need you to convince everyone, namely Mama Laverne, that I'm fine and that I'll be in good hands."

Blade smiled as he thought about Luke's request. He remembered how at the family reunion last year Mama Laverne had kept an eye on everyone; especially on Mac and Luke. The old gal was both smart and observant so there was no way she would not know that Luke was in good hands. She was also determined to marry off all of her grands and great-grands before she took her last breath. Those were her words and not his. "Okay, I'll do that. They're waiting for me to get back to them with an update on your condition anyway," he said. "I told them earlier that you were okay, and even went so far as to tell a little white lie, that we had talked when we hadn't, just to calm their fears. Especially when I heard Mama Laverne had ordered Uncle Jake to get his jet fueled and ready to fly."

He couldn't help but laugh when he heard Luke's groan. "Don't worry. I convinced them you were okay. Just a busted knee and a few scrapes. I didn't mention anything about the cracked rib."

"Thanks, I owe you one."

"And I plan to collect." And in a low voice he said, "I want the name of that nurse who tried getting in bed with you." Blade chuckled when he heard Luke groan again.

"I see Cam didn't waste any time calling to tell you about her," Luke said.

"No, he didn't," Blade said. "He knows I like the daring type. But on a serious note, it's a good thing Cam and Mac walked in when they did or this time next year you'd be receiving a Father's Day card informing you that you were some baby's daddy. A woman with a get-rich-quick scheme will try just about anything." The thought of something like that happening to Luke or any single man for that matter actually made him shudder.

"So when are you leaving the hospital?" he then decided to ask Luke. "Aunt Carrie and Mama Laverne will want to know."

"In the morning. Mac is picking me up. Cam and the others left this morning for the rodeo in Phoenix."

"Okay. Have Mac call me after she gets you settled in tomorrow. I'll be the go-between so the two of you won't get a lot of calls from the family. They will want to know how you're doing for a while. And I talked to Slade and Skye. They got back this morning from Maine and like everyone else they were worried about you. But I assured them that you would live."

Luke chuckled. "Gee, thanks."

"Don't mention it. And once I tell them that you'll be crashing over at Mac's place they'll know that you're fine."

"And how will they know that?" Luke asked.

Blade laughed. "Trust me, they'll know. Look, I got to go. My lady friend is already in bed and I hear her calling my name. I don't want her to wait too long."

"Sorry if I held you up."

Blade smiled. "No harm's been done. I'll just make up for any lost time."

As Mackenzie prepared the guest room for Luke's visit she couldn't fight off this weird feeling that she was making a grave mistake. If she had been in the mood to laugh she would have found the entire situation rather amusing. For the past five years she had avoided Luke, or at least she'd tried to, whenever she was invited to Madaris family gatherings, and she'd been invited to practically all of them—to Christmas sleepovers at Whispering Pines, the huge ranch owned by wealthy rancher Jake Madaris and his movie-star wife Diamond Swain Madaris, to the numerous birthday parties and baby showers. Just last month she had attended the christening of Alex and Christy Maxwell's beautiful baby girl whom they had named Alexandria.

The Madarises considered her as one of their own. From the first, after she had been introduced as Ashton's cousin, they had made her feel welcome and part of their clan. So it seemed the least she could do was to return the favor by taking care of Luke for a little while, at least until he was on his feet. Even though, as she had told him, she wasn't sure how much help she could be since she had a full-time job. That meant she wouldn't be with him around the clock.

Closing her eyes, she held her breath as she remembered their kiss. Why had he done that? It was their first kiss and she hated admitting it but her lips hadn't been the same since. It didn't take much to remember his taste, the texture of his lips, the expert way they had taken hers and focused on giving her pleasure. She had gotten so wrapped up in the kiss that for a moment she had lost all sense of time, place, and control. All she had been able to think about was the feel of his broad, masculine chest pressing against hers and the slow, purposeful way his mouth had moved over hers.

She opened her eyes after experiencing a shiver that had gone straight to her core. Without thinking she took her fingertips and touched her lips, knowing the kiss they had shared was one she wouldn't forget.

Deciding that she needed a cold shower, she was headed toward the bathroom when the phone rang. She glanced at the clock. It was past ten and nobody called her this late unless it was one of her partners at the law firm needing her advice about something. Samira Di Meglio and Peyton Mahoney were friends she had met in law school and they had been more than ready to form a law practice with her. It still amused the three of them when clients walked in expecting to find three men by the names Mac, Sam, and Peyton and then to discover three women instead. She was proud to say that since the law firm had opened nearly five years ago, their business had increased and they were winning more cases than they were losing.

She reached for the phone. "Hello?"

She heard someone on the other line but no one responded, so she repeated her greeting. "Hello?"

When the person continued to breathe in her ear but

refused to say anything, Mackenzie decided she had more to do with her time so she hung up the phone. She continued toward the bathroom thinking that some people evidently had nothing better to do than to play games on the phone.

The caller hung up the phone, satisfied. They had the right phone number. The next step would be to make sure they had the correct address.

Chapter 3

"Nice place, Mac."

Mackenzie leaned against the closed door and watched Luke, who was standing in the middle of the floor after his gaze had given her living room one wide sweep.

"I'd heard you had a pretty large spread, but I didn't expect all of this," he added.

She shrugged, thinking that most people didn't. Her parents, Colt and Anita Standfield, had known each other for a long time. He was a full-blooded Cherokee and she was a Black Cherokee known as a Cherokee Freedman. After college they had married and settled here on land in Oklahoma that Colt's grandfather had given them. And yes, it was a large spread that encompassed over a hundred acres of land along with the ranch house where she had been born. But compared to some ranch houses, hers was rather small. The only thing her parents had wanted under the roof of the modest stone structure was what they'd considered the necessities: three bedrooms, two baths, a kitchen, living room, and dining room. And just like her parents, Mackenzie thought the size of house fitted her needs perfectly.

The land was another matter. It had been too much for her to handle, so when she had moved to Louisiana after college to work at a prestigious law firm, she had leased portions of the land and its upkeep to several Cherokee families.

After returning home and opening the law office in

town, she had purchased several horses, and Jake Madaris had helped by providing her with a few heads of cattle. And then with Ashton's assistance, she'd hired several men whom she could depend on to keep the ranch running and operating smoothly. That had been five years ago and since then she had come to realize just how much being back home meant to her. With every day that she spent here, the more she appreciated the legacy her parents and grandfather had left to her.

She took a deep breath as she moved away from the door. "I'm glad you like it. No matter where I went I considered this home and had always wanted to return."

Mackenzie then pointed toward a door. "That's the guest room where you'll be staying."

"Thanks," he said, and headed in that direction. And not for the first time she studied him, thinking he had a nice body in a pair of jeans. The best she had ever seen.

Tall, broad-shouldered, and with a lean waist, firm stomach and thighs. And he had a tush that was worth drooling over. Without a doubt Luke Madaris, rodeo rider extraordinaire, was one hundred percent all man, pure testosterone and solid muscles. The upper part of his body, which was covered with his chambray shirt, was bandaged up and he was walking with a limp, but not once had he complained during the ride from the hospital, although she'd known he'd been in pain. She had gotten one of her men to help bring his things in the house, but he'd been determined not to accept any assistance for himself. At the hospital yesterday when he'd told her about his grandmother and great-grandmother, she'd gotten the distinct impression that he didn't care to have anyone hovering over him. And that was fine with her.

As if he'd known she was watching him he looked over his shoulder at her and smiled. "Coming?"

Her heart pounded in her chest. "Excuse me?"

His smile widened at the corners of his lips. "I asked if you were coming in here with me. To show me around."

She fought the temptation to roll her eyes. It was a

bedroom, for Pete's sake. What was there to show around? It had a king-sized bed, a dresser and mirror, a five-drawer chest and nightstand. "You don't need me to show you around, and I can vouch for the furniture being sturdy since it has endured the likes of the Sinclair triplets on more than one occasion."

He grinned as he turned back around to face her. "I heard you keep them sometimes."

She chuckled. "If truth be told, they probably do a good job of keeping me. Those three have to be the most active four-year-olds I know. They certainly keep you on your toes. There's never a dull moment while they're here."

"I can imagine," Luke said, before turning to enter the room.

"But now if you need my help getting settled then I—"

"Thanks, but I don't need your help."

"If you change your mind about that, let me know," Mackenzie called after him.

"I will."

She knew that he wouldn't and that irritated her to no end. The doctor had explained that for the next few days he would probably be in quite a bit of pain and not to hesitate to take his pain medicine if he needed it, but she was yet to see him take a single pill although she suspected he'd been pretty uncomfortable on the drive over. Yet he never complained, which she figured was the cowboy's creed—take your aches and pain like a man, anything else was a sure sign of weakness.

She rolled her eyes thinking the opposite sex's thought processes were beyond reason at times. She knew that Luke was to begin physical therapy in a few weeks and he'd even been ordered to start doing a few motion exercises that were intended to strengthen the knee. Although he had argued against it, she intended to transport him to and fro to physical therapy. He said he didn't want her to miss any time off work because of him. He'd soon discover the hard way that when she made up her mind about something, then that was it. She would give in and let him have his way about some things but with others she would stand her ground. She had talked to Blade and Slade that morning and they said if Luke tried being difficult just to give them a call.

She appreciated their support but intended to handle Luke her way. If he thought for one minute that he would be a difficult patient then he had another thought coming.

Luke leaned against the bedpost and gritted his teeth against the sharp pain that tore up his leg. Taking a deep breath he eased down on the bed, appreciating the feel of the soft mattress beneath him.

He hated lying but when Mac had asked if he needed her help, he'd said he didn't, when actually he had. But his pride had kept him from telling the truth. Damn. And as a result, it had taken him a full hour to unpack the few things he'd brought with him. And moving around on his leg had irritated his knee somewhat. He needed to chill a bit, he thought, rubbing his thigh. Or else he'd run the risk of causing his body more harm than good and he'd have to kiss the Reno rodeo goodbye. And that was one thing that he refused to do.

"Just what do you think you're doing?"

"Sitting on the bed," he answered without bothering to look up. He knew who it was. Besides, at the moment there was an intense throb through most of his body and the last thing he needed was to increase that throb somewhere else.

Mac had taken a shower. He could tell. She had that fresh scent of soap, powder, and woman. The latter was what his mind latched on to and not for the first time. The nickname "Mac" didn't sound at all feminine and certainly didn't do justice to the woman it was applied to.

"And why aren't you in the bed?" she asked, coming into the room and making a point of standing in front of him, right in his line of vision.

He couldn't pretend not to notice her so he looked up and instantly felt sweat bead his forehead and an increased throbbing in his body as his gaze met hers. He took a deep

breath and stared back at her while thinking he'd probably
made a grave mistake by asking to stay here while recuperating. She had changed out of her jeans and tank top
and was wearing a printed top and matching skirt. Evidently she was staying inside for the rest of the day since
he couldn't see her doing anything significant outside the
way she was dressed.

Her body was what male dreams were made of, and her
looks were as drop-dead gorgeous as any looks could get.
She had a stunning face, a set of beautiful dark eyes, lips
he knew were of the kissable kind—although at the moment they looked pouty and irritated—and silky black hair
that hung past her shoulders. Her high cheekbones were
evidence of her Native American ancestry and her creamy
chocolate skin an attribute of her African American side.
He'd heard her mother's people had joined the Cherokee
tribe as free men back in the eighteen hundreds. He also
knew her mother had family living in the North and that
when her parents and grandfather had died she had been
sent to live with an aunt in Boston for a while.

"Luke?"

It was then that he realized he hadn't responded to her
question. "The reason I'm sitting on the bed, Mac, is because I just finished putting my things away."

"It took you that long?"

He cocked his head. "Yeah, it took me that long."

She placed her hands on her hips and stared back at
him, her expression one of annoyance. "Why didn't you
call for me? I could have helped. I did offer my services."

"I know," he said. "And I appreciated it," he added. "But
I preferred doing things myself," he pointed out.

"Fine. So look what you have to show for your stubbornness. You're in pain and don't try denying it because I can
tell. Now I'm going to have to help you after all."

He frowned. "No, you don't."

"Yes, I do," she said, straightening her shoulders.
"And if I were you, I wouldn't try giving me a hard time,
especially not now."

He lifted a curious brow. "Why especially not now?"

"Trust me, you don't want to know."

"Trust me. I do."

A frustrated sigh escaped from Mackenzie's throat before she said, "Someone wrecked my mailbox."

He lifted a brow. "What do you mean someone wrecked it?" He remembered seeing her mailbox earlier when they'd arrived. It was a huge brick roadside structure that had been erected at the gate leading onto her property.

"Just what I said. From the time I got home until a few minutes ago when one of the ranch hands noticed the damage, someone must have hit it with their car and kept on going."

He shook his head. "That certainly wasn't a very nice thing to do."

"No, it wasn't. That mailbox had fond memories for me since my dad built it for my mom. I remember the day he did it. I was eleven at the time. They had visited some friends in Denver and had seen one and Dad knew how much she liked it and decided to build her one himself."

Luke reached out and cupped her cheek. He could hear the sadness in her voice. "I'm sorry about that, Mac."

He could tell from her expression that his touch surprised her. Without being obvious about it, she eased her face away from his hand and plastered a smile on her face. "No big deal."

He knew that it *had* been a big deal, although she was pretending otherwise, and it bothered him. "Before I leave I'll make it my business to replace it," he said.

"You don't have to do that. It's not your fault that someone was thoughtless and reckless."

"Doesn't matter. Besides, I'm pretty good when it comes to bricks and mortar. Whenever I came home and they were shorthanded, Blade and Slade were notorious for putting me to work at one of their construction sites." He then stood and wished he hadn't. A sharp pain shot up his leg and he gritted his teeth to keep from cursing.

"When was the last time you took your pain pills, Luke?"

The sharpness in her voice was as deep as the pain he'd just felt in his leg. He glanced over at her. "Not sure."

"Not sure?"

From the look on her face evidently that hadn't been a good answer. "Before I left the hospital," he decided to come clean and say.

Her eyes narrowed. "The doctor told you to take a couple more of them when you got here."

"Yeah, but I've been busy."

"Only because you were too stubborn to accept my help," she said, moving toward the bed to turn the covers back. "All men are bullheaded to a certain degree but cowboys are the worst."

He felt the need to lean against the bedpost again. "Why cowboys?"

"I don't know. You tell me since you're one of them."

Yes, he was one of them and proud of it. He got distracted for a moment when she leaned over and fluffed the pillow, presenting him with her profile, which looked as good as the rest of her. "You don't have to do that."

"Too late. I just did," she said, before walking away from the bed and back to him. "Now I need you to sit back down so I can help you."

He lifted a brow. "Help me to do what?"

"Take off your clothes."

I don't think so. He had never liked having a woman undress him, refusing to give a female even that much control. On the other hand, he'd never had a problem undressing a woman and hadn't yet met a woman who'd complained about him doing so. "I can undress myself, Mac."

"I don't doubt that, but the quicker it's done the sooner you can get some rest."

Getting rest sounded good, he thought.

"And once you take a couple of pain pills you won't hurt for a while," she added.

And as far as he was concerned that sounded even better. But still. "Don't you have anything better to do?" he asked.

She blew out a frustrated breath as she looked up at him. "Yes, several things, but I won't be able to concentrate on them until I know you're okay."

Luke pressed his lips into a tight line and said, "I didn't mean to come here and cause you trouble."

"You're not. But I have to admit that I wish you had dropped the stubbornness at the door before you entered."

He frowned. "I'm not stubborn," he said defensively.

"Yes you are. You keep it up and I'm going to nickname you 'mule.'"

He lowered himself on the edge of the bed, amused by her words. "I'm not that bad."

"So you say."

When she reached for the front of his shirt he automatically grabbed her hand. "What do you think you're doing?"

She rolled her eyes. "Taking off your shirt. I need to check the bandage."

"Oh."

He tried remaining calm as her fingers went to work at his buttons and found it difficult to do so. He tried looking at the paintings on the walls, the various live plants in the room, and the toy box that sat in the corner. But none of those things could hold his attention like the woman standing in front of him. So he thought, *What the hell*, and he looked at her.

Thankfully, she wasn't looking back. Instead her full concentration was on working his buttons free, and it took everything he had not to groan out loud when her tongue darted out of her mouth to moisten her lips.

"There. All done." He watched as a slow, satisfied smile slid over those same lips when she eased the shirt off his shoulders and down his arms. His guts immediately clenched. He felt a shiver touch his body.

"You okay?" she asked with concern.

"Yeah. Sure. I'm fine." That was another lie. He wasn't fine. His body seemed to be on automatic throb around her. Ashton would probably do him in if he had any idea what thoughts were running through Luke's mind about everything he'd like to do to his cousin. And they weren't thoughts that had popped up suddenly. Hell, if he were completely honest then he would admit he'd been attracted to Mac from the first. But he'd been smart enough not to start anything he knew he couldn't finish. And his only goal in life, his main focus, was staying in good standing with the PRCA and doing everything possible to regain his title this year. One thing he knew for certain was that serious relationships and rodeos didn't mix. Women had this thing about men being gone away from home most of the time while competing. In the end they tended to see the rodeo as competing for their time and ultimately they became jealous. He didn't have time for such foolishness. He was not a forever kind of guy and was definitely not looking for a forever kind of woman. rodeo was the only mistress he wanted. Granted, his injuries were a setback but he would not let them get the best of him.

"Your bandage looks fine but you're going to have to make sure it stays dry when you shower," Mac said, reeling his attention back in. "It won't get changed until tomorrow. Now for your pants."

My pants? Is she kidding? Does she really think I'm going to let her take them off me? He forced himself to lean forward to stare into her eyes and said in a tone that could not be misunderstood, "Trust me, Mac, taking off my pants is the last thing you'd want to do right now."

It wasn't difficult to hear the catch in her throat when she glanced down at his lap and took note of what he was kindly trying to say. Hell, what did she expect? He was a man. She was a woman. Some things a person couldn't hide. He had kissed her a couple of days ago so he was well aware of how she tasted. She was standing pretty close so he knew just how she smelled. In his book all those things equaled desire with a capital *D*. It then occurred to him that other than the day she had been with him in his hospital room while Camden had stepped out, this was the first time the two of them had ever truly been alone. At other times people had been around.

"All right, you can finish things up on your own," she said, easing back. And he could hear the forced steadiness of her voice. "But at least let me help you with your boots."

That seemed like a reasonable request, and considering the pain in his leg, it was one he could appreciate. "Okay. Thanks." He inhaled deeply, thinking the next six weeks here with her should be pretty interesting.

Stooping down, Mackenzie willed her fingers not to tremble as she tugged Luke's boots off his feet, trying to keep her gaze off his crotch. Was sex all men ever thought about?

She knew the answer to that one rather quickly. No. Some spent their time thinking of ways to be deceitful, and she immediately thought of Lawrence. Knowing it wouldn't do her any good to dwell on the past, she pushed thoughts of her former boyfriend and his betrayal aside.

Instead she decided to focus her thoughts on Luke. Even though he was not in the best of health the man looked good, but she didn't want to think about his good looks. The room had gotten quiet. Too quiet. She could feel him staring at her but refused to look up and confirm her suspicions. Instead she decided to start talking.

"Tell me about Camden."

"What is it you want to know?"

She shrugged. "I can't help but notice that his eyes are the same shade of gray as your cousin Dex's."

She heard him chuckle. "There's a reason for it. My aunt Marilyn, Dex's mother, was a Bannister before she married Uncle Jonathan. She has two brothers, Stuart Jr. and Roland. Cam is Stuart's second oldest. All the Bannisters have charcoal-gray eyes."

"So in essence Camden is not your cousin. He's the cousin of some of your cousins," she said, and glanced up in time to catch Luke's smile.

"Yes, that's right. But every once in a while we claim we're kin on the rodeo circuit, just for the hell of it."

He didn't say anything else for a second and then, "I
guess it can get kind of confusing trying to keep up with
who is a Madaris and who's not, since my family is so big."

"Yes, but having a big family has to be nice."

He chuckled. "And it has its moments. I can remember
when I made the decision to become a rodeo rider. All hell
broke loose at my parents' house. All they could think about
was that they had sent me to college to become more than
just a cowboy. And then they literally freaked out after what
happened to Blaylock."

She knew who he was referring to. Blaylock Jennings,
a man in his late sixties, worked as cook, housekeeper,
and all-around man at Whispering Pines, Jake Madaris's
huge ranch on the outskirts of Houston. She had heard the
story even before meeting Blaylock. He had once been a
rodeo star competing on the national circuit until a mean
and nasty bull decided to plow into him one night. In the
end, like Luke, Blaylock had been rushed to the hospital.
But Luke's injuries were minor compared to what had
happened to Blaylock. He hadn't been quick enough and
the bull had bruised one of his kidneys and as a reminder
had left a deep, long slash on the side of his face. The
slash was now a horrendous-looking scar that got a lot of
attention when people saw him for the first time. But once
they got to know Blaylock and saw how warm and caring
he was, they looked beyond his features. She knew that
Jake, his wife Diamond, and their two kids, Granite and
Amethyst, simply adored the man.

"How did you get them to look past that?" she asked,
thinking what a nightmare it would be to receive a call
saying your son or daughter had been injured critically
while performing. It was the same call they could have
gotten a few nights ago if Luke's injuries had been more
severe.

"I didn't. It was Uncle Jake, Blaylock, and my cousin
Dex who did. They reminded my parents and grandpar-
ents of the importance of letting someone go after their
dream, no matter what it was. Besides, I'd been trained by

the best. Uncle Jake taught me how to rope a steer while I was still a toddler, starting me off with a calf, and Blaylock taught me the rest. He showed me how not to make the mistakes that he had."

Mackenzie nodded. "What happened the other night?"

Luke sighed deeply. "Don't know, but it wasn't due to a mistake that I made. Someone got careless. And unfortunately for me with the wrong bull. Scar Face and I go way back. We've had a face-off a number of times and that damn bull despises me. Its intent was to plow into me in a real good fashion."

Mackenzie shuddered at the thought. Changing the subject, she asked, "Where did you go to college and what was your degree in?"

He smiled. "Slade, Blade, and I are Morehouse men. It was nice living in Atlanta those four years."

And she could bet that being such a long way from their homes in Texas without the prying eyes of their families gave them the opportunity to get into plenty of mischief, especially with the all-girls college, Spelman College, so close by. Slade had gotten married last year, but everyone knew that Blade was definitely a ladies' man.

After removing his last boot and tossing it aside, she straightened up and met Luke's gaze. "I've prepared dinner. Let me know when you're ready to eat it. You might want to wait and take the pain pills on a full stomach."

He nodded. "Okay."

She turned to leave and he called out to her. "Mac?"

She turned back around. "Yes?"

"Thanks for everything."

"You don't have to thank me, Luke."

"Yes I do."

She decided not to argue with him. "Okay, then. You're welcome."

And when he smiled she felt a pull in her stomach at the same time she felt a weakness in her knees. He didn't smile a whole lot, but when he did he always managed to bring out the one thing she was trying so hard to ignore around him. Sexual awareness. The kind that could leave you mesmerized. Unfocused. Emotionally scared.

The latter was what made her pull in a deep breath. She was way out of her league with Luke. The kiss they'd shared a few nights ago had proven that. She didn't think he was anything like Lawrence, but still. Every once in a while a particular lesson had a greater impact than others, and some things she could never forget.

"I'll see you later. Call me if you need anything."

And before he could make another comment that would unnerve her she eased out of the bedroom and closed the door behind her.

"And you're absolutely sure that Lucas doesn't need us?"

Blade leaned against the table as he gazed at the two older women sitting before him. The eldest was his great-grandmother, whom everyone affectionately called "Mama Laverne." The other was his aunt Carrie, Luke's grandmother. He was trying to keep his word to Luke and assure them that Luke was doing fine and they didn't need to go trekking to Oklahoma to see for themselves.

"Yes, ma'am. I'm sure. I talked with him again this morning, just moments before he left the hospital. The only thing on his mind was making it to Mac's house and getting into her bed."

Blade flinched, decided those words didn't quite sound right. He definitely hadn't meant them that way. The last thing he wanted was to give either woman any ideas, whether accurate or otherwise. He gazed at Mama Laverne and Aunt Carrie under hooded lashes to see if they had noted his blunder and was relieved when it appeared they hadn't.

"I feel a lot better knowing Mackenzie is there with him. She's a nice girl with a good head on her shoulders," Mama Laverne was saying.

"But do they get along?" Aunt Carrie asked, wanting to know.

"Better than Clayton and Syneda ever did," Mama Laverne said up to reassure her.

Blade couldn't help but smile. It wasn't that his cousin Clayton and his wife Syneda didn't get along, because they did. In fact, he thought they got along just fine, recalling the many times he'd walked in on them while they were exchanging a hot and torrid kiss. It was that the two of them were attorneys and usually didn't agree on anything. And because of it, a lot of family gatherings became the scene for their debates.

He pushed away from the table. "I'll give you both periodic updates since I plan to keep in touch with Luke on a regular basis. And I'll even go see him for myself this weekend."

"Thanks, Blade. You're a good boy," Mama Laverne said, slowly coming to her feet. "You can get into a lot of devilment with women, like Clayton used to do when he was single, but for the most part, you're a good boy."

He chuckled. "Thanks, Mama Laverne."

"Now I could use a ride over to Christy's," Mama Laverne went on to say. "I'm spending the night to help her with the baby while Alexander is out of town. She needs me."

"I'll be glad to take you," he said, grinning. Then to his aunt Carrie, he asked, "What about you? Is there any particular place you'd like to go?"

She smiled over at him. "Yes. I'd like to go home."

Relief flowed through Blade. The two had caught a ride over to his place with Luke's brother Reese, surprising the heck out of him. He had just started getting dressed to go out for the evening. Reese had walked them to the door and had hauled ass big-time. No doubt he'd been more than ready to discharge them to Blade's care.

Blade was grateful they didn't want him to chauffeur them around the city to visit other relatives. He had a hot date with Lucinda and had no intention of missing it. Nor did he want to be late picking her up. He remembered all that had happened at her place the last time they'd been together. The woman was as easy as they came, had a number of her own ideas how things should be done in the bedroom, and all of them he more than liked.

"Is there any reason why you're standing over there smiling, Blade?" Mama Laverne was asking.

He quickly wiped away his smile as he pulled the car keys out of his back pocket. "No, ma'am there isn't a reason. No reason at all."

Chapter 4

"I have a question for you, Mac."

Mackenzie glanced across the dinner table at Luke. Although she had tried convincing him to stay in bed and rest for a little longer, after showering, eating the dinner she had prepared, and taking a short nap, he had gotten up and come to sit in the living room with her. She had just finished making notes on a case she'd been working on and had asked if he wanted a slice of the pie she'd baked earlier. When he said that he did, they had moved from the living room into the kitchen.

"What's your question?" she asked.

"I've known you for five years now and I've yet to hear about your involvement in a serious relationship. Why?"

His question left her a bit surprised and at the same time wondering how he knew whether or not she was in one. Had he gone so far as to question someone about her? The only person who knew what she was or was not doing in her life was Ashton, and she didn't see him sharing any information about her to anyone.

She couldn't help but wonder if perhaps he was playing a guessing game, trying to feel her out for some reason. And if he was, did it really matter? The bottom line was that he was right. She hadn't been involved in a serious relationship for almost five years. She had moved back to Oklahoma right after things had ended with her and Lawrence. Was it any of Luke's business as to why?

"Why do you want to know?" she finally asked him.

"Just curious."

She absolutely hated being one of those people who couldn't accept things at face value. And with his comment, she didn't. There had to be a reason other than plain old curiosity that was driving him to dig into her personal business. But still, this time she would do something she had stopped doing with other men and that was to give him the benefit of the doubt and believe it was just curiosity like he said.

"The reason I'm not involved in a serious relationship is probably the same reason you aren't," she said as a smile touched her lips.

"And what do you think is my reason?" he asked, leaning back in his chair.

"You haven't yet met that one person who's worthy enough to become the center of your world. That one person you can trust implicitly, love unconditionally."

He chuckled. "I don't think such a person exists for me."

"And I don't believe one exists for me either." And then under her breath she added, "At least not anymore."

Her words hadn't been low enough for him not to hear, and he asked, "But you did at one time?"

"Yes, but it was an incorrect assumption on my part, one I won't make again. I learned a lesson in doing that the hard way." Deciding she'd told him enough, even possibly too much, she decided to steer him to another subject. "How are the rest of your family doing?"

He gave her a look that said he was well aware of what she was doing. "Last I heard everyone was fine. As you know I'm on the road a lot so I don't get to go home as often as I'd like. Slade and Blade keep me informed of anything important."

"You didn't make it home for the christening of Alex and Christy's baby."

He nodded. "No, and I hate having missed it. I was doing a rodeo in Florida that same day, but I understand you were there."

She lifted a brow. "How would you know that?"

"Blade mentioned it."

She couldn't help wondering why Blade would mention anything about her to him. A lot of people had been there that day, so why was she singled out? The Madarises were well known and had a slew of friends, and it was one of those get-togethers that drew practically everyone, including famous movie star Sterling Hamilton all the way from Hollywood, and Sheikh Rasheed Valdemon from the Middle East.

She sighed. Maybe she hadn't gotten singled out after all and her name was just one of many Blade had mentioned to him. Luke had gone back to eating his pie, and she could tell he was getting tired. "Don't you think we should go to bed?"

He lifted his head, met her gaze, and held it. "I don't know. Should we?"

Too late she realized what she'd said and how it sounded. But he knew what she had meant. "What I meant to insinuate is that you should be the one in bed."

He glanced over at the clock on the wall. "It's late. Both of us should be in bed. Separate ones, of course."

"Of course. But I still have plenty of things to take care of tonight. Since most of my men don't work on the weekends, I meet with Theo Graves, my foreman, a couple of times of week to make sure things are running smoothly. Your uncle Jake is using some of my land to expand the breeding program for his Red Brangus cattle."

"I heard. How is that working out?"

"Great. The partnership between us has been wonderful. Around five of his men work here to assure everything is done as per Jake's specifications."

Luke stirred his coffee and said, "I don't doubt that."

She chuckled. "He's pretty intense when it comes to the quality of his beef."

"Always has been. Jake is not only one hell of a financial advisor, he's also a businessman extraordinaire. The man is simply brilliant and I'm not saying that because he's my uncle."

Mackenzie nodded. "What was it like growing up as Jake's nephew? I'm sure you get asked that a lot."

"I do. Growing up I always thought my uncle was bigger than life, and now that he's married to Diamond, all I can say is, wow!"

A grin touched Mackenzie's lips. She fully understood. The former Diamond Swain was still the most sought-after movie star in Hollywood and her beauty was so vivid, it was past the point of stunning. Men drooled after her. Women both adored and envied her. She was respected by many for her charity work. And when she had married wealthy Texas rancher Jake Madaris, it was the marriage dreams were made of. Somehow they had managed to keep their marriage a secret from the media for almost two years. Mackenzie thought whenever she saw them together that not only did she see a power couple, but also two beautiful people who were perfectly matched and deeply in love. You could just feel the love radiating from them. After her marriage to Jake, Diamond had stopped making movies and just concentrated on being Jake's wife. Now two children later, Diamond on occasion returned the spotlight but only to work with her close friend actor/producer Sterling Hamilton.

"But seriously, I owe most of what I know to Uncle Jake. I told you how he helped to convince my parents about me following my dream. Well, Uncle Jake is also the person who let me know it was okay to dream and that if you worked hard enough you could make your dream come true. I think he knew I wanted to get into the rodeo before I did. He's the one who taught me how to ride my first horse and rope my first calf."

Mackenzie sipped her coffee while listening to him. "Is it true that your cousin Clayton is the only one in the family who doesn't know how to ride a horse?" she asked.

Luke grinned as he stood up from the table with his plate in his hand. "Clayton knows how to ride a horse, he just doesn't like doing it. I heard it was because he was thrown once, but according to Clayton that never happened."

He stared at her for a moment before saying, "I'm going to take a couple of those pain pills and then I'm off to bed for the night. Don't say up too late."

"I won't, and I'll probably be gone when you get up in the morning. Everything you'll need in the kitchen should be easy to find. If something comes up, my work number is keyed into my phone as number four. Just try and get some rest tomorrow."

"I will."

As she watched him leave after he placed his plate and cup in the sink, she hoped he'd take her advice and get some rest. He was determined to compete in the Reno rodeo, which meant his body needed to heal—but it needed to heal properly. She didn't want to imagine what might happen if he participated in an event and he wasn't one hundred percent well. What if . . .

She sucked in a deep breath. "The last thing I need to do is care too much," she murmured out loud. "Luke is a grown man and is free to do whatever he wants."

But still, she couldn't deny that the thought of him getting injured again bothered her.

Hours later, Luke lay in bed wide awake. His body was numb because of the pain pills he'd taken but he hadn't been able to drift off to sleep. He turned his head and glanced over at the illuminated clock on the nightstand. It was almost midnight and he knew that Mackenzie was still up. He couldn't help wondering what kind of case she was working on that would keep her up so late. Maybe tomorrow he would get her to talk about it.

In fact, he couldn't help wondering about Mackenzie, period.

She wasn't involved with anyone seriously; he had pretty much confirmed that but he still wanted to know why. From the remark she'd made, the one she'd probably preferred he not hear, he could only assume the parting between her and the last guy she'd been seeing had not ended well. He couldn't help wondering what had gone wrong. Men didn't easily give up women who looked like Mackenzie. And it wasn't just her looks. It was evident that she was smart and intelligent. The man probably had a few screws loose, definitely wasn't operating with a full deck. But still, five years was a long time not to get back into the swing of things, get your life back together and move on. Had she loved the guy so much that whatever he'd done had scarred her for life? Was she even capable of falling in love again?

And why am I losing sleep over it?

He shifted in bed the same moment his cell phone went off and he quickly reached up and retrieved it off the nightstand. "Hello."

"I thought I would check with you one more time before calling it a night."

Luke smiled when he recognized the voice. It was his cousin Slade. They had talked earlier that day before he had left the hospital. "Thanks, but I'm fine. Experienced a few painful moments earlier today, but that was because I hadn't taken my medicine the way the doctor instructed. Mac almost chewed my head off about it."

"I'm glad she's taking that approach, Luke. We want you well."

Luke laughed. "Hey, I want myself well. I still plan on competing in Reno in September."

"That's pushing it, man, but if anyone can do it, you can."

"Yep, and I don't plan to lose focus," Luke said.

"It was nice of Mac to put you up for a few weeks. According to Blade, Aunt Carrie and Mama Laverne are happy with the arrangement. They think Mac has everything under control, which means they won't have to go to Oklahoma."

"Glad they think that way," Luke said, grinning. "How's Skye?"

"Skye is doing fine. She just went off to bed a short while ago, leaving me up to finish the paperwork on this project we're about to bid on. It's a new outlet mall in Dallas."

They talked for several more moments before Slade ended the call by saying he and Skye would be joining Blade and coming to see him that weekend. Luke was staring up at the ceiling trying to find sleep when he heard the door to the bedroom open and he immediately picked up on Mackenzie's scent.

He closed his eyes pretending to be sleep and knew the exact moment she came to stand beside his bed. And then he felt her fingertips feather across his forehead to check his temperature. To his way of thinking, if he didn't have a temperature before, he probably had one now with the heat invading his body from her touch. It was taking all he could do not to groan out loud when the heat trailed lower, going straight to his groin.

And if that wasn't bad enough, it seemed the entire bed was suddenly sweltering and he was tempted to kick back the covers. A part of him wanted to grab hold of her hand and push it away and another part wanted to hold it there, pressed to his skin.

Then she pulled her hand away, stepped back from the bed, and left the room. He opened his eyes when the door closed shut behind her, feeling an acute moment of loss with her departure. Luke wondered what the reason for it was. The only answer he could come up with was that because of the time he had spent training for the rodeo, he'd neglected having a social life lately, although until now he hadn't really missed one.

He wasn't sure what else it could be, and he sure didn't know what he could do about it. Nothing, he quickly decided, since he wasn't in shape to pursue his sexual needs with any woman, even if he'd wanted to do so. But still, there was something about Mackenzie's care and concern for him that he found touching. And for that reason he couldn't help but wonder about the man who undoubtedly had broken her heart.

Chapter 5

"Okay, Mac, stop trying to hold back and tell us about that hunk who's living under your roof."

Mackenzie glanced across her desk at the two women who stood there. She knew if she wanted to get any work done she'd have to answer their question so they'd leave her office. Sam and Peyton were two of her closest friends and had been since college when they had shared an apartment for four years. Of the three, Mac considered herself the least outgoing, probably because she'd been an only child and seldom interacted with other kids. This was especially true while she was living on the reservation after her parents' death. Even while living in Boston with her aunt she hadn't had many friends.

She loved the two women like sisters and had appreciated their support when things with Lawrence had turned sour. Although they had planned to work together after college, it hadn't happened. She had gotten an offer from that law firm in Louisiana and it had been too good to pass up. After seeing she was fighting a losing battle, Sam had given in to her filthy rich family and had gone back to New York to work at her family's law firm there. Peyton, who had grown up on the Southside of Chicago, had wanted to return home and work in the community as an attorney for neighborhood economic development. They always kept in touch and tried to get together for fun and relaxation at least once a year for a weekend of beauty—Sam's idea—at a day spa.

When Mackenzie had made the decision to leave Louisiana, Sam and Peyton had been ready to move on to other things as well. Using the money she had received from her trust fund, Sam had financed the mortgage on the perfect building in downtown Oklahoma City for the three of them. That had been almost five years ago and now after a very humble beginning, they were considered one of the top-notch law firms in Oklahoma, often championing those who'd been taken advantage of by major corporations, as with the case Mackenzie was presently working on—Coroni versus the Whitedyer Corporation.

Not surprisingly, it was Sam who was doing the talking and as usual Peyton was holding up the rear, taking everything in. Mackenzie would answer their questions, but not before giving them a hard time for the interruption.

"You two act as if we don't have an important case we need to be working on," she said, taking a sip of her coffee. "It's our firm against one of the largest developers in the country, and all you want to do is talk about a man with a nice set of biceps and abs."

Sam placed her rear end on the edge of Mac's desk while Peyton was satisfied to lean in the doorway. "Yes, that's about it. Besides, we have all the confidence in the world that you will take on the Whitedyer Corporation and win, so we aren't worried," she said. She then glanced over her shoulder. "Are we, Peyton?"

Peyton could only nod her head and grin as she crossed her arms over her chest. "Of course not, Sam."

Mac laughed and wondered why Peyton was so agreeable all of a sudden, when she loved being argumentative most of the time. And Sam could be soft as cotton but tenacious as a bulldog when needed. Born to wealth herself, Sam knew how the wealthy thought and didn't hesitate to use that knowledge to benefit their clients time and time again.

"Okay, you've both seen Luke before, so why the questions?" she asked.

"Yes, but not in the flesh, just in magazines and in the newspapers. So tell us," Sam was saying. "How is he up close and personal? Is he really that hot? Can he really make a woman with a dry mouth actually drool? Can he ride a woman the way he does one of those bulls?"

"Sam!"

"Just asking."

Mackenzie shook her head. "I have no idea how the man rides a bull or a woman since I've never seen him in action other than on a horse."

"Boy, you're slow."

"No, I'm a perfect hostess and I have no intention of taking advantage of an injured man. Besides, Luke and I don't have that kind of relationship."

"Now is your opportunity to change that. If he was under my roof, I would."

Mac chuckled. "Yes, you probably would, but then I'm more considerate. You would be dangerous to any sexy man."

"So you're admitting that he's sexy?" Peyton asked, moving away from the door and walking into the room.

"Of course. I'll definitely give him that, since the man can do wonders to a pair of jeans. But he's also a man who is already married . . . to his profession. He's no more interested in a relationship with a woman than I am with a man."

"If you tried hard enough you could make him forget all about being a cowboy," Sam interjected, before turning her attention to a magazine on Mackenzie's desk that featured President Barack Obama on the cover.

Mac smiled, thinking Sam's confidence in her was boundless. "Thanks, but no thanks. Luke has his goals and I have mine. They don't mix. Being a rodeo rider is his career, one he is as dedicated to as I am to mine. Besides, you both know my history with men."

Peyton snorted as she took the chair opposite Mac's desk. "We know your history with only one man, but he's a casualty of blatant stupidity and doesn't count and has no place in this discussion. Don't you think it's time for you to dust yourself off and get back on the horse for another ride? It's been what . . . five years since you've seen Lawrence?"

"Yes, but he calls from time to time."

Sam snapped her head up and stared at her. "You've never told us that."

"Only because the calls weren't of any importance. Most of the time he calls to gloat about some victory in the courtroom."

"And what about his wife? Does he ever mention her? The one he dumped you to marry so he could get a piece of her father's wealth when he thought the old man was on his deathbed, only to discover the man had nine lives," Sam said with anger in her voice.

"No, he never mentions her, but I know they're still married, and from what I hear, she gave birth six months ago to their second child. But to put you at ease, his betrayal doesn't bother me anymore. If he had not done what he did, I would probably still be in Louisiana. I would not have had any reason to move back here and convince you two to join me."

"That's true," Peyton said, smiling. "So let's get back to the hunk. Lawrence is water under the bridge. The little wife deserves him." She smiled. "The hunk—Luke Madaris—exactly what sort of guy is he?"

Mackenzie leaned back in her chair. "Um, although he's close to his family, he's still a loner in some ways. I'd say he doesn't offer friendship easily and goes about choosing his friends carefully."

"Smart man," Sam said, smiling.

Mackenzie nodded. What she remembered about the time after the auction, when she had gone out with him, Slade, and Blade for drinks at one of the hot spots in Houston, was that the twins had done most of the talking. Luke had just leaned back in his chair with his eyes on her, barely saying much of anything.

And what she would not share with them was the fact

that he had kissed her at the rodeo. Although it had been a kiss that had made her toes curl and her stomach clench whenever she remembered it, she couldn't place a lot of importance on it.

"Well, if I were you, I would let him heal up really good, then before I sent him off, I would have my way with him," Peyton said.

Mackenzie rolled her eyes. "Whatever." When it came to men, Peyton was all talk. Sam was another story—she was full of action.

Later that day as Mackenzie opened the door to her home, she felt strange knowing a man was on the other side. She had called to check on Luke during her lunch hour but when he sounded rather drowsy, she had made the conversation quick, satisfied he was at least getting some rest.

When she glanced toward his bedroom she saw the door was closed, so after kicking off her shoes, and tossing her purse and briefcase aside, she decided to check on him before starting dinner. She knocked a couple of times on the door and called out his name softly in case he was still sleeping.

"Come in."

She slowly opened the door and her gaze automatically went to the bed but found it empty.

"I'm here."

Mackenzie followed the sound of his deep, husky voice, and when she saw him she had to fight back her reaction. He was standing at the window in bare feet, shirtless, and his jeans riding low on his hips. She thought he had to be, without a doubt, the sexiest, best put-together man she'd ever seen.

"Luke," she said, forcing his name out past a dry throat.

He met her gaze. "Mac. And how was your day?"

She shrugged, trying to ignore the deep penetration of his eyes. "It was okay. What about yours?"

"I slept through most of it."

She nodded. "You removed the bandage."

"Yes. It began irritating my skin so I called the doctor and he said it would be okay to take it off. Wearing it wasn't a requirement since either way the body will heal itself. But he did warn against doing anything that could aggravate it."

"I see," she said, trying not to focus on his muscular chest and the flat planes of his abdomen.

"I went ahead and threw something together for dinner," he said, moving away from the window.

She frowned. "You didn't have to do that, Luke. Besides, didn't the doctor tell you not to aggravate your injury?"

"It was no big deal, Mac."

Yeah, no big deal, she thought, and wished her body felt the same way. It seemed that being around him for any period of time caused flutters in her stomach. She wished her physical attraction to him wasn't so strong.

She cleared her throat. "What did you cook?"

A proud smile touched his lips. "A casserole."

"Wow," she said, smiling back. "I'm impressed. What kind?"

"Shepherd's pie."

She leaned in the doorway in her stocking feet. "So in addition to being a cowboy, you also know your way around the kitchen."

He chuckled softly, as if careful not to cause himself pain. "I can get by. All Madaris men can, thanks to Mama Laverne. Cooking lessons were required."

She'd heard that. "Well, as long as you didn't overdo things."

"With a shepherd's pie? Are you kidding? I could make one of those in my sleep. Let me know when you've gotten settled and I'll put dinner on the table."

"Luke, you don't—"

"Mac, will you stop saying that? You're wrong—I do have to do it. I'm not a person who can lie around and do nothing. I have to feel useful."

She nodded. He had made his point. "All right. Let me

change my clothes. After dinner I need to check with Theo to see how things went today. More cattle were supposed to arrive this morning from Jake."

"They did. I heard all the commotion outside but at the time I was too doped up on pain medication to move."

"So you were hurting some today," she said.

She could tell from his expression he hadn't meant to let that part slip. "A little. No big deal."

Just like he had set her straight on telling him what he didn't have to do, at some point she needed to set him straight about saying things weren't a big deal. "Okay, give me a second to change, I'll be back."

Luke couldn't ignore the tight feeling in his chest when Mackenzie walked away, disappearing down the hall. Hell, what was wrong with him? The moment he had felt her presence and had turned from the window to see her standing there, he'd felt a sense of satisfaction that only came after he'd competed at the rodeo and won.

He rubbed his hand down his face and blew out a frustrated breath, thinking that wasn't good. He'd never known a woman who could give him the same adrenaline high that he got from performing in the rodeo. Such a thing just couldn't be possible. There had to be a reason for it. Hell, he knew the reason. He clearly needed a woman in a bad way. But as far as he was concerned, Mackenzie was off limits. No matter how attracted he might be to her, he would never allow himself to act on it. If things didn't work out between them—and he had no reason to think that they would, given his goals in life—there would be plenty hell to pay. For starters, Ashton was her cousin and, like the Madarises, family mattered to him. On top of that, she was now a business partner of his uncle's. And finally, his family liked her, especially Mama Laverne. The old gal had made sure he'd known it more than once.

That kiss they had shared had been his idea and a bad one. Now whenever he saw her mouth move he thought of how her lips tasted beneath his and how she had felt in his arms. Mac was definitely the kind of woman who could make a man lose his common sense, and he wasn't about to let that happen.

Walking over to the chair, he slowly put his shirt back on, making sure he took his time. One wrong move and the pain could start up again. After taking a long nap he had awakened feeling a lot better, but he knew it wouldn't be wise to stop taking his medication. Besides, the last thing he needed was for Mackenzie to get on his case about anything. The woman was as bossy as they came.

He couldn't help but smile. He'd never liked bossy women. Until now.

"This is simply delicious, Luke."

He grinned and Mackenzie noted he seemed pleased that she thought so. "Thanks. I'd give you the recipe but it's a family secret."

"Really?" she said, amused. "Just like the tea recipe."

"Oh, you've heard about that, have you?"

She chuckled. "Yes. I've heard about it."

"Well, if it's any consolation, I don't know the ingredients to that tea any more than the women in the family. A Madaris man has to be at least thirty-five so I have two more years left. But honestly, it wouldn't bother me one bit if no one ever shared it with me. Then I wouldn't have to worry about Syneda buttering me up trying to get it, and the men wouldn't worry about me being a traitor and giving it to her."

Mackenzie smiled. Over dinner her gaze had kept straying to Luke. Although he had assured her a number of times that he was doing okay, she couldn't help noticing how he would occasionally grit his teeth when he accidentally moved his body in a position that obviously caused pain. But she was determined not to say anything. The very idea that a person had that much pride was just plain ludicrous.

"Since you talked to the doctor today, did he say when you'd start physical therapy?"

She saw him frown. "Not as soon as I would like. They do have a therapist willing to come here and work with me so I won't have to travel to the hospital each time. The Reno rodeo is in September and I need to start getting into shape."

When he glanced back down at his food, she couldn't help but roll her eyes. Was that blasted rodeo the only thing he could think about?

"Blade mentioned that he, Slade, and Skye were coming this weekend," he said.

Luke's words reclaimed her attention. She could tell from the tone of his voice that he was looking forward to seeing the three. "Yes. I talked to him yesterday. I guess they want to see for themselves that you're doing fine."

"Yes, I suppose so," he said as he reached across the table for another piece of bread. "Damn."

She quickly gazed up at him, just in time to see him ease back in his chair and take several deep breaths. "What's wrong, Luke?"

"A sharp pain," he admitted. "I shouldn't have tried reaching so far."

Mackenzie narrowed her eyes as anger swept through her. "You could have asked me to hand you some bread."

"It was no big deal."

Okay, that did it. She placed her fork beside her plate. "I'm warning you, Luke Madaris, if you say those words one more time, I'm going to clobber you."

The woman had a temper. If he hadn't known it before, he sure knew it now, Luke thought as he slowly walked beside Mackenzie while they headed toward the barn. Jeeze. She had threatened to clobber him, for crying out loud. And the glare in her eyes and the pinched corners of her lips had indicated she had been dead serious. Thinking about it, he couldn't help but chuckle a little, even if it did make his chest ache.

She glanced over at him. "What's so funny?"

"Nothing."

The look she gave him said she wasn't fooled. Whatever had him amused had something to do with her. Refusing to make her any angrier than she already was, he said, "Nice evening, isn't it?"

"What's so nice about it?" she asked, opening the barn door.

Luke's lips twitched as he followed her inside. It seemed she had already gotten angrier. Now he had to do whatever it took to smooth her ruffled feathers. "The breeze is nice. It's no longer hot and— Holy cow! Where did she come from?" he asked, stopping in his tracks the moment his gaze latched on to the most beautiful buckskin paint mare he'd ever seen.

And he didn't miss Mackenzie's smile as she walked over to the horse. He saw immediately just how proud she was of the animal and he couldn't help but smile as well.

"This is Princess," she said. "Her father was my horse right before I left for college." Suddenly a bout of sadness crossed her features but she quickly pushed it away before adding, "When I returned to Oklahoma, knowing I would get a horse sired by Prancer made coming home worthwhile."

The smile slowly left Luke's face. From the little things she had said and from the little bits and pieces that he'd heard over the years, returning to Oklahoma had had something to do with the man who'd hurt her. The man who was the reason she couldn't get on with her life. The thought that any man could not appreciate her did something to him inside.

"And I can see why," he finally said, ignoring his limp as he walked slowly over to her to pat the mare's neck. "She's a beauty. I can't imagine what Cisco is going to think if he ever sees her."

She lifted a brow. "Cisco?"

He smiled. "Yes, my horse."

"That big, black mean-looking stallion?"

He chuckled. "Yes, he's the one."

She laughed. "I don't know what Cisco will be thinking but I have a good idea what will be on Princess's mind."

"What?"

"Just how quick she can run for cover and hide."

Luke couldn't help but laugh, which immediately caused his chest to ache. His laughter suddenly became a groan.

"Luke, are you okay?"

He opened his mouth to tell her that yes, he was okay, no big deal, but after her threat earlier, he said, "I shouldn't have laughed."

"Sorry, I shouldn't have made you laugh."

"No—" Catching himself, he stopped short and then said, "Nothing."

Mackenzie chuckled, knowing what he'd been about to say. "I need to add a few more slang words to your vocabulary."

It then occurred to Luke just how close they were standing. She was pinned between him and her horse. He started to back up but when she nervously nibbled at her lower lip for a second, before taking her tongue and sweeping it over that same lip, all he could think about was that tongue mingling heatedly with his. Even the air surrounding them suddenly seemed charged with an element that was seeping into his pores, causing his heart rate to increase.

Maybe, just maybe, if he could have found his voice, he would have suggested that she go into the house while he hung back a while to get himself together, regain control of his senses. But he didn't find his voice. What he found instead was that he was slowly and carefully reaching out and pulling her to him while lowering his mouth to hers.

The moment their lips touched all the reasons why he should not taste her, right then and there, vanished from his mind. Instead his mind filled with all the reasons he should proceed, go as deep as he could and get as much as he could handle. Desire, the last thing he needed to feel at that moment, flared within him with the intensity of a typhoon tearing across the ocean as a force so powerful, he felt the surge in every part of his body.

And he felt her.

He felt the way her chest rested against his, the way she was responding to his kiss, as if, like him, she had been waiting for this to happen again. And he felt how perfect she was in his arms. And when he deepened the kiss even more, he felt how she quivered in his arms, how her mouth vibrated beneath his. A burning sensation was erupting deep in his gut but it had nothing to do with pain, and had everything to do with a need that had never affected him this way, not with any woman.

And when she latched onto his tongue, heat flared in the pit of his stomach, and without realizing he was about to do so, he let out a deep moan and felt an intense outpouring of desire that consumed him completely. He was finding it impossible to pull his mouth back. His mind refused to recall that earlier he'd decided he should not have kissed her that first time. It was a moot point now. He would deal with this weak impulse later. The most important thing was that he held her in his arms and was enjoying every tantalizing moment that her lips were joined to his, her tongue mingling with his own.

No telling how long he would have stood there and taken her mouth like a starving man if Princess, who was jealous for losing Mackenzie's attention, hadn't decided to reclaim it by nudging her. Mackenzie pulled her mouth away from his and then she leaned back to stare at him.

He decided to speak first, having an idea what she would say. Bringing his hand to the side of her face, he said, "If you can't say anything nice about what we just did, then don't say anything at all."

Instead of saying anything, she lowered her head to gently rest it against his chest. He instinctively wrapped his arms around her waist again. "That should not have happened, Luke," she said softly, against his shirt. But he heard her loud and clear.

"Whether it should have happened or not, Mac, it was bound to happen again, sooner or later," was his response.

She lifted her head and met his gaze. "Why?"

Her question, asked in a quiet tone, nearly robbed him of breath. She was staring at him with those big, beautiful dark eyes. And in their depths he actually saw confusion, like she really didn't have a clue. It was as if she didn't fully understand the impact of sexual chemistry.

He decided to try and break it down for her. "The reason why can be summed up in several different words, Mac. Hormones. Testosterone. Sexual need. Desire. Temptation. Take your pick."

She took a step back, at least as far back as Princess would allow, which wasn't much. "I don't want to pick any of them. Why can't we just remain friends?"

A smile touched his lips. "That might be easy enough if we'd ever been friends. Think about it. That night of the auction, you had met Slade and Blade a few months earlier. Because of my extensive travels on the rodeo circuit, our paths had never crossed until that night. The twins were comfortable with you. I wasn't. Not sure if I'm even comfortable with you now."

He could tell from her expression that his words had surprised her. Not only had they surprised her, he sensed by the stiffening of her spine that they had also offended her. "You wanted to come here and stay in my home while not being comfortable with me?" she asked, as if such a thing were clearly an insult, not to mention illogical.

"That's not what I meant. The reason I'm uncomfortable with you has nothing to do with trust, Mac. It has everything to do with control. Let's be real here for a moment. From the first, we were attracted to each other. Admit it, because I certainly can and will. The moment I walked out on that stage and saw you in the audience I was attracted to you. I homed in on you like nobody's business, and the reason my gaze kept coming back to yours is because I felt something being reciprocated."

He waited for her to deny such a possibility and when

she didn't, he continued. "And the reason I didn't act on it then is the same reason I don't want to act on it now. To develop a relationship with you that goes beyond mere friendship is not possible It's not anything I want and I doubt it's something you want either. You're married to your profession like I'm married to mine. I don't want a woman in my life and I've sensed that you don't want a man in yours."

She nodded in agreement. "Then what was that kiss about?"

He smiled again. "I've told you. Hormones. Testosterone. Sexual need. Desire. Temptation. They're all there, here, between us, making us think crazy. Making us lose control. Making us want to share kisses." He decided not to mention what other thoughts were running wild and rampant through his mind whenever he kissed her.

Instead of looking at him, she stared down at the ground for a second, as if trying to come to terms with what he'd said. She then looked back at him. "All right. Since we can admit we don't want an involvement of any kind, what do you suggest we do to make us not want to share kisses?"

Hell, he wished he knew. He had a feeling he would always want to kiss her. But since she had asked, he stated what he thought was the only solution. "We can try working on developing a friendship, not a relationship. And when we do that, all those things that tempt us, make us want to kiss, or take things further than that, will eventually fade."

Luke heard his own words. They sounded good, easy enough, and plausible. And to his ear they made perfect sense. But when he was around her he discovered that he had a tendency to throw perfect sense right out the window. And around her he wanted to take kissing to another level. It was a temptation he would have to fight like hell to overcome.

He gazed down at her. She was studying the ground again. "Talk to me, Mac. Tell me what you're thinking."

She glanced up, met his gaze. "I was wondering if it

will be possible for us to become friends, I mean *real* friends. One thing I've picked up on is the fact that you're not overly friendly."

He stared at her for a moment and then he couldn't help but chuckle, although doing so made his body ache some. "You're right, I'm not an overly friendly person, at least not in the same way you might consider Slade and Blade as friendly. In their line of work it pays for them to be friendly. It's a part of who they are. It's a natural ability and one they have perfected over the years. With me, my job doesn't require friendliness. It requires concentration and total control. Therefore, I tend to blot a lot out. I also make the mistake of not taking things at face value."

Mackenzie opened her mouth and was about to say something, but at that moment Theo walked in with his cell phone. "Sorry to interrupt, Mac, but it's Ms. Sam. She's been trying to reach you. Says it's important."

Luke watched as she immediately took the phone from the man. "Yes, Sam, what's going on?"

He watched her eyes widen before a fierce frown clouded her features. "Okay, I'm on my way."

She handed the phone back to Theo and then she turned to Luke and said in an angry tone, "That was one of my partners at the law firm. Someone has broken into our office and ransacked the place."

Chapter 6

What a mess.

That was the first thought that entered Mackenzie's mind when she walked into her office and glanced around. What was the reason behind this? And who would do such a thing and why? Had it been a burglary or outright mischief? And why had her office been the only one targeted?

The law firm of Standfield, Di Meglio, and Mahoney was located in downtown Oklahoma City in a very busy part of the city. In fact there was a popular restaurant a few buildings down, so the first thing Mackenzie wondered was whether anyone had seen or heard anything.

Trying to push aside the anger that was trying to boil inside of her, she glanced across the room and saw Sam and Peyton. They were talking with two police officers. They glanced her way and she wasn't surprised when their gazes moved beyond her to the man standing by her side. She had tried convincing Luke to stay at her place until she returned, but he had answered her with two words in a firm voice. "No way."

So here they were and she knew her partners' anger had momentarily been replaced by outright male appreciation and awe. The way they were looking Luke up and down was clear evidence of that. She suddenly felt a distinct chill sweep through her body and couldn't understand the reason for it. Sam and Peyton were her two closest friends, so there was no reason for the feeling of jealousy that twisted sharply inside of her. Why on earth was she feeling territorial toward a man who less than an hour ago had suggested they work on developing nothing more than friendship between them?

At least that's what she was pretty sure he had suggested. But the protective arm he had placed around her waist the moment they entered her office was undoubtedly sending a different message to Sam and Peyton. She knew those two and could just imagine what they were thinking.

She also knew if she didn't do something about Luke, he could become the primary focus instead of her ransacked office, so she turned to him and said, "Are you sure you're okay? This place is a mess. Don't you want to sit outside in the lobby until—"

"I'm fine, Mac. Come on. Let's see what the police officer has to say."

Seeing that he wasn't going to leave her side, she said, "All right."

Stepping over clients' folders strewn on the floor, and ever mindful of Luke's slight limp, they crossed the room to where the others were standing. Sam smiled then made introductions to the police officers. "This is our other partner, Officers, the one this particular office belongs to. Mackenzie Standfield. And this hun—man"—she quickly amended what she had clearly been about to say—"is her friend Luke Madaris."

After the policemen shook hands with Mackenzie and Luke, Sam's smile widened as she said, "And because we haven't been officially introduced, Luke, I'm Samari Di Meglio and this is Peyton Mahoney. We've heard a lot about you."

Mackenzie rolled her eyes when Luke shook hands with the two women. "All nice things, I hope," Luke said, smiling, presenting both women with a killer-watt smile.

"Of course," Peyton said, beaming brightly. And Sam's smile, Mackenzie noted, was just as radiant.

"Luke Madaris?" one of the officers was saying. "Are you *the* Luke Madaris, who's a rodeo star?"

Luke's attention then switched to the officer who'd asked the question. "Yes, I'm a rodeo rider."

"Hey, come on," the officer said, chuckling. "Stop being so modest. You're more than just a rodeo rider; you're one of the best with all those titles under your belt. My dad and brothers are into rodeo big-time. We even follow the circuit. We were there the other night in the arena when you got pinned in with that bull. That was a pretty nasty predicament. Are you doing okay?"

"Yes, I'm healing nicely, thanks. I hope to be back in the chute in Reno in end of September."

Mackenzie sighed. That's all they needed, a cop who was one of Luke's fans. From the hero-worshipping look in the officer's eyes, she had a feeling she'd have to interrupt if she wanted any answers. "Excuse me, Officer, but do you have any idea who might have done this?"

It was the second officer who spoke since the one who was Luke's fan still appeared too stunned by having Luke in his presence to answer her question. "No, ma'am, but according to your partners there doesn't appear to be anything taken. It seems the person just wanted to make a mess for some reason."

"And I think I know the reason and who that person might be, or who the person could be working for." Sam crossed her arms over her chest, frowning.

"Who?" Luke's adoring fan asked.

"In my line of business I hate accusing anyone of anything, but Mac is working on a very important case, one that could cost this corporation plenty of money if they lose. I bet they had something to do with it."

"And what corporation is that, Ms. Di Meglio?"

It was all speculation on Sam's part and they knew it. But still, the officer jotted down the name supplied by Sam.

"And what about you, Ms. Standfield, since this was your office and the only one that was messed with. Do you know of anyone who would do such a thing? Do you think

Whitedyer Corporation is involved, like your partner has insinuated?"

Mackenzie shrugged. In all honesty, she didn't know what to think. "I'm not sure. I know I was somewhat threatened—but in a joking kind of way—by their company attorney. I was told to find another case to work on or I'd wish I had. But I took it to mean in the courtroom."

"What about your client? Has he reported harassment of any kind?"

"No, but then Mr. Coroni is in the hospital and has been for about two weeks."

The officer lifted his brow. "What's wrong with him?"

Mackenzie understood what the officer was thinking and quickly assured him that was not the case. "Mr. Coroni is in his seventies and is dealing with a lot of health issues right now. There's nothing more to it than that."

The officer nodded. "My partner and I will check with the restaurant a few doors down," he said. "There's a possibility someone may have noticed something when they parked their car."

Less than thirty minutes later, the officers had left and Mackenzie, Sam, and Peyton, with Luke's help, began straightening up the office, doing as much as they could. They would have to hire a cleaning company to come and take care of the mess made from overturned plants, the computer ink smeared in the carpet, and the substance the officers used to get fingerprints.

"I can't believe someone would do such a thing," Peyton said angrily as she attempted to refile a bunch of their clients' folders. If Whitedyer is responsible for this, then they will be sorry."

Mackenzie and Sam nodded in agreement.

On the way back to the ranch Luke noted Mackenzie was pretty quiet and figured she was still upset about the break-in at her office.

Although she had tried to convince him otherwise, he had helped with the cleanup. At the moment all he felt was a little soreness, although he might pay a price for his stub-bornness later tonight. But he didn't care. There was no way he could have stood aside and not helped.

As he rubbed the back of his neck to ease a bit of the tension he felt there, he couldn't help but think about Mac's partners. It was pretty obvious the three women were close. He gathered from their conversations they had met while in college and had remained friends over the years. Samari was the feistiest of the three and he could tell that she'd be quick with an attitude and was the type of woman a man would either tame or let run wild if he was up for the challenge. Tall, with shoulder-length, black curly hair, a caramel complexion, and a pair of dark eyes—that he doubted missed much—she was a mixture of Italian and African-American ancestry and was very attractive.

Peyton was also an attractive woman but she didn't have much to say and only spoke when she had a specific purpose. She definitely wasn't one to waste her time with words. She was the tallest of the three women and wore her thick black hair in dreads to her shoulders.

He couldn't help mulling over what Sam had told the police officers regarding her suspicions about that corpo-ration having something to do with the break-in at Mac's office.

Luke glanced over at Mac and stared at her for a few moments before saying, "If Sam's suspicions are true about that company, why would they go to such an extreme just to get a piece of land?"

She glanced over at him. "It's not just a piece of land. Mr. Coroni owns a huge tract that Whitedyer would like to use to expand their mining business. Some of the people in town are for the expansion because it could mean more jobs and that would provide an economic boost. But others see it for what it really is: another example of how some corporations are not taking steps to protect the environ-ment. When Whitedyer came to town four years ago they promised to work with the community to preserve the ecosystem, but all they've done is use under-the-table tactics with some of our politicians to ease environmental regulations."

Luke didn't say anything for a moment and then asked, "But if Coroni doesn't want to sell what can Whitedyer do?"

Mackenzie glanced over at him when she brought the car to a stop at a traffic light. "At the moment they're still working under-the-table, trying to get Mr. Coroni's land rezoned. They've already tried increasing his property taxes to an amount he can barely afford to pay. To counteract that, a fund was established by concerned citizens to offer him assistance. Now Whitedyer is trying to force him off his own land by abusing eminent domain. That's where I come in. My job is to stop them and it hasn't been easy. Their company attorney, Lewis Farley, is nothing but an asshole, and unfortunately he has several members of the development council and city chamber backing them. They are trying to take the property away under an amendment that allows for the taking of property for private development if doing so can create jobs or raise revenue."

"If expanding the plant will create more jobs then how can you have a case?"

Mackenzie sighed heavily as she put the car back into motion. "By proving that's not their intent. Whitedyer just want their hands on the land. We got an anonymous tip telling us that once they get their hands on the property they intend to drop it in the lap of a third party who wants to build a resort; a resort they plan to bring their own people in to run and operate."

"Do you have proof of that?"

"No, but I still plan on fighting them with the laws we have on the books now."

Luke didn't say anything for a moment and then he asked, "And Sam thinks this Farley guy is responsible for what happened at your office tonight?"

"Yes, that's what she thinks, but I'm not so sure. I can't see Farley getting his hands dirty by being part of something like that. But who knows? Desperate people will do just about anything, and I know for a fact they want me to get off the case. However, that won't happen."

Nodding, Luke didn't say anything until they came to another traffic light. "If not Farley, then who?"

Mackenzie shrugged as she stared straight ahead out the windshield. "Who knows, Luke? There are some people who see what we're doing as a negative because they think it's stopping the expansion of a company that's willing to offer needed jobs. To them, we're the bad guys, not Whitedyer."

Lost in his thoughts, Luke hadn't realized they were back at the ranch until she brought the car to a stop. He couldn't help but recall what had happened around ten years ago to Caitlin, his cousin Dex's wife. Blade, Slade, and Luke had been away in college at Morehouse at the time but had heard about it when they came home on break.

From what he'd heard, Caitlin had owned a piece of property that a certain developer had wanted, and they had been desperate enough to try just about anything to get it. They went so far as to try and threaten her into selling it to them. Their tactics backfired when they were confronted with the likes of Dex Madaris, who had just reentered Caitlin's life. The bad guys found out the hard way that Dex was a force to reckon with.

"Luke, are you okay?"

He glanced over at Mackenzie. She sat there watching him. "Yes, why do you ask?"

"Because I'm home and you're just sitting there and not saying anything. Nor are you making an attempt to get out the car. Are you sure you're not in any pain?"

He couldn't help but smile. "Yes, I'm sure. I was just lost in my thoughts, remembering a time around ten years ago when a developer tried forcing Caitlin to sell her land to them. It was land that had been in her family for generations."

"I gather they didn't succeed," Mackenzie said, taking the key out of the ignition.

Luke chuckled as he unfastened his seat belt. "No, they didn't succeed. They had to deal with Dex."

He saw Mackenzie's gaze fill with understanding. Anyone who knew Dex Madaris would appreciate what Luke was saying. Dex, who was almost twelve years older than Luke, was the Madaris who was known not to play—not even the radio. The majority of the time he was as serious as a heart attack, and when it came to anyone messing with those he loved, he kicked ass first and asked questions later.

Moments later Luke was walking beside Mackenzie across the yard to the house. "Nice night," he decided to say, just to see if her response would be any different than the one she'd given earlier.

She stopped walking and looked up into the sky. The stars seemed to shine brighter tonight. Her voice was low when she spoke. "Considering everything that happened, I would say yes, it's still a nice night. I refuse to let anyone take that away from me." She then turned to him. "Do you understand what I'm saying, Luke?"

He nodded. Yes, he understood. If he didn't before he certainly did now. What happened tonight had made her angry, but it had also made her more determined. If the person behind tonight's chaos figured that would be a way to get Mac out of the picture, they were sadly mistaken. The memory of how she had looked when she had walked into her office tonight and seen the mess was etched in his brain. She had looked angry, hurt, yet at the same time fired up, fighting mad.

She began walking again and he fell in step beside her thinking it was a good thing she was moving. Otherwise, he would have been tempted to pull her into his arms and kiss her again. And hadn't they decided earlier this evening, before she'd gotten that call from Sam, that they would just be friends, that they would build a friendship and not a relationship?

Mackenzie unlocked the door and Luke followed her inside. After stepping over the threshold, he tossed his hat on a nearby hat rack and watched as she headed toward the kitchen. He decided to keep his distance from her for a while. The car ride had been murder on his body in more ways than one. Sharing space with her had caused heat to run through him even when he'd tried not thinking about her. He never wondered how it would feel to have a woman to call his own. A woman whom he could claim as his possession, to do with as he pleased and whenever he pleased. As long as she was willing, of course. And she would be willing, he would make sure of it. That would definitely be an important factor. She would also have to be enticing, provocative, and filled with as much sensuality as any one woman could manage. And all for him.

The thought of having a woman like that had certain parts of him throbbing to the point he could no longer just stand there. But instead of taking the nearest chair he decided to stroll around the room to walk off the need he felt all the way to his groin. After circling the room several times, he began to wonder what Mackenzie was doing in the kitchen. She had been in there for a while now.

He headed in that direction but came up short when he passed through the doorway and saw she stood staring out the window with her back to him. And from the silent quaking of her shoulders he knew she was crying.

Luke realized he should turn away, go back into the living room, and give her this private time alone, but for some reason he couldn't make himself do that. She was mad. She was upset. Her tears were tears of fury. And at the moment she needed a good shoulder to release them on.

She needed his.

That would put him in a role he wasn't used to. Hell, the last thing he wanted was for some woman to cry all over him, get all emotional. But he ignored those thoughts as he crossed the room to her. After all, they were working on this friendship thing, weren't they?

He stood close, at her back, deciding not to wrap his arms around her just yet. Even from where he was standing he could sense the anger vibrating from her. So instead he said in a soft tone, "It's okay, Mac. Things are going to be all right."

Her breath escaped in surprise. Evidently she hadn't detected his presence. Without turning around she said in a broken voice, "I'm okay."

At that moment he decided to make sure that she was and reached out and circled his arms around her waist, bringing her back against the solid wall of his chest and only winced a little when he did so. He rested his chin on the top of her head. "Yes, you're okay, and do you know why you're okay, Mac?"

She shook her head negatively before saying, "No."

"Because you have guts. And because you also have the drive to do the right thing and fight for a cause."

"But what if I lose?" she asked in a mere whisper.

He leaned forward, close to her ear, and said, "You won't. Didn't anyone ever tell you that the bad guys never win?"

It was then that she turned in his arms and met his gaze. "Never?"

She was looking up at him with those big gorgeous dark eyes of hers and there was no way he could tell her anything different. Besides, he actually believed what he'd said. Bad guys never won. "No, never."

She sighed as if she believed him, and when he pulled her closer to the fit of his body, she came willingly and snuggled even closer. His hands moved higher and began gently massaging her back, to ease the tension. This was what she needed, rather than the kiss he desperately wanted to give her.

Her face was buried in his shirt but for some reason his chest didn't feel any pain or discomfort. What he felt at that moment was something a lot more emotional than sensual. It might seem ludicrous but he was mesmerized by the woman in his arms in a different sort of way.

Remember, Lucas Garen Madaris III, it's all about

building a friendship and not a relationship. He wanted to push that particular reminder away but it seemed unmovable and he knew why. A relationship wasn't compatible with his life goals. Friendship was all they could ever share.

She lifted her head and met his gaze and he felt his gut clench when he focused on her lips. A part of him wanted to taste them but another part, his common sense, told him not to do it.

"Thanks, Luke. I'm fine now," she said softly.

His gaze shifted to her eyes. His voice seemed to have dipped an octave when he asked, "Are you sure?"

"Yes."

They stood staring at each other for a few quiet moments longer before she said, "It's getting late. I'd better go."

Instead of responding, he released her and took a step back. "Good night, Mac."

"Good night, Luke. Make sure you take your medication before you turn in."

He nodded.

And then she was gone and he was left there, standing alone, and wondering just how he had managed to get himself in such a fix.

Chapter 7

Blade and Slade Madaris, fraternal twins and owners of Madaris Construction Company, were handsome men, Mackenzie concluded as she stood in her doorway watching them get out of the car. She observed Slade offering his hand to his wife, Skye, who swung her legs out of the car to join the brothers. Not for the first time she thought that Slade and Skye made a beautiful couple, and she really liked Skye. She had such class and she was a very friendly and outgoing person.

Her gaze then shifted to Blade. To say he enjoyed being a bachelor was an understatement. Over the years she had heard a lot about him and his philandering ways, his long list of affairs. He was a heartbreak just waiting to happen for any woman who thought she could tame his womanizing heart. She bet a number had tried, but so far none had succeeded.

Suddenly her heart began throbbing against her rib cage and heat began spreading through her lower extremities, an indication that Luke was near. In fact, she was consciously aware of the moment he came to stand directly beside her.

Out of the corner of her eye she saw he had changed into another pair of jeans and shirt. He had that just-showered smell along with his usual masculine scent. The combination was tormenting her senses and reminding her of just what an enticing male specimen he was, something she tried not to dwell on. Especially these past three days since the night she had practically made a fool of herself by crying in his arms.

The day after that humiliating incident she had left home before he had gotten out of bed, convincing herself she was doing so to be there for the cleaning crew. They'd be coming to clear out the mess in her office from the night before. And she had returned late that night since she had scheduled a meeting with a client.

It had been close to ten by the time she had gotten home to find Luke had prepared dinner again—another casserole—that was just as tasty as the one he'd made the night before. He had been in the bedroom but had gotten up to join her in the kitchen, inquiring whether the police had made any progress in their investigation. She had told him the police still didn't have a clue who had ransacked her office, but they were still obtaining more information. Of course Whitedyer denied any involvement and so far none of the customers at the restaurant that night had reported seeing or hearing anything suspicious.

He had asked her how her day had gone, but when he saw she wasn't very talkative he had gone back to bed.

That night had pretty much set the pattern for the following two days. They only had a conversation when they thought they had something to say; otherwise they seemed to be distancing themselves from each other. She sighed deeply at the thought of that happening. So much for them trying to be friends.

"If your frown gets any deeper everyone is going to wonder what I've done to you, Mac," Luke said in a low voice, interrupting her thoughts.

She couldn't help but glance up at him, taking in the handsomeness of his features, especially his sensual mouth. She had noted that he was getting around better these past three days. His limp was less pronounced and he didn't wince as much when he moved around. He had mentioned at breakfast that morning that he had cut back on his pain medication a few days ago and was getting along just fine without them. She had been glad to hear that, but she wasn't glad to hear what he'd just said.

"I'm not frowning," she countered, forcing a smile to her lips.

He chuckled as he glanced back up at her. "Now you're not, but only because I just mentioned that you were. The last thing I want them to think is that I've been a bad patient."

No, he hadn't been a bad patient. In fact, he'd been just the opposite. It wasn't his fault that his very presence caused havoc to her central nervous system, producing some sort of physical response whenever he was near. Instead of responding to what he said, she took a step on the porch when Skye quickly moved in her direction. Sexual tension seemed to be swirling in the air between her and Luke and the sooner she put distance between them, the better.

"I don't know how the rest of your body is holding up, but I'm glad to see your eye sockets are still in pretty good working order where Mac is concerned."

Luke shot his cousin Slade a frown "What are you talking about?"

Slade chuckled. "I'm talking about the fact that when it comes to Mac, Blade and I do all the talking and you still do all the looking. Just like you were just doing. Just like you've been doing since we got here. She moves, your eyes move. They're like radar that keeps track of her."

Luke silently admitted that he had been staring at Mac, and probably had been doing so frequently. But then she was pretty, and damn, he was a man who appreciated beautiful things, especially women.

"We're trying to be friends," he finally said, thinking that statement would explain everything.

"Why?" It was Blade who asked.

The three of them were sitting on the porch while Skye and Mac were out in the yard near the corral. Theo had brought out an easygoing gelding for Skye to ride. Luke couldn't help but smile at the thought that the first time Skye, a New Englander, had been on a horse was after she'd met Slade. And now she was a city girl who was determined to adjust to the western life she was a part of.

Luke glanced over at Blade. "Why, what?"

"Why are you trying to be friends with Mac? Slade and I are her friends. We always figured you would shoot to be something more."

Luke's frown returned. "How could the two of you think something like that? You of all people know I don't have time for relationships. I just got time for rodeos."

Blade chuckled. "How often do I have to tell you, Luke, that a man makes time for it all? Especially a woman."

Luke rolled his eyes. "Everybody doesn't have your stamina, Blade, or your desire to hit on any woman not already taken."

Blade smiled. "Speaking of a woman not already taken, if you're not placing a claim on Mac, then I know a couple of guys who're interested in her. I've been keeping them at bay by saying she was yours, but if you're going to relinquish any serious interest then—"

"Who are these men?" Luke asked, feeling his shoulders stiffen as well as a tightening in his chest that had nothing to do with his injury. He knew some of Blade's friends. They were womanizers like him, and the prospect of Mac being exposed to any of them didn't sit too well with him.

"Wyatt is one and Tanner is the other."

Luke was out of his chair so fast that he winced at the pain he felt in his knee. "Wyatt Bannister and Tanner Jamison?"

At Blade's nod, Luke scowled deeply. "Keep them away from her. They would mean her no good."

"Mac's a grown woman, Luke," Blade said.

"And those two friends of yours are nothing but horny-ass men," Luke all but growled. "Do like I said, Blade. Keep them away from her." Without another word, Luke limped into the house.

Slade glanced over at his brother. "Well, I think you've done it now. You got him pretty pissed."

"Damn, I hope so," Blade said cheerfully. "What I told him is true. Wyatt and Tanner are itching in the crotch to hit on Mac. The only thing keeping them at bay is Luke. They don't want to infringe on his territory. I thought I'd prepare him since Wyatt and Tanner are attending the graduation party the folks are giving QT next month and Mac plans to be there too." QT was the nickname for Quantum Talon Madaris, Blade and Slade's twenty-five-year-old brother, who had recently graduated from Howard University Medical School.

"Luke needs to come to terms with what Mac means to him. If he's determined to pick rodeo over her then he should move aside," Blade said, smiling, knowing there was no way Luke would do that. However, it was something Luke would have to discover for himself.

Slade looked over at his twin. "Why do I get the feeling that you, of all people, are trying to play matchmaker?"

Blade chuckled. "Mainly because I like Mac, and like Luke, I don't want Wyatt or Tanner to come anywhere near her. Hell, they're my home boys so I know what they're about. I consider Mac like a sister. Besides, I would hate for Ashton to get involved if one of them were to get out of line with her."

Slade shuddered at the thought. Ashton Sinclair, a colonel in the marines and a former Recon man, was as tough as they came. Like Mac he was part Cherokee and part African American and rumor had it that he even had some sort of mystic powers. "Hopefully, Luke will make some sort of move before the party," Slade decided to say.

Blade nodded. "Yeah, we can both hope so."

Luke stood at the kitchen window watching Skye and Mac. Both were good-looking women. One was spoken for and one was not. His vision was concentrated on the one that was not.

Mac.

He frowned when he remembered what Blade had said a few moments ago. There was no way in hell that he was going to let Wyatt Bannister or Tanner Jamison get anywhere near her. He knew Wyatt a lot better than he knew Tanner since Wyatt was one of Camden's brothers. And he'd heard enough about Wyatt's exploits from Cam to know just how Wyatt operated. Besides, Wyatt was one of Blade's closest friends which in itself said it all. Blade and a few of his "buddies" were affiliated with a sort of private all-male fraternity called the Notorious Gentlemen's Club, and although Blade had never acknowledged it, Luke had heard the members would periodically hold secret meetings and they were even contemplating opening a nightclub in Houston with that same name—Notorious Gentlemen's Club—as if any of them could ever be considered true gentlemen.

Mac was a beautiful woman and he couldn't blame any man for being interested in her, but as far as Luke was concerned, those men could effectively count her out as a possible conquest. Whether he laid claim to her or not, she would still be off limits to any of them.

As if she could feel him thinking about her, he saw Mac glance first at the porch and then scan the area before looking at the kitchen window and seeing him standing there. Their gazes met and held and immediately he felt an intense stirring in his midsection before his entire body began to throb. They had been avoiding each other lately, living under the same roof but exchanging few words over the dinner table. In the beginning he had been fine with that, finding the arrangement acceptable. But now . . .

Hell. He wanted her. And he wasn't quite sure how to go about getting his body to understand that he couldn't have her. She was off limits to him just as much as she was to Wyatt and Tanner, but for different reasons. He didn't see her as a conquest. He saw Mac as a threat. She was a threat to everything he had worked so hard to achieve for the past eight years.

All he had ever wanted in life was to be a rodeo star and

he was determined to keep climbing to the top for as long as he wanted. Thanks to Uncle Jake he had a trust fund as well as a number of successful investments. In other words, at thirty-three he was pretty well off and could afford to live his life however he chose while enjoying his passion. And his passion was the rodeo. But lately he found his passion trying to shift to something else. Or, more precisely, to someone else.

When Mac finally broke eye contact with him to listen to something Skye was saying, he released a deep sigh. The main thing he needed to concentrate on was getting better so he could pack up and move on.

Moving on wouldn't be easy, but it was something that he had to do.

Mackenzie didn't get a lot of overnight guests at her ranch so she was having the time of her life. The twins were always fun to be around and Skye was a jewel. She had assisted her in preparing dinner and she had been pleased at how the three men had eaten it all up, even asking for seconds.

Because her ranch house was small, sleeping arrangements had been a challenge. She had insisted that Slade and Skye take her room, and she would sleep on the love seat that converted to a bed in her office. Blade had agreed to the sofa in the living room.

She had always known how close Luke, Blade, and Slade were, and she always enjoyed seeing them together and being part of the camaraderie they shared. After dinner they had watched one of those reality shows, and while she and Skye had enjoyed it, the cousins had basically pulled it apart, speaking out and saying what they hadn't liked about it.

Afterward, they sat around eating bowls of popcorn while Slade and Blade told them about this new construction job they were bidding on. Skye, an accountant, was working full-time for Madaris Construction, and from what

Mac could gather, she enjoyed being part of her husband's company.

"I understand you had a bit of trouble this week, Mac. Luke told us about it," Slade said when the room had gotten quiet.

She sighed. "Yes, and I'm hoping whoever did it thinks he's made his point and will keep on trucking."

"But what if they don't? Especially since you're moving ahead with the case. What if they decided to strike again?" Blade asked.

Mac hadn't wanted to think of that possibility. "Let's just hope that they don't. The police are investigating, and although they say they don't have any leads, I'm hoping they'll eventually find the person responsible."

Later that night while lying in bed, Mac couldn't help but think about Slade and Skye's relationship and wish she could have found something similar for herself. It was obvious that Slade adored his wife, that she was his world and that he loved her the way a man was supposed to love a woman. At the same time, she could tell that Slade was the most important person in Skye's life. The one person she could depend on if others failed.

Mackenzie could now admit that was the kind of relationship, the kind of ever-lasting love, she'd thought she had found with Lawrence, only to discover that for him, it had been about his ego first and opportunity last. During the two years they'd been together he had enjoyed having her by his side, putting her on display as his token girlfriend. But then, when opportunity came knocking and he got the chance to marry into wealth, he had dumped her like yesterday's garbage. He didn't mind being the spoiled rich girl's "yes" man if it meant he would one day inherit daddy's money.

Sometimes she wondered what she'd ever seen in the jerk in the first place.

Her thoughts then shifted to what Blade had said regarding the break-in at her office. What if the person decided to strike again? She shifted in bed, telling herself that she couldn't worry about that possibility, that things wouldn't go that far. Besides, she had taken on cases before where the opposing side had tried using scare tactics. It hadn't worked then and it wouldn't work now.

Mackenzie wasn't the only one thinking about what Blade had said. Long after everyone had retired for the night Luke lay in bed thinking about it and wondering if the person would attempt something else annoying.

To ease the slight ache in the upper part of his body, Luke shifted position. Although she had gotten pretty upset by what had happened, Mac hadn't let the incident deter her from representing her client. She'd even revealed a vulnerability that she probably wished she hadn't, especially in front of him, but still her inner strength and fierce determination would ensure that justice was served. Mackenzie Standfield was one gutsy woman and he couldn't help but admire her.

However, what Blade had said still troubled him. He just hoped the responsible party would leave well enough alone, but for some reason, Luke wasn't entirely convinced he would.

Chapter 8

"Mr. Madaris, are you trying to be difficult?"

Luke's eyebrows shot up as he looked at the person the hospital had assigned as his physical therapist. The woman had to be his mother's age, or close to it, which was around fifty-one. But the similarity stopped there. Sarah Madaris was petite, soft-spoken, and easygoing. This woman, who had shown up a few hours ago and introduced herself as Margaret Stone, had to be a descendant of Attila the Hun. No one wanted to see progress more than Luke, but if he didn't know any better he'd think the woman was trying to kill him.

Since she asked the question he decided to provide her with an answer. "No, ma'am, but you're asking me to put my knee in a position that hurts like the dickens."

She frowned. "It all hurts, Mr. Madaris. In the end your entire body is going to hurt. But then you'll get better. And I assume you want to get better, don't you? Or will you be satisfied with using a cane for the rest of your life?"

An image flashed in Luke's mind of being in the arena, but standing on the sidelines, leaning on his cane, while he watched other rodeo riders compete.

A fierce frown touched Luke's brow. This woman definitely had it all wrong. There would not be a cane in his future. He intended to compete again, not stand on the sidelines. "I won't be using a cane," he said in a firm and decisive tone. "I'm competing in the rodeo in September."

"Not at the rate you're going, you aren't. I don't want you to impel your progress more than you should, but you'll have to bite the bullet and take a little pain."

His frown deepened. She was goading him, trying to make him mad. And it was working. He'd been pretty pissed off for around an hour or so now. "With all due respect, ma'am, I *am* taking pain and I've been taking more than just a little. Hell, I'm doing the best I can here"

"Not good enough. I want more."

He stared into her eyes and found not one ounce of pity. Not even a gram. "Fine, I'll give you more," he all but snarled. Even after saying the words he wasn't sure how he would give her more, but dammit, he would even if it killed him, which was a very strong possibility judging from the way his knee was aching.

Suddenly, she smiled. Actually smiled. And then she chuckled and said, "Now we're talking, cowboy."

"How did your physical therapy go today, Luke?"

Luke glanced over the dinner table at Mackenzie. They were following their regular routine. She had come in from work. He had fixed dinner—a casserole—and then they had sat down and eaten together. Afterward they would share kitchen duty before going their separate ways. Usually he would go back to his bedroom and watch ESPN, and she would check with Theo to see how things had gone on the ranch that day. To say they were deliberately putting distance between them was an understatement.

But tonight he intended to put an end to it. They both knew the root of their problem and needed to talk about it. This was one situation where he didn't buy into the theory that with some things you needed to leave well enough alone.

"It was rough going at first," he finally answered. "I thought the woman wanted to kill me. But once I figured out she was actually trying to help me, that she and I had the same goal, then Margaret and I got along beautifully."

He watched Mac's brows lift as she momentarily stopped eating. "Margaret?"

"Yes."

"The two of you are on a first-name basis?" she asked.

"Yes."

She resumed eating, at least she put some ground beef on her fork before asking, "Umm, how old is she?"

"I didn't ask. But fairly young." Okay, so he was stretching it a bit. But she didn't have to know that he was comparing her to his great-grandmother's age, and compared to Mama Laverne, Margaret was fairly young.

Mac stopped eating again and met his gaze. "And she's able to handle you all by herself."

He thought about all the goading and prodding Margaret had done that day and he couldn't help but smile. "Oh, yeah, she's able to handle me . . . all by herself."

It must have been the smile, Luke figured, that had given Mac the wrong impression. Or it could have been the tone he'd used when he made the comment or the way he'd said the words. All he knew was that a flash of fire suddenly appeared in her eyes. And it was the kind of fire a man recognized when a woman was pea green with envy.

It stirred his insides to see that there was a chance she wasn't as indifferent to him as she wanted him to think. But that worked the other way around too. He wasn't indifferent to her as well. In fact, he'd been trying like heck for the past week not to pull her into his arms and give her the kiss he thought they both needed. He could go even further and imagine something else they probably both needed, but he refused to go there. The thought of a kiss was all he could handle for now.

"Does the thought of Margaret being my therapist bother you?" he decided to ask after the room got quiet, except for the sound of her fork hitting against her plate each time she scooped up some of the casserole. A sure sign that she was upset.

"No, why should it bother me?" she asked, not looking up at him.

"I don't know, you tell me." For some reason her little bout of jealousy didn't rile him the way Nadine Turner's had. In fact, he found it endearing because Mac had nothing to be jealous about. If he had a mind to be interested in a long-term affair with a woman, she would be his choice, hands down. Unfortunately, Nadine had been used to getting whatever she wanted—her daddy had made sure of it—and she had assumed Luke was her possession, so it had come as a blow to discover that he wasn't.

"I'm not telling you anything," she said, interrupting his thoughts. He inwardly smiled. She hadn't denied that what he'd said about Margaret had bothered her, just that she wasn't going to tell him why it did.

Luke met her gaze. He studied her expression. She was mad. And she probably didn't have a clue as to why. But he did. He knew the meaning of sexual frustration. At least he'd gotten a whopping taste of it being around her. How long had he been here with her? Three weeks?

"I could get it out of you if I want."

She blinked as if confused. "Excuse me?"

He had no problem repeating himself. "I said that I could get it out of you if I want."

She narrowed her gaze. "You can try," she said mockingly, her tone haughty.

Suddenly, he felt blood rush through his veins, felt heat settle right smack in his groin. Since she had invited him to do so, he would. There was nothing wrong in trying. Without taking his eyes off her, he pushed his chair back and stood up. He knew the moment she realized that she had made a mistake.

Too late.

"I think I will try, Mac. What do I have to lose?"

She placed her fork down and stood as well. "Luke . . ." She said his name as if to calm him down, make him see reason. But what she evidently didn't realize was that he was calm and he did see reason. Especially now that he had made his mind up about what he was going to do.

He watched her back up another step. "I think we should talk about this," she said.

He gave a crooked smile. That was cute. Now she wanted to talk. "I don't want to talk."

"Well, I do. And you don't scare me," she said, backing up even more when he moved around the table.

"I'm not trying to scare you, Mac," he said, taking a step toward her and noticing that his limp, even after such an intense physical therapy session, was less profound.

"If you're not trying to scare me then what are you trying to do?" she asked, taking yet another step back.

"Get myself in a position to work off a bit of frustration."

Her back was against the wall, literally. She had misjudged things and there were no more steps backward for her to take. Just as well, he thought. He had her just where he wanted her. And when he saw her stiffen her spine and tilt her head to glare at him, and then said, "In that case, call Margaret," he deepened his smile.

He came to a stop directly in front of her. "I like you a whole lot better," he said, and watched an angry pout take shape on her lips.

"Besides," he decided to say before she took a notion to kick him, especially in his bad knee. "You're a lot younger than Margaret. She's old enough to be my mom."

He saw the moment she understood. "Your mother?" she asked incredulously.

He leaned in a little. Damn, she smelled good. And her lips looked so ripe, like they were made for kissing. "Yes, my mother."

"But you had me thinking she was a young woman."

He shook his head. "No I didn't. You jumped to conclusions."

Her glare deepened. "You could have set me straight."

His smile widened even more. "Yes, I could have but I chose not to. You've been acting skittish around me for weeks now. Trying to put distance between us. That little bout of jealousy was the first sign you've given that you cared."

"I'm not jealous and I don't care," she denied hotly.

"Liar."

She placed her hands on her hips and her spine stiffened even more. "Well, you haven't exactly been the friendliest person lately."

No, he hadn't. In trying to build a friendship with her instead of a relationship, he had created animosity between them. "Sorry," he said, bracing both hands against the wall, effectively pinning her in. "But I'm about to change that, starting now." And then he lowered his mouth toward hers.

Mackenzie saw it coming and knew without a shadow of a doubt that Luke was about to kiss her. And she knew without a shadow of a doubt that she wanted him to kiss her, in a bad way.

Although she should resist, just a little. But the moment his lips touched hers, any thought of resisting escaped her mind. Instead she concentrated on his scent—sensual and provocative—and then on the way he pulled her tongue into his mouth and began mating with it with an intensity that made her purr.

She quickly decided there was definitely something intrinsically erotic about kissing Luke. This was their third kiss and each one got better and better, went deeper, became more succulent and mind-blowing. Just plain wonderful. Heat was thrumming through her stomach and what felt like bolts of lightning were flashing in her body. Being pinned up against him, feeling her taut nipples pressed into his chest, wasn't helping matters either. Sensations she had never felt before, didn't think were possible, were steadily eroding her defenses, overwhelming her to a degree that was just plain unreal. Then there was the heat of his body that she could actually feel through his clothes. Luke Madaris was definitely a red-hot male with a masculine scent and he was doing crazy things to her mind. Like enticing her to inch her body even closer to his, wrap her arms around his neck, and kiss him with the same intensity that he was kissing her. She and Lawrence had kissed, but never like this. Never had the air surrounding them been charged like it was now. And she'd never been involved in a kiss that required so much tongue interaction. And when he increased the pressure and began taking the kiss to another depth, she actually felt weak in the knees. Her breasts, which were pressing against him, began to tingle, the nipples hardened. And then not surprisingly, she heard herself purr again.

She had no idea how long the kiss lasted. She wasn't keeping track of time but figured they had to come up for air sometime. And when they did it was only for a second— no, a half a second—before Luke was back at her mouth with a hunger that astounded her and at the same time shattered any restraints she might have had.

Only half mindful of what she was doing, she removed one of her arms from around his neck and her hand went to his belt, eased the buckle free before sliding down his zipper. Luke broke off the kiss and with a low murmur close to her ear he asked, "Are you sure you're ready for that, Mac?"

Weakly, still filled with sensations she didn't quite understand, she raised her eyes to his, regarded him for a moment while wondering why he would even ask her something like that. How many men would? They would seize the opportunity to indulge in their wildest fantasies. A willing woman was something they would not question, just thank their good fortune.

But a part of her knew Luke Madaris wasn't just any man. He was a man who knew what he wanted out of life. He also knew what he didn't want and a long-term relationship with a woman was one of them. rodeo was his life. The only mistress he desired. Anything else was just wasted time. Besides, she knew although he desired her that she wasn't his type. She had seen the kind of women who threw themselves at the rodeo riders. Bold, brassy, and assy. That had been Cam's way of describing them, not hers.

"Answer me, Mac."

She blinked, remembering he was waiting for her response. No, she wasn't ready for it although her body was singing a different tune. She wasn't one to indulge in trivial affairs. She couldn't be just another notch on any cowboy's bedpost, just another itch he had to scratch. An easy lay.

She dropped her hands from him and shook her head. "No," she finally said softly. "I'm not ready."

Accepting what she said, he took a step back and she felt the heat of embarrassment when he rezipped his jeans. "All right. But if you ever change your mind—"

"I won't."

He smiled. "If you ever do, you'll always know where to find me."

Yes, she knew. All she had to do was follow the PRCA circuit. Instead of saying anything, she nodded. And then before she could take her next breath, he leaned in and kissed her again. This one was different. There was a tenderness to it that vibrated emotions all the way through her.

It only lasted a minute and then he was walking away and all she could do was inhale softly as she watched him go.

Chapter 9

The next morning when Luke got up, Mac had already left for work. He smiled, thinking she probably assumed it was business as usual, but boy was she wrong. He would be turning up the heat and more than just a little.

He had accepted her decision that taking things to another level was something she wasn't ready to do, but he intended to get her primed so when the time came and she was ready, it would be a very smooth transition. Friendship was no longer an option for them. Even a committed player like Blade had been able to see that. The only excuse he could come up with for not seeing it himself was the fact that when it came to life he had tunnel vision. The rodeo was the only focus he had in his future. It had always been primary. Anything else was secondary.

Nothing had really changed in that regard, but he was willing to indulge in a short-term affair with Mac, just as long as she understood short-term meant short-term. "Forever" was not a word in his vocabulary. Neither was the word "love." Both had been the downfall of many good rodeo riders, who were probably sitting at home, watching the rodeo on their television, and regretting having given up the chance to experience the profound adrenaline rush that came with the sport.

He would not be one of them. Once Mac understood that and accepted how things had to be between them, his conscience would be clear and they'd be free to move on, enjoy the moment and create beautiful memories.

His cell phone rang, interrupting his thoughts. He quickly picked it up. "Yes?"

"Luke, it's Reese."

Luke couldn't help but smile at the sound of his brother's voice. There were two years between them. At thirty-one Reese was following in their cousin Dex's footsteps, and after getting a degree in geology, he was presently working as a geologist at Madaris Explorations, the company Dex owned.

Luke's brother Emerson, who was twenty-nine, was a criminal attorney working for Houston's state attorney's office; and his brother Chancellor, who was twenty-seven, had joined the military after high school, and after giving Uncle Sam five years as a U.S. Army Ranger, he had returned home to try his hand at ranching. He owned a small spread outside Houston not far from Whispering Pines and enjoyed ranching as much as Jake did.

"How's it going, buddy?" Luke asked Reese. He was close to all three of his brothers.

"That's what I want to know about you. Blade suggested we wait a few weeks before we call, to give you time to adjust."

"Yeah, I know and I appreciate it. That first week was a killer. I was in a lot of pain most of the time. Now I'm undergoing physical therapy." He chuckled when he thought about his first day with Margaret. "Hell, I'm still having pain, but at least I know it's a means to an end and I'll be back in the chute in September."

"Just don't overdo it, Luke."

"I won't."

He spent the next half hour talking to Reese, getting caught up on what was happening with his other two brothers and figured that he would probably be hearing from them before the week was out.

"So, how are things with Mac?"

Luke lifted a brow. "Mac is fine. Why do you ask?"

"I was over to Uncle Jake's place on Sunday and the womenfolk were there. And I overheard a few things."

"A few things like what?"

Reese cleared his throat before saying, "I think they assume that something is going on between you and Mac. Said they had picked up on it a while back and it would be just a matter of time before you got hooked."

"Hooked?"

"Yes. I think they meant it would be just a matter of time before you fell in love with Mac and walked away from rodeo."

Luke snorted. Evidently they had lost their minds if they thought that. "Trust me, Reese, it's not going to happen. The only thing I love is rodeo. There's not a woman alive who can compete. rodeo is the number one thing in my life." There was no reason to admit that Mac was a very close second.

"That's what I thought but I figured how they were thinking was something that you should know."

"Thanks for sharing."

After ending the call a slow smile touched Luke's lips. He could just imagine who was the ringleader of the Madaris Women's Movement. Syneda. She thought the only good Madaris was a married one and probably felt that way only because Clayton, when footloose and fancy-free, had had a reputation as a ladies' man that made Blade's looked tame. And the thought of that was pretty scary considering Blade's reputation. Hell, after Clayton had settled down and married Syneda, he had given the case of condoms he'd kept in his closet to Blade. And Blade had been quick to tell him and Slade about the assortment of shapes, styles, and colors, but all guaranteed to be highly effective. And as per Clayton they didn't have an expiration date, which meant they hadn't been cheap. That had been nearly five years ago and knowing Blade they had probably gotten all used up by now.

Luke glanced at the clock on the wall. Margaret would

be arriving in a couple of hours. That would give him a chance to go out and share a cup of morning coffee with Theo. He liked the older man and had been surprised to learn that he'd had dreams of being a rodeo rider, but an unexpected pregnancy that had resulted in a rushed marriage had ended those dreams.

Luke shook his head. As far as he was concerned the worst kind of dream was one that ended before being given a chance to come true.

"Finally, a hickey."

Mackenzie's hand flew to her neck before recognizing the shrewd smirk on Sam's face. She frowned. "I don't have a hickey!"

Sam chuckled. "I know. Gotcha!"

Mackenzie rolled her eyes. "That's not funny."

"Yes it is," Sam said, coming to place her rear end on the edge of Mackenzie's desk. "The mere fact that you reacted as if you could have had one is definitely a telltale sign. Evidently you're not too tired when you get home late in the evenings to mess around with the hunk."

"But not what you think."

"Hey, cheer up. It's bound to happen sooner or later," Sam said, smiling. "And make sure you pass on to me any new positions. For me it's been a while."

"Longer for me," Mackenzie couldn't help but say.

"Has not," Sam countered.

"Has too."

"Has not."

The two women then simultaneously laughed at the ridiculousness of their conversation. "But seriously," Mackenzie said, wiping tears of laughter from her eyes. "It's been over five years for me."

"Damn, Mac, it's been only two for me. Didn't you do what I suggested after you broke up with Lawrence?"

Mac gave her friend a stern look. "No, I didn't. I couldn't do something like that." Not surprisingly, Sam was the one who'd suggested that she get back at the entire male race—especially those with the word "player" written on their forehead—for what Lawrence had done by setting up a few for heartbreak . . . only after she had gotten her use out of them.

"Hey, don't pity the players of this world. They deserve every bad thing that comes their way."

Since she'd always known Sam was a player-hater, especially after that episode with Guy Carrington a few years back, Mackenzie decided not to waste her time getting into an in-depth discussion about it. There was no need. The bottom line was that on occasion, Sam enjoyed setting up players by pretending to be an airheaded, ultra-needy, spoiled little rich girl. By the time the players discovered the truth, it was too late.

And all because of Guy.

Guy Carrington was the man who had caused what should have been Sam's beautiful wedding day to end disastrously when two women showed up, claiming they were Guy's other women . . . and with babies in tow—three of them. Talk about baby-mama-drama. Mackenzie wasn't sure who'd screamed the loudest—Sam, her mother, the women, or the babies. Luckily, all of that had taken place before Sam had gotten the chance to say "I do," so instead she'd said, "I don't," and had been a true-blue player-hater ever since.

Deciding to avoid the subject of Sam's love life or lack thereof, Mackenzie said, "So, what brings you to my office? Don't tell me you've run out of cases."

Sam grinned. "Not on your life. I met with Amanda Johnson today and she's determined to go ahead and bring a lawsuit against that dealership for selling her that car knowing the speedometer had been tampered with."

Mackenzie nodded. "If they were smart they would try and settle out of court."

"That's the problem, they aren't smart. So how are things going on the Whitedyer case?"

Mackenzie shrugged. "We're waiting for the judge to set a date for the initial hearing and I'm hoping it will be sometime next week. The sooner we can take it to court, the better." And then she asked, "Where's Peyton?"

"She had a lunch meeting with one of her clients. And speaking of lunch, what are your plans?" Sam asked as she slid off the desk to stand.

"Haven't made any."

Sam smiled. "In that case, how about if we go and grab something at that deli on the corner?"

"Sounds good but I can't eat much," Mackenzie said, opening a desk drawer to pull out her purse. "Luke prepares dinner every evening. He's good at making casseroles."

"You're lucky he's making something. Some men wouldn't think of lifting a finger in the kitchen. They would expect us to come home and throw something together after working all day." Sam then gave a suggestive grin and said, "You might want to keep him around."

Mackenzie stood and led the way out of her office. "And I've told you a dozen times that he's moving on as soon as he's better," she threw over her shoulder.

"And I've told you that if I were you, I'd do whatever I could to make him change his mind."

Mackenzie looked at Sam when they reached the door that led out of the building. "I have no reason to do that."

"Umm," Sam said, giving Mackenzie a serious smile. "It wouldn't hurt if you were to think of a few."

The person sitting on the bus stop bench put down the newspaper he had pretended to be reading when the two women walked by. He leaned over to ask his companion, "Which one?"

The companion smiled and said, "The one in the brown pantsuit."

"You sure?"

"Positive."

The person nodded before tossing the newspaper into a garbage bin nearby. The two individuals then stood and parted ways.

Chapter 10

Luke nodded into the phone for the umpteenth time before he finally got a chance to say, "Yes, ma'am, Mama Laverne, I won't overdo anything and I promise not to return to playing cowboy until the doctor says I'm good and ready."

He couldn't help but smile when his great-grandmother began talking again, trying to call the shots all the way from Houston. He loved the old girl dearly. She was the matriarch of the Madaris family and one tough lady who kept everyone in tow . . . at least she tried. It might have been easy with the second generation of Madarises—the grands, namely his father and all those older cousins like Justin, Dex, and Clayton, but he knew she definitely had her work cut out for her with those in his age group, the great-grands who were the Madaris new wave.

He couldn't help but think of the family legacy his great-grandparents, Milton and Felicia Laverne Madaris, had started so many years ago with their seven sons— Milton Jr., Lee, Nolan, Lucas, Robert, Jonathan, and Jake. After Poppa Milton's death, Mama Laverne had raised her sons while overseeing the huge family spread, Whispering Pines. All her sons were alive and healthy except for Robert who had gotten killed in the Vietnam War.

Luke was proud of his family; always had been and always would be. They were a close-knit group who were taught to look out for one another.

"Luke, are you listening to me?"

Luke felt guilty because in all honesty, although he had heard her words, he hadn't been listening "Yes, ma'am, I *heard* every word," he said.

"So, you do agree it's time for you to settle down with a wife and children?"

Luke almost dropped the phone "No, ma'am, I don't agree with that. I love my life just the way it is. I don't need a wife and children. I plan to do like Uncle Jake and wait until I get into my forties before thinking about marrying" He smiled. "Heck, I might even wait until I'm fifty."

"Need I remind you that Jake was married for a short while years before Diamond?"

"Yeah, but as far as I'm concerned, it didn't last long enough to be considered a marriage. Hell, I never laid eyes on the woman. None of his nieces and nephews in my generation did. So as far as we're concerned he was a single man until he married Diamond. Marrying late seems to have merits."

He breathed in deeply and was tempted to hold the phone away from his ear when she began giving him a blistering and scolding retort. But he couldn't do anything but stand there and take it like a man As soon as he was able to get a word in he told her he had to use the bathroom, expressed how much he loved her, and quickly ended the call.

Moments later he found himself pacing the floor waiting for Mac to come home. Usually she arrived like clockwork around eight o'clock, saying she preferred remaining at the office finishing up everything instead of bringing any work home to do. He wasn't all that crazy about her working late, especially since the police hadn't gotten any leads on the person responsible for ransacking her office. However, he had felt relieved after she'd informed him that she, Sam, and Peyton had hired a security guard to be there whenever they worked late. Also, those two police officers had agreed to patrol the area more. But still, she wasn't home yet and it was eight-ten already.

He stopped pacing and rubbed his hand down his face. Why was he feeling so antsy about seeing Mac? Had that kiss they'd shared yesterday affected his brain cells or something? Although he usually thought about her every day, today had been worse than usual. She had been on his mind practically every second.

She hadn't been aware of it but he'd been awake when she had left that morning and he had stood by the bedroom window and watched her leave. She had looked real nice in her brown pantsuit, a pillar of professionalism. But what he liked most about the pantsuit was the way it had emphasized the soft curves on her body. And they were curves that he very much wanted to become acquainted with.

He took a deep breath when he heard a car door slam and couldn't force back the smile that touched his lips. Mac was home.

Mackenzie entered her home and gasped when Luke suddenly appeared seemingly out of nowhere. She placed her hand over her chest to slow down the rapid beating of her heart. "Luke! My goodness. Why were you standing by the door?"

"I've been waiting for you to come home."

Her eyes widened fractionally. "You've been waiting for me? Why?"

"For this," he said, reaching out and stroking her jaw, just seconds before tilting her chin up and lowering his mouth to hers.

The moment their mouths connected Mackenzie dropped her briefcase to the floor and wrapped her arms around Luke's neck. She hadn't expected this, but she definitely planned to take full advantage. She had thought about their kiss most of the day. In fact when Sam had walked into her office and teased her about the nonexistent hickey, she had been thinking about it.

Now she was getting another kiss to think about tomorrow Wow! Is this how it was when you truly bonded with someone? Was married to that person? Coming home and being greeted at the door with a kiss was certainly a pretty nice benefit.

What was even nicer was the time he was taking to kiss her. He wasn't doing a rush job but was drawing things out with every lick, suck, and entanglement of their tongues. And she was plastered so close to him that she could feel every tight muscle on his masculine frame.

There was no doubt in her mind that Luke Madaris was an experienced kisser. The man certainly had a way with his tongue. It had to be a gift. Even now she could hear the tiny whimpers coming from deep within her throat and could feel the heat throbbing all through her body. And she could feel the deep pounding of her heart in her chest and the hardening of her nipples.

Finally, he lifted his head, just barely, and went for her neck, placing soft kisses there, and she knew she would definitely have a hickey tomorrow because she felt the exact moment he branded her.

The thought of him claiming her that way sent shivers up her spine, and when he captured her mouth again, she became the aggressor and began stroking her tongue inside his mouth, using that same erotic technique he had used on her earlier, and felt a moment of satisfaction when she heard his deep guttural groan. When he lifted his head this time it was to rest his forehead against hers and take several deep breaths.

"What was that all about?" she asked, barely able to get the words out.

He pulled back slightly and let his gaze roam over her face, focusing on her just-kissed lips. She could feel it like it was a caress. "It was about the fact that I missed you today."

That was good to hear because she had missed him too. But she was still curious. "Why today?"

He shrugged and then smiled and that smile caused

ripples of sensation to pass through her. And it didn't help matters that he looked good in his jeans, shirt, and bare feet. "It must have been that kiss yesterday," he said, placing kisses at the corners of her lips. "I couldn't think of anything else most of the day."

She was surprised he would admit such a thing and decided to see if it was true that confessions were good for the soul. "Same here. I couldn't think of anything else most of the day either." There, she had said it. She had admitted it. And the comprehension of what she'd done was like a huge awakening of some sort.

"Only thing about kissing, Mac," he leaned in and murmured in a deep, husky voice close to her ear, "is that sometimes it's not enough. There has to be more, and desiring more can lead to other things."

She knew what he was saying; what he was hinting at. Yesterday he had asked her if she was ready to take their relationship to another level and she'd said no. Today she still wasn't ready, although she was definitely feeling it more than yesterday.

"Come on, dinner is waiting for you," he said, taking her hand and leading her toward the kitchen. She adjusted her stride to keep up with his slow pace. She could tell he was improving since his limp was becoming a lot less noticeable.

"Umm, another casserole?" she asked as they passed through the living room.

He smiled over at her. "No. I found out from Theo what your favorite meal is."

Her eyes lit up. Theo would know. "Did he say pork chops smothered in thick gravy over wild rice?" she asked excitedly.

Luke chuckled before leaning down and placing a quick kiss on her lips. "Yes, that's exactly what he said, so wash up while I put dinner on the table."

Mackenzie couldn't help but smile as she headed toward the bathroom. She wasn't sure what was going on in

Luke's mind, just what his intent was. But if he was trying to impress her then he was doing a pretty good job at it

Whispering Pines Ranch

Jake Madaris glanced up from reading the documents in front of him when the sound of his office door opening caught his attention. He smiled at the beautiful woman who walked in. Tossing the papers aside he got to his feet.

"The kids are tucked in?" he asked as he reached for her, thinking she always managed to look sexy even without really trying.

Diamond Swain Madaris went to him, walking straight into her husband's embrace. "Yes, but they're waiting for you to come in and say good night."

"I will after this."

Without any preliminaries, for no particular reason, he leaned down and captured the mouth of the woman he loved to distraction. The kiss filled him with exhilaration, it was one of passion and as usual it was one that sent his heart into overdrive.

"Umm, what have I done to deserve such ardent attention, Jacob?" she asked, arching her body even closer to his when he reluctantly broke off the kiss.

Jake chuckled softly, knowing her question was a joke, because he always gave her attention, anyplace and anytime. He loved and adored his wife and didn't care who knew it. But then a number of men loved and adored her as well since she was one of the most successful, as well as popular, actresses in the country. And he could proudly claim this very beautiful and sexy woman as his. She was his wife, lover, best friend, partner in a number of business ventures, and the mother of his children—six-year-old Granite and three-year-old Amethyst.

"Just because you're you," he murmured huskily close to her ear.

"Oh. In that case . . ." She wrapped her arms around his neck and on tiptoe joined his mouth back with hers. And when he slid his tongue deep inside her mouth he could actually feel her body ooze into his like hot, melted solder. And like before, a shudder passed through him.

Moments later when she leaned away from him, she smiled into his eyes and whispered, "And that, Jacob, was because you are *you*."

He gave a low laugh and pulled her into his arms, liking the feel of having her there as aways. There was a time he'd thought the ranch was all he'd ever need but she had proven him wrong.

The ring of the phone intruded and without removing his hand from around her waist he used the other hand to reach across his desk to answer it. "Hello."

"Jake, this is Rasheed."

A smile touched Jake's lips. Sheik Rasheed Valdemon was someone Jake considered a friend. "Rasheed, how are you?"

"I'm doing well. Did I call at a bad time?"

Jake's hand moved from around Diamond's waist to glide up and down the length of her spine before returning to curve around her waist, pulling her even closer to him. He kissed one corner of her lips before saying to Rasheed, "No, in fact it's a *good* time. What's up?"

"I'll be visiting your country again in a couple of weeks and was wondering if I could stay at the cabin for a few days. I need time alone to contemplate an important decision I need to make."

Jake's eyes scanned Diamond's features and zeroed in on her lips before speaking into the phone. "Sounds serious."

"It is one of the most serious decisions I'll be making in my entire lifetime."

Jake lifted a brow and swiftly switched his concentration to the call. "In that case, the cabin is yours for as long as you need it, my friend. I'll make the arrangements. It will be well stocked when you get here."

"Thanks, Jake."

After hanging up the phone Jake pulled Diamond even closer into his arms, smiled, and said, "The sheik is coming for a visit."

Chapter 11

"So, what do you think?" Luke asked.

Mackenzie lifted her gaze from her plate and glanced over at him and smiled. And not for the first time, nor the second, he thought she had beautiful eyes. Ebony eyes. Deep, dark, and sexy. They were the kind a man would want to be looking into while reaching an orgasm of the most intense kind. The kind a man would want to wake up to each and every morning.

He swallowed deeply. Hell, why would he think of something like that? He wasn't someone who contemplated a future of waking up beside a woman in the mornings.

"I think you're wasting your time on the rodeo circuit. You'd fit perfectly in anyone's kitchen, Luke. Evidently, you were one of your great-grandmother's most ardent students."

With difficulty he transferred his attention off her eyes and back to the conversation. He couldn't stop the smile that touched his lips. "No, in fact on several occasions she almost kicked me out of the cooking classes. Blade was her most devoted student."

He watched her lift perfectly arched brows. "Blade?"

"Yes. He figured he could use the expertise of how to whip up a good meal as a tool of seduction."

Now it was her time to smile and the one she bestowed upon him sent sensations straight to his gut. And before his stomach could recover she picked up her wine glass and took a sip. He couldn't help how his gaze zeroed in on her lips and the way they touched the rim of the glass, reminding him of how those same lips had been devoured by his mouth earlier.

"And I thought it was men who loved women who could cook and not the other way around," she said, putting the glass back in place beside her plate.

Luke grinned. "Blade figured anything was possible and wanted to cover all bases."

She studied her plate for a moment before lifting her gaze and asking, "Do you think Blade will ever settle down and get married?"

Luke chuckled. "Well, I wouldn't put my money on that happening any time soon. He's determined to remain a devout bachelor and break Uncle Jake's record as the oldest Madaris to ever marry. Some of us in the family don't consider his first marriage as valid since it didn't last that long."

She nodded. "And what about you, Luke? What do you plan to do in regards to marriage?"

He met her gaze thinking that question was the perfect opening for a conversation he needed to have with her. He knew what he wanted from her and he also knew the parameters he intended to stay within to achieve his goal. "I plan to give Blade a good run for his money for that same record. In other words, I don't plan to marry until I'm too old to sit on the back of a horse."

There, he'd said it. Directly to her. She had heard it straight from him. There could not be any misunderstandings about expectations. No misconstrued notions or wrong assumptions. If she was a woman with marriage on her mind he had just informed her that he was not a candidate. Prime or otherwise.

She looked away from him to gaze out the window before returning her eyes to meet his. She smiled lightly and said softly, "I feel the same way, Luke. Although for me, my ability to sit on a horse won't be the determining factor for marriage." She then went back to eating her meal.

He should have been overjoyed at her words since it took a lot of the pressure off. But still, he picked up his wine glass and asked, "What will be the determining factor?"

She shrugged and lifted her gaze again and he immediately felt sensual awareness skitter across his skin to the extent that it felt like a physical caress. He broke eye contact with her to glance down at his arm, just to make sure he was imagining things. Satisfied that he was, he glanced back at her and still felt that pull, that unexplained electrical charge that floated across the table between them. By the darkening of her eyes he suspected that she felt it too, but he doubted she would mention it.

She tossed her head back as if that act alone would negate what was taking place between them. For what it was worth, he believed that sexual tension was sexual tension and for them it seemed to be all over the place. "I'm not sure there's a determining factor," she finally responded. "I discovered five years ago that love isn't all that it was cracked up to be."

He didn't say anything for a moment and then he leaned back in the chair and decided it was time to ask. "Who was he?"

"He?"

"Yes, *he*. The man responsible for making you feel that way."

Mackenzie felt her heart lurch in response to Luke's question.

"Why do you want to know? He doesn't concern you."

Luke gave her a smile that didn't quite reach his eyes. "I disagree. He does concern me. Even after five years, his memory . . . or his nightmare is the reason I can't make it to first base with you."

Mackenzie broke eye contact with him to glance out the window again. He was so wrong. He'd already made first base, even second, and was slowly inching his way toward third. But the problem for him was the fact that she would not let him make it to home base. He would strike out before that happened.

"It's no big deal," she said, and regretted the words the moment she'd said them. The lifting of his brows reminded her that she had declared those words off limits to him, and so he was declaring the same for her.

"Let me be the judge of that, Mac."

For whatever reason, she decided to let him be just that. Maybe then he would understand the depth of her reluctance . . . her refusal to let another man into her life, the way Lawrence had gotten into it and messed it up. She pushed her plate aside, took another sip of her wine, and then leaned back in her chair. To relax. Share her soul. Relive her pain.

"His name is Lawrence Dixon and we met the first day I began working for the Rivers, Salvatore, and Graham law firm in Baton Rouge, right out of law school. I felt lucky to have been chosen to work for such a prestigious firm. Lawrence was already employed there, working his way up to the top toward a partnership in a few years. I thought he was brilliant, intelligent beyond reason, debonair to a fault, and handsome as sin."

She chuckled slightly. "He probably won cases just on his looks alone. He could walk into a courtroom and grab the attention of any woman there. And usually he did. I was young, inexperienced, and felt totally elated that I was the one to capture his interest. We dated for two years."

Luke nodded. "What happened?"

Mackenzie sighed deeply. Even after revealing all of that history, she actually considered not telling him. Not that it was still too awfully painful, but because a part of her was somehow convinced she should have seen the signs. How could a man be involved with two women and the other not know it? "What happened is that I discovered there was another woman. The kicker is that I didn't make that discovery until a few weeks before his wedding to her. She lived in Dallas so she never had reason to drop into the office unexpectedly. And he knew exactly when she would be coming to town. For him it was very simple to rearrange our schedule to make it work for them. I was very flexible. And she was very rich. All I had to offer him was my heart. She could offer him a place in her father's law firm, the possibility of a political career, and to be set financially for the rest of his life. He grabbed all that over love."

"That was almost five years ago. I assume right before we met that night."

"Yes. Standfield, Di Meglio, and Mahoney had only been open a few months. That bit I handled for Ashton that night in Houston at the auction had been the firm's first official assignment."

"And you haven't seen or heard from the guy since?" Luke asked.

She smiled weakly. "I've run into him a few times at several law conferences, but I've managed to avoid speaking to him directly. And he calls me from time to time just to gloat whenever he wins a big case."

"He never talked about the two of you getting back together?"

"No, that would have been impossible anyway. I can forgive and forget some things and others I can't. Besides, he needs to show himself as a dedicated family man."

"Why?"

"Because it's my understanding from mutual friends that he's thinking about running for political office in Texas. He hasn't officially announced his candidacy, but they expect him to."

Sighing deeply, she ran a hand through her hair, pushing a bang off her forehead. "So there you have it, Luke Madaris, the story of my love life and the end of it as well."

"I don't think so."

She watched his eyes light up in a challenge as he pushed his chair back and stood. "Dixon is something that I definitely am not," he said in a husky tone as he came around the table.

She tilted her head back to look up at him as he stood beside her chair, purposely invading her space. The depths of his dark eyes were filled with so much intensity it almost took her breath away; and the broad, muscular shoulders beneath his shirt were provoking images in her mind and she'd rather not go there. Especially since they were naked images.

"And what is he that you're not?" she asked, forcing the words from between lips she wanted to use to kiss the underside of his jaw with instead.

"A fool."

To Luke's way of thinking, his statement had left Mac at a loss for words, and for a heartbeat of a moment, his dark eyes locked with her darker ones. She said she wasn't ready to move forward into an affair with him, but he planned to continue his crusade to get her there. By the time they shared a bed, which he figured would be sooner rather than later, she would be wondering why it took them so long.

"Have you been intimate with anyone since Dixon, Mac?"

Taking a deep breath, she said in an agitated tone, "Do you think that's any of your business?"

He smiled and thought if she only knew. It seemed that he would have to break it down to her. "Yes, I'm making it my business. So have you?"

Reluctant to admit the truth, Mackenzie didn't say anything for a moment and then she said, "No."

He smiled. "That's good."

The man was confusing her. "And just why is that good?" she asked. As soon as the question was spoken she wished there was some way she could take it back. Especially when she saw the heated desire that suddenly formed in his eyes.

"It's good because I plan on giving you a taste of passion that's almost five years overdue. I'm talking about real passion, Mac. The kind that will get you as ready for an involvement with me as you'd ever be."

Chapter 12

Mackenzie's eyebrows rose, thinking Luke couldn't be serious. How had they gone from building friendship instead of a relationship to tasting passion? She took a deep breath. He looked serious. Dead serious. That meant it was time for her to set him straight.

"Didn't you hear anything I've said? Were you not listening to what I shared with you about Lawrence? If not, then let me spell things out for you, Luke. I don't do casual involvements. I detest affairs. At this stage of my life I'm not even interested in happily-ever-after. I don't need a man to sustain. I've gotten set in my ways. I like not having to worry about raised toilet seats, stinky socks, or dishes left in the sink—although I will admit that since being here you've proven that not all men are guilty of those things. But still, the fact remains that I like my life the way it is. Don't you?"

He was still towering over her. And he was frowning. "Don't I what?"

She rolled her eyes. "Don't you like your life the way it is?"

"Sure."

"Well, then. The same holds true for me."

"But I will admit that I do need a woman every once in a while," he said.

Mackenzie chewed on the inside of her lip thinking

she really wasn't surprised. "Only because you probably have a high testosterone level."

"Are you saying that in the past five years you've never desired a man, Mac?"

Mackenzie broke eye contact with him to look out the window again. How could she explain that, in essence, she hadn't until the night she had gone to that Brothers Auction and had seen *him*? Seeing him hadn't really made her realize what she'd been missing, because in all honesty, once she had the chance to sit back and analyze her two-year relationship with Lawrence, she saw that their sex life had left a lot to be desired. What meeting Luke had done that night was open her eyes to all the possibilities and a whole lot of fantasies. But being the responsible and logical person that she was, she had eventually put both the possibilities and fantasies out of her mind. She felt if there actually were such things as red-hot passion, multiple orgasms, and all-night marathons, she was better off not knowing about them.

"Mac?"

She met Luke's gaze and eased her chair back and stood up. "It's getting late, Luke. I have to go to work in the morning and I still need to meet with Theo tonight as well as help you clean up the kitchen."

He crossed his arms over his chest and gave her an agitated look. "You're not going to give me an answer?"

She mimicked his stance by crossing her arms over her chest as well. "No, because it's really none of your business, no matter how you've convinced yourself that it is. My life—with or without a man—is my life. And whether I desire one or not is *my* business."

She made a move to walk around him and he reached out and touched her arm. She immediately felt the sizzle, the heat, and the sensual sensations that injected through her body from his touch. She drew back and shot accusing eyes at him. "What are you doing?"

"Proving a point," he said, taking a step closer to her. "What you just felt is sexual chemistry of the most potent kınd. You desire me, Mac, the same way I desire you. You can't deny ıt."

Mackenzıe nervously licked her bottom lip and knew that, no, she couldn't deny ıt. Not when the object of her desire was rıght here, staring her in the face in the form of Luke Madaris. She suddenly realızed just how close they were standıng, and how heat seemed to be radıating from his body straıght to hers. And then there was his masculine aroma. All male.

"Mac?"

She met his gaze and then wished she hadn't. His eyes had darkened and the sound of his voıce was deep and husky. Their bodies were close. Not too close but close enough. "Just what do you want me to say, Luke?" she asked shortly.

"What you know is the truth," he supplied easily.

She still wasn't sure that was the best thing. "But why does ıt matter to you? You admitted earlier that you're not looking for anythıng long-term."

"Yes, and you admitted to that same thing. You even said you don't want happily-ever-after. Make no mistake about ıt, Mac, I don't want happıly-ever-after either. Maybe I wıll someday in the distant future, but no time soon and definitely not before I'm fifty."

He took a step closer and she felt his solıd muscular form press against her. She forced herself not to breathe in sharply, not to let hım get next to her. But it was too late. He had gotten next to her and from the look in his eyes she could tell he knew that very fact.

"I'm not asking any woman to wait for me, so what I'm saying is that anything we share has to be short-term," he continued. "I'm already married to the rodeo so when I leave to return to ıt, things between us will be over. If and when you do decıde that you're ready, all we'd be embarking on ıs an affair to satisfy our needs and wants. To work each other out of our systems. We can both honestly admit there has always been this burning fire between us. Don't you thınk it's time to put it out? And will you be able to handle an affair that you know won't have a future? One where I won't make you any promises?"

Mackenzie knew things couldn't get any plainer than that. In other words, Luke was telling her in frank terms that he was not the marrying kind. But she had already admitted that she wasn't looking for anything long-term. And he was right. Although she didn't engage in casual affairs, five years was a long time to go without sharing intimacy with a man. Her body did have needs. She felt them each and every time she dreamed about Luke. So why was she hesitating? Why not jump into an affair this one time with him? An affair that would end the moment he walked out the door to return to the rodeo world. What was stopping her?

The answer was simple and she was faced with it each and every time their gazes met. She had fallen in love with him. It wouldn't do any good to try and figure out when it happened. The bottom line was that it had happened. Bigtime. And the one thing she was faced with admitting was that life was short. It could be taken away from you at a moment's notice. Luke could have lost his life when that bull had tried to attack him. So why not have an affair with him? Why deny herself the very thing she wanted, the very person she loved? The one man who could make her life totally complete . . . even if it would only be for a little while.

"Fine, I see you're still not ready to make any decisions," Luke said, interrupting her thoughts and taking a step back.

He was about to walk away when she reached out and placed her hand on his arm. Immediately, she felt the heat gathering in a hot and sensuous rush in the lower part of her body. Their gazes locked and desire was sprinting through her just as fast and furious as the blood that was gushing through her veins. But she kept her hand on him when she said, "I *am* ready."

As if he needed to make sure they were talking about the same thing, he asked her, "And just what are you ready for, Mac?"

She was ready for her hands to touch him all over. Ready for her tongue to taste the passion he had promised, and ready for her body, which seemed to suddenly develop this intense hunger for him to get satisfied.

"What I'm ready for, Luke," she answered in a quiet yet clear and distinctive voice, "is you."

Chapter 13

As far as Luke was concerned, Mackenzie didn't have to say any more than that. However, to be certain she knew what being ready for him meant, just what it entailed, and to what degree she affected him, he reached out and eased his arms around her waist before shifting them lower to close over her bottom. He then urged their bodies closer and watched her eyes widen with the evidence of his arousal pressed hard against her stomach.

"I've been concentrating on winning the title back this year so it's been a while for me too," he explained in a low voice.

And because he knew she probably wouldn't ask, he said, in a lower voice still, "Almost a full year." He decided not to mention that he hadn't touched a woman since he'd seen her last at the Madaris family reunion. For some reason he hadn't wanted to.

And because he thought they had done enough talking for a while, he lowered his head and let his tongue sweep across her lower lip before boldly sliding into her mouth. He felt the exact moment a shiver raced through her body. His heart was pounding in his chest. And when he deepened the kiss, a voracious sensation erupted in his gut and he responded by kissing her with a hunger he had never known before. Her mouth seemed to open wider and he took advantage by tasting every area of it that his tongue could touch. He captured her tongue, entwined it with his, sucked on it hard.

He reluctantly dragged his mouth away and took a step back to roam his eyes over her, seeing how good she looked in her pantsuit and thinking of the quickest way to get her out of it.

"Luke?"

He glanced down into her face and saw the question in her eyes. "I want you naked."

He doubted he needed to explain further. She had to be fully aware that the air surrounding them had thickened and the temperature had risen a notch.

"Uh, Luke, we're in the kitchen."

He smiled. "I know. What better place to cook up a little heat? What better place to give you your first taste of *real* passion?" It might be a bit presumptuous on his part to assume Dixon hadn't fulfilled his job in that area, but he had a gut feeling the man had failed miserably. Luke could tell by the way Mac had returned his kiss. It was as if she weren't sure how far she could go, and he intended to show her there were no limitations.

With a blush visible on her cheeks, she tilted her head at an angle that would hold his gaze. He watched as she slowly began unbuttoning the suit jacket to reveal a chocolate-brown colored camisole underneath. She let her arms slide out of the sleeves of the jacket and held it in her hand while she pulled the camisole over her head. He tried to remain calm and in control, but felt his body throb all the way to his bare feet when moments later she tossed both items of clothing aside, clad only in her pants and a chocolate-brown bra.

Even with the lace bra covering her breasts he could tell they were perfect, full and firm, and would be a total delight for any man's hands and mouth. He could just imagine stroking his finger all around them ever so lightly before lowering his head and replacing his fingers with his mouth, taking a nipple between his lips and having his way with it.

His gaze shifted lower when she dropped her hand to her waist to unsnap her pants and he struggled to keep his ragged breathing under control.

"How am I doing, Luke?"

He jerked his head back up to her face. It was hard to get air through his lungs as he said, "You're cooking rather nicely. Trust me. I don't have any complaints about how this meal is going to turn out."

She smiled as she stepped out of her shoes and kicked them aside. "Glad to hear it."

His gaze then lowered to her hands as she eased the pants down her hips, thighs, and legs. She stepped out of them and for a moment he nearly lost his breath. She was standing directly in front of him, in the middle of her kitchen, wearing nothing but her bra and matching panties—and a very sexy pair at that.

"Should I stop now?"

"No." The word sliced through the air.

At her raised brow, he said in a low, husky tone, "Please continue."

And she did while steadily holding his gaze. He leaned against the kitchen counter for support, fearful he would lose his balance when she tossed her bra and panties aside. He could only stand there with his hands in the pockets of his jeans and stare. She had to be the most beautiful woman ever created. Her breasts were so flawless that he wondered why she bothered wearing a bra and the dark area between her thighs had his entire body throbbing.

"Are you interested in joining me in the bedroom?" she asked in a quiet voice.

Oh, he was interested all right but he doubted he could make it that far. He wanted her now. "Come over here, Mac."

They silently stared at each other a moment before she took her first step. When she began walking toward him he withdrew his hands from his pockets and pushed away from the counter. His gaze continued to roam all over her, zeroing in on the area between her legs. Never had he seen anything so beautiful and thought of all the things he wanted to do there. He groaned just thinking about them.

When she came to a stop in front of him, she reached out and grabbed the front of his shirt She then looked up into his eyes and said in a seductive voice, "You called, Luke?"

Oh, yeah, he had called all right. Now if he could only get out of his clothes real quick and in a hurry. But first . . .

He leaned toward her mouth and she opened it the moment their lips touched. He immediately deepened the kiss, went on a taste frenzy, almost gobbling her up, practically devouring her. His mouth was hot and hungry, the taste of her was driving him wild, nearly insane. The thought of making love to her had him weak in the knees. Her scent filled his nostrils, made him want to taste her all over.

She drew back from the kiss and whispered, "Now you're the one who needs to get naked."

He had no problem with that and nearly ripped the buttons on his shirt trying to take it off. He tossed it aside and then sucked in a quick breath when she leaned down and kissed the area of his chest that displayed a bruise from his injury. She then lifted her head, met his gaze, and said in a soft tone, "I'm sorry you got hurt, Luke."

The sincerity in her words made an ache that he couldn't define ruffle his emotions. He had to clamp down on his lips to keep from saying something really stupid, such as he wasn't the least bit sorry because if he hadn't gotten hurt he would not be here with her. Although he wouldn't say it, he was thinking it and that was just as bad.

Needing to get out of his jeans quick, he went for the belt, unbuckled it, and eased it through the loops before placing it on the counter. He then took the condoms that he'd placed in his back pocket earlier and put them on the counter as well.

He saw her gaze at the condom packet and then waited for her to say something, but she didn't. Instead her attention was drawn back to his hands and how they were easing down his zipper.

His gut tightened at the way she was licking her lips. He didn't want to think about what that could possibly mean. In fact, he thought it best to eradicate that thought real fast or he wouldn't be able to slide the zipper down over his erection.

"Need help?"

He was tempted to tell her that, yes, he needed help but decided this time around he would do it for himself. He would give her the same kind of strip show she'd given him. "Thanks, but I'll manage."

And he did. He heard her sharp intake of breath when he eased the zipper down and, like a Jack-in-the-Box, his erection, not hindered by any type of underwear, sprang forth like it had been eager to be freed from the constraints of his tight jeans.

He smiled when he felt himself getting harder. "It has no shame."

"Umm, I can see that."

Luke removed his jeans and straightened his body just seconds before reaching out and pulling her to him, capturing her mouth and devouring her like she was his dessert. He touched her bottom. The feel of her soft skin beneath his fingers only escalated his arousal, which was pressing into her stomach, desperate like heck to get inside of her.

When he knew he couldn't take any more, he broke off the kiss and snatched a condom pack off the counter and proceeded to put it on, aware that she was watching. Finished, he looked up at her.

He noticed how she released a slow breath before asking, "Now what?"

He couldn't help but grin at the thought that she had to ask. Instead of answering he grabbed a chair and eased his naked body down into it. At her bemused expression he met her gaze and said, "And now, Mackenzie Standfield, you get a chance to ride."

Chapter 14

Was he kidding?

Mackenzie studied Luke's face and then decided apparently he wasn't. He was in her kitchen, sitting wide legged in a chair as naked as naked could be, fully aroused and she meant fully, with a look on his face that all but asked . . . *What are you waiting for?*

And that was a good question given the fact the area between her legs had begun to tingle, not to mention he was sitting there looking incredibly sexy, undeniably hot, and definitely ready. He came across as every bit of a rugged cowboy, untamed, virile, and edible. Yes, he was definitely Luscious Luke.

"Now it's my time to ask if you need help," he said.

His words brought her attention back to the matter at hand and her gaze automatically went to his lap. She hadn't known they made them *that* big. As if he'd read her mind, he said, "You can handle it."

She wished she could say his faith in her abilities was reassuring but it wasn't. He wasn't the one who hadn't been sexually active for five years.

"That's why I'm letting you do the riding, Mac, so you'll have full control. I'll be at *your* mercy," he went on to say.

Luscious Luke at her mercy? Now that was a thought and a very hot one. Deciding she had wasted enough time, she slowly moved toward him. When she came to a stop in front of his legs, their gazes held and her nipples hardened and he reached up and placed his arms at her waist before saying in a husky voice, "Come on, babe. Straddle me."

She glanced down. The thought of doing what he asked sent sensuous chills through her body and without hesitating further she eased into his lap facing him, and knotted her hands in his shoulders. He deliberately shifted to place his erection right at her feminine opening, but went no further.

He stared down at their bodies and then lifted his gaze to meet hers again. "I'm going inside of you now," he said in a low, husky voice. "Ready?"

Instead of speaking, she nodded. Already she felt her body getting hot from the feel of her bare thighs clamping his waist and her breasts pressing into his chest. Lawrence had been of the mind that any type of lovemaking should be restricted to the bedroom. It was plain to see that his and Luke's opinions differed vastly on that notion.

Slowly Luke began easing into her and she felt how her body began to stretch to accommodate him. It wasn't easy. Several times he had to stop along the way, breathing in deep before starting again. She knew he was trying not to hurt her and she appreciated the effort. She watched his features, saw the tension in his face the deeper he tried to go. Sweat was forming on his forehead and his lower lip was quivering. Knowing the reason he was making it such a long-drawn-out process was because of her, she decided to help speed things up by pushing him over the edge— just a little.

She leaned in closer and took her tongue and licked his lips at the same time she squeezed his shoulders.

"What do you think you're doing?" he asked through clenched teeth while glaring straight into her eyes.

She met his gaze and said, "Helping." And then without wasting any more time she forced her body down on him and gasped sharply when he penetrated her to the hilt.

He cursed low but she still heard it. "Why did you do

something like that, Mac? You could have gotten hurt, bruised inside," he said, frowning fiercely.

She inhaled deeply, not believing what she'd done. Overwhelmed by the feel of him inside her so deep, and the way her body had taken him in, as if inside of her was where he belonged.

His hand was gripping her hips in a tight hold and she glanced down and saw how they were intimately joined. It was then that she lifted her gaze back to his face to answer his question "The reason I did it was because you were taking too long and I'm ready to ride."

And before he could draw his next breath, she began moving.

"Shit."

Now *that* she heard clearly and decided he needed his mouth washed out with soap, but figured her tongue was the next best thing. So she proceeded to attack his mouth in a way that made him shudder, had him moving with her. He thrust upward with every downward stroke she made. Effortlessly he took her weight and each time she came down on him he rose high enough in the chair to take her deeper and deeper Their bodies would withdraw and then rejoin again. Over and over.

When she began riding him faster and harder, he matched her pace, which made all kinds of sensations rush through her. She moaned. He groaned. She was working him and he was definitely working her, making her feel things she had never felt before, making a driving need consume her to the point where it had every nerve inside her body, every single molecule quivering. It was as if he were unleashing a tidal wave of passion that would eventually drown her. Suddenly, she couldn't fight the raging tide any longer and jerked her mouth free of his to release one loud scream when a climax tore into her, touched her very soul while at the same time it rocked her senses into the next hemisphere.

He quickly buried her face in his chest to smother the

sound and whispered, "Easy, baby, Theo is going to think I'm killing you in here or something."

As far as Mackenzie was concerned, what Theo or anyone else thought didn't matter. The only thing that mattered at that moment was how Luke was making her feel. Her inner muscles were clamped down hard, clenching him tight. And no sooner was she able to suck air into her lungs, than she felt him buck wildly beneath her, nearly lunging out of the chair with their bodies connected when he was struck with his own intense orgasm.

"Mackenzie!"

He said her name through clenched teeth and in a guttural moan and she tightened her hold on his shoulders. And when he leaned in and kissed her with an intensity that touched her everywhere, more sensations exploded inside of her and she was hurled into another mind-shattering orgasm.

When he released her mouth her body went limp against him. She was simply amazed. Never in her life had she experienced the sensations and emotions Luke had just made her feel. If anyone had told her such feelings and emotions were possible, she would not have believed them. She was literally gasping for air, closing her eyes against the sexual aftermath that actually had her feeling light-headed.

"You okay, Mac?"

She said nothing. She couldn't get a single word out even if she'd wanted to. She barely had the strength to nod her head. Instead he made sense of her response by the motion of her hands on his shoulders.

In acknowledgment, he pulled her closer to him, not caring that their bodies were still intimately connected. And then he said her name in a low whisper just seconds before taking her mouth in a long, slow kiss that she thought she would remember for the rest of her life. In fact, she doubted she would ever forget any of what they had just shared. She loved him and memories of this moment would remain with her, keep her warm on those cold nights when he was no longer a part of her life.

Moments later he pulled back from the kiss and she immediately felt a sense of loss. But the moment she met his gaze she knew the feeling would be short-lived because Luke Madaris planned to keep them fairly close for the rest of the night.

And he proved that theory true when he leaned down to whisper against her moist lips, "Now we take it to the bedroom."

Long after Mackenzie had fallen asleep, Luke lay there holding her in his arms and staring at her while she slept. He closed his eyes and sighed heavily against the pull he felt in his gut. Even after making love to her several more times once they had made it to her bedroom, he still wanted her with a hunger that seemed insatiable.

This was the first time something like this had happened to him. Bedding a female was something to do when those male urges hit; nothing to really get caught up in to the point where you lost control. However, things hadn't been that way with Mac. He had gotten caught up to the point where he *had* lost control. One time he hadn't even remembered to put on a condom until the very last minute, for Pete's sake.

Her mouth had to be sore from all their kisses, and he was fairly certain she had used muscles that hadn't seen that kind of vigorous action in a long time, if ever. And what was with him wanting to beat on his chest like a damn caveman after every lovemaking session? Even now his leg was thrown possessively over hers, as if he didn't intend to let her go.

Their bodies were positioned so that once she awoke he could ease right on inside of her. Hell, he'd thought it would be a smart idea—as well as handy and pretty darn convenient—to go ahead and put on a condom so he wouldn't slip up and forget again.

He opened his eyes and gazed down at her thoughtfully. She had to be the most giving woman that he knew. Simply incredible. Even now his aroused body part was hard, throbbing with anticipation of making love to her again.

Knowing she needed her sleep, yet at the same time knowing he wanted to get as close to her as he could, he pulled her to him, being careful not to wake her up, and then tangled his hand in her hair. Satisfied he had her just how he wanted her, he closed his eyes and joined her in sleep.

Mackenzie slowly opened her eyes and squinted to adjust them to the light coming into her bedroom from the hallway. Her heart began pounding in her chest when she felt the heavy weight of a leg across hers and Luke's fingers in her hair. It was a good thing she didn't need to use the bathroom because if she had, she would need to free herself from Luke's hold without waking him first and she would have a tough time doing so.

To say Luke had a strong sexual appetite was an understatement. Just thinking about the intensity of it had hot sensations shooting in the area between her legs. And to think she hadn't made love to man in five years. But Luke wasn't just any man. He was the man she loved.

She looked over at him. Like her he was completely naked. As she studied his features she saw how relaxed he appeared while asleep. She then closed her eyes and recalled how earlier that night, in her kitchen, she had straddled her thighs across him in the chair. It was a good thing the chair had been made of solid wood and had been strong enough to support both their weight, as well as the action the two of them had given it. She doubted she would ever be able to walk into her kitchen without thinking about what had taken place between them there. Those memories would certainly come in handy when he left.

When he left.

There was no doubt in her mind that when he got better he would be leaving. He had told her that he would and she believed him. She knew the score when it came to Luke. He had made sure of it. He had spelled things out for her so there would not be any misunderstandings, and there wouldn't be. She had made her decision knowing how he felt, even with all the love for him she had in her heart. She realized now that what she'd felt for Lawrence had been more fascination than love. Luke was pulling emotions out of her that she'd never experienced before.

"You're awake."

She stared over at him. If she didn't know better she'd think he'd been waiting for her to do that very thing. "Yes, I'm awake."

"Good."

And then he pulled her closer and she felt him slide into her body. Automatically, she bent a knee to give him better access to what he evidently wanted. She watched his face as he went deeper inside of her and saw the satisfied smile that touched his lips when he made it to the hilt. He then tightened his leg over her as if to hold their bodies in place, locked in that position.

"I love being inside of you," he whispered.

"I gather as much. And just for the record, I like having you inside of me." She then thought of something. "Protection?"

He smiled over at her. "Already in place."

She chuckled softly. "Boy, aren't you efficient."

"I try to be." A few moments later he said, "Did I tell how much I like your breasts?"

"Not with words, no. But your actions proved that point," she said, remembering. The memory of what he'd done to them had quivers going through her body.

"Umm, but just to make sure," he said, before reaching up and cupping a breast with his hand.

Her breath caught at his touch. "I'm not sure you want to do that, Luke."

He met her gaze. "Why not? Are you tender?"

"No. Eager. I'm eager for you to put your mouth there."

He smiled. "I like a woman who doesn't mind letting me know what she wants." And then he shifted slightly and captured a nipple in his mouth and tugged.

"Luke!"

Her entire body seemed to be melting and there was no
way he couldn't feel it. But he kept up what he was doing,
performing all kinds of provocative acts to her breasts
with his mouth. He then switched breasts and started the
torture all over again.

"Now to put the icing on the cake," he whispered moments later, when the lower part of his body began moving
as he began thrusting back and forth into her. The man was
tearing away at her senses, overloading her body with sharp
sensations. His hands were on her, touching her, pressing
her closer to him, keeping her in tune to the rhythm he had
set. And when she felt him buck, she clamped down hard on
him with her inner muscles.

"Mac!"

The sound of Luke calling out her name triggered a
climax inside of her and then everything seemed to explode. His mouth left her breasts and moved to her neck
and kissed her there and she knew he had left his mark.
She moaned at the thought.

He kept thrusting inside of her, pushing them both toward another orgasm, and he took her mouth and relent-
lessly mated with it. And when another climax struck, she
knew in her heart that the day Luke Madaris walked out
of her door that he would be taking a huge chunk of her
heart with him.

Hours later when dawn broke, Mackenzie woke up in her
huge bed with Luke all but sprawled across her. She needed
to get up and go to the bathroom and there was no way she
could do so without waking him.

She glanced over at the clock. It was time for her to get
dressed for work. She sighed deeply when she recalled that
because of her and Luke's activities last night, she'd never
had the chance to check in with Theo, although she and
Luke had managed, in between lovemaking sessions, to go
back into the kitchen to collect their scattered clothes,
clean off the table, and wash the dishes.

She was about to wake up Luke when there was a loud pounding on her front door.

"What the hell . . ." Luke woke up immediately and was already out of bed and sliding into his jeans.

"Mac, it's Theo. I need to talk to you. It's important."

When Mackenzie heard the sound of Theo's voice she quickly moved out of bed and slipped into Luke's shirt. "That's Theo. I wonder what's going on."

Luke reached the door but she was right on his heels. If Theo thought it strange that they both had come to the door wearing very little clothing, it didn't show in his expression. "Theo, what is it?" Mackenzie asked, seeing the angry look in the man's eyes.

"The cattle. The ones belonging to Jake Madaris. Someone has poisoned some of the herd."

Chapter 15

"Here, Mac. Drink this."

Mackenzie stopped pacing and stood still long enough to look at Luke and the cup he held in his hand. "I don't want any coffee."

He met her eyes, saw the anger, and then said, "It's not just coffee. It's something a little stronger. Go ahead. You need it."

She placed the cup to her lips and after taking a sip she glanced up at him over the rim of the cup. "Brandy?"

A slight smile touched his lips. "Yes."

She took another sip before crossing the room to sit down on the sofa. He followed and sat down beside her and placed his arms around her shoulders.

"How could anyone do such a thing? I can't believe someone would be that—that vile," she said angrily.

He nodded, understanding just how she felt. The vet and sheriff had come and gone. The vet had confirmed the cattle had been poisoned and the only evidence the sheriff had come up was a set of tire tracks near the corral gate. All the men working at the ranch had been questioned and no one recalled hearing or seeing anything strange.

"I'm mad, Luke."

He looked at her. "I know you are."

She took another sip of coffee. "I won't be satisfied until the police find the person responsible."

"I won't either," he said, playing with a lock of her hair.

She took another sip. "You know who I think is responsible, don't you?"

"Whitedyer?"

"Yes, and I won't let them get away with it," she said, trying to get up off the sofa. His arms around her shoulders held her in place.

"Relax. And you don't have any proof."

She pulled away from him and glared. "Fine. I'll get proof and then I'll put them out of business."

She started to take another sip of coffee and then decided against it. "I forgot I need to get dressed for work," she said, placing the cup on the table in front of her.

"No you don't," he said gently. "I called Samari and explained everything."

Surprise lit Mackenzie's eyes. "You did?"

"Yes, and she told me to tell you not to come in, that she and Peyton had everything under control and to call if you needed them for anything."

Mackenzie met his gaze and for the first time since getting the news about the cattle, she smiled and Luke took a deep breath, not wanting to admit just what that smile did to him just then.

"Thanks for taking care of that—I *am* too upset to go into the office," she said.

"Figured that you would be," he said, picking up her unfinished cup of coffee and taking a sip. Then another one. "I have a suggestion," he said, putting the cup down.

"What?"

"Let's go into town and do something and—"

"No, Luke," she said, shaking her head and standing. "I have too much to do here. Besides, I need to call your uncle Jake to tell him what happened."

Luke came to his feet as well. "After you talk to Uncle Jake then you can tell me what you need me to do."

She shook her head again. "You're not completely well and—"

"No. I want to help, Mac. Let me. There has to be something I can do that's not real strenuous."

She evidently saw the determined look on his face and said, "All right. I'll check with Theo. If nothing else we need to take the stock numbers of those cattle out of the system."

She then walked across the room to look out the window and he followed her and pulled her into his arms to give her the hug that he knew she needed. Whoever was trying to get on her last nerve had gone too far. That was Madaris cattle and knowing Jake, he would be just as upset as Mac and wouldn't be satisfied until the person responsible was arrested.

The man in the dark sedan seemed extremely pleased with the phone call he'd just gotten. Now it was time to report to the person who had hired him to take care of a few matters. He punched into his cell phone the numbers that were becoming familiar to him.

"Yes?"

"We've taken care of things for now. I believe it's safe to say that we've gotten her attention."

"Okay, Luke, what is going on out there that I need to know about?" Jake Madaris asked his nephew while standing at the window in his office and looking out. He had gotten a call from Mackenzie earlier and she didn't have much to tell him other than the fact that six head of cattle had been poisoned.

"Not sure, Uncle Jake," Luke was saying. "A couple of weeks ago someone broke into Mac's office at work and ransacked the place real good, and now this. Mac thinks the two are connected and believes someone at the Whitedyer Corporation is trying to scare her off a case she's handling."

"And Mac's sure nothing was taken from her office?"

"Yes, she checked everything thoroughly the next day. They didn't even bother to take the cash box that was in one of Mac's desk drawers, so it's evident they weren't trying to take anything of value. It was as if the person wanted her to know the reason for the break-in was personal, and that's what I don't like about this whole damn thing."

For the next ten minutes Luke told his uncle everything Mackenzie had told him about the case, including why she suspected Whitedyer.

"When it comes to land rights some companies get outright foolish," Jake said. "I know Henry Whitedyer. He's a Texan and we run in the same social circles on occasion. I don't know him that well so I don't know what he's capable of doing, and I don't want to accuse him of anything, but at the same time, I don't want anyone messing with my cattle."

"I understand."

"I think I'll send a few more of my men to keep an eye on things, at least until we get that first group of cattle to the market," Jake said.

"That probably wouldn't be such a bad idea." Luke knew how astute Jake's men were. They would be quick to notice anything suspicious. Besides, he wanted assurance that Mac would be protected whether he was there or not. Right now whoever was behind this seemed satisfied with just rattling things up for Mac by indulging in mischief. But Luke was determined that it wouldn't go any further. He would tear apart anyone who tried to hurt Mac.

"While your men are here I want them to keep a close eye on things, Uncle Jake. I'm going to talk to Theo and make sure everyone stays alert in case whoever is behind this decides to turn his attention to Mac personally."

"That's a good idea," Jake said. "Has Ashton been apprised of what's happened? I think he'd want to know," Jake went on to ask.

"Not yet. He's in Houston for the summer. I tried contacting him earlier but it seems Sir Drake is in town and Ashton, Trevor, and Drake left to spend a few hours on the gun range." Trevor and Sir Drake—as he was fondly called by everyone—were friends of Ashton. The three had served in the Marines Special Forces together and were as close as any blood brothers could be. And Luke knew Trevor well since he had been a close friend of the Madarises for as long as Luke could remember.

"Well, I plan to visit soon and I'll let you know in advance as to exactly when. I promised Mom I would be coming to check on you anyway, I don't think she's taking Blade's version of how well you're doing at face value."

Luke chuckled. "I'll look forward to seeing you."

Luke hung up the phone and went in search of Mackenzie. He found her at the kitchen table knee-deep in papers. The moment he walked into the kitchen he was assaulted with pleasant memories of what had happened in this very room yesterday.

Mackenzie glanced up and met his gaze and from the look in her eyes he knew she was remembering as well. "Hey," she said, smiling over at him. "Margaret's gone?"

"Yes, she left a half hour ago." Mac had finally gotten to meet his physical therapist. Not surprisingly, she liked the woman.

"How did things go today?" she asked, pushing her papers aside.

"Pretty good. Margaret said I'm coming along nicely and she sees no reason for me not to be ready to compete in September if I continue at the rate I'm going." As he slid into the chair across from her he suddenly realized that getting better meant moving on and leaving her behind. The thought of that bothered him for some reason.

"What you got here?" he asked, glancing at the papers she had spread out.

"Research papers on other eminent domain cases. I can't believe how that law has shifted over the years."

"In what way?"

"It's amazing how many corporations have managed to take over land owned by private citizens. That was not the original intent of that law."

Luke leaned back and listened to Mac explain the law in detail and why she was determined to make sure her client wasn't taken advantage of. As he listened he couldn't help but be impressed with not only her vast knowledge of the law, but also with how dedicated she was to her client.

"This case is important, and now more than anything I can't let Whitedyer think their scare tactics are working. I've gone over these papers a dozen times but I feel there's something here that I'm missing. I only wish there was someone a little more familiar in this area, with whom I could run by some of my ideas before the hearing next week."

"May I make a suggestion?" he asked.

"Yes."

"Why not give Clayton and Syneda a call? Although their specialty is family law, I know for a fact they're well informed in other areas, even corporate law. Blade and Slade use them all the time. I'm sure they'll be glad to answer any questions you might have."

Hope shone in her eyes. "You think they will?"

"You'll never know unless you ask," he said, standing to take the cell phone out of his back pocket to hand to her. Luke knew that his cousin Clayton and his wife Syneda, a power couple if there ever was one, were fast becoming two of the most sought-after attorneys in Texas. "Go ahead and call them."

Mackenzie smiled as she took the phone from him. "I think that I will."

Syneda Madaris walked into her husband's office, and when she saw he was on the phone she sat in the chair across from his desk. He glanced over at her and smiled and then returned to the call, but only giving whoever he was conversing with part of his attention. She knew she had the other part. Just to be sure, she crossed her legs and watched the movement of his eyes. With regard to his wife he was very observant. In other words, he didn't miss a thing.

And he was definitely a good-looking man. Always had been, and the years had definitely been kind to him, overly generous was more like it. He could still turn female heads when he walked into a room. Only difference was, nowadays he didn't look back. He only had eyes for her. Just like she only had eyes for him. Pathetic? No, actually she thought it was wonderful that after nearly nine years of marriage she could still put that sparkle in his eyes, and he could make her appreciate being a woman. Anyplace and at any time. She couldn't help but smile thinking about some of those places and times. Scandalous. Exciting. Typical Clayton and Syneda.

"Hey, beautiful, you're smiling," Clayton said, interrupting her thoughts and hanging up the phone. "What's up?"

She shifted position in the chair and his gaze followed her every movement. She grinned. "I just talked to Mac."

He lifted a brow. "Ashton's Mac?"

She shook her head. "No, Luke's Mac."

"What do you mean, Luke's Mac? You talk like there's something going on between them."

She couldn't help but smile. His keen sense of observation was limited to her at times. "There is."

He leaned forward. "There is?" he asked in a disbelieving tone.

"Yes, you sound surprised."

"I am. How could I have missed that?"

"The same way you missed Alex and Christy," she said smartly, grinning at the frown that appeared just then on his face. "You need to pay attention more. There's been some interest between them ever since the night of the Brothers' Auction at Sisters."

Clayton shook his head. "Hell, the only thing I remember about that night is Corinthians going into labor."

He didn't say anything for a moment and then asked, "Hey, wait a minute. Do you know for certain that something is going on or are you just speculating?"

"Speculating, but I'm willing to bet."

"Not with my money. I need every penny to keep you and Remington in clothes. Now why was Mac calling?"

"She needs our help for a case she's working on. An eminent domain issue. It sounds interesting."

"You want to come over here and fill me in?" he asked, pushing away from his desk and patting his lap.

She laughed. "I'm fine just where I am, Madaris. Besides, sitting in your lap always gets me in trouble."

"I promise to behave."

"Ha!" she said, sending a mass of golden bronze hair flying around her shoulders. "Sweetheart, you don't know the meaning of the word."

He laughed. "Do you?"

Umm, he had her there. "No."

"Okay, then come over here and lose the skirt. And for heaven's sake, don't forget to lock the door."

She chuckled, knowing why he'd made that request. The last time their secretary had been out to lunch, but they hadn't counted on Clayton's brother Dex, who also had an office in the Madaris Building, nearly walking in on them.

"Don't you think we're getting too old for this?" she asked, getting to her feet, stepping out of her heels, and unzipping her skirt.

"No. I'll still be thinking about different ways to make love to you when I'm in a wheelchair."

Syneda smiled. She had no reason not to believe him.

Luke stood in the doorway of Mackenzie's bedroom. She had taken a shower while he was outside talking to Theo, and was now wearing her bathrobe and sitting in the middle of the bed—Indian-style—while reading something from a huge book. Seeing her affected him the way it always did.

She had the ability to stir something hot and elemental within him to the point where it became an uncontrollable blaze. Last night had been proof of that. Desire for her had raged through him, stoked an inner fire that made his need to mate with her that much more intense. She had reciprocated, hung on to him, wrapped her legs around him to lock him inside of her—as if he would actually try and go somewhere else. Hell, he had used nearly half a dozen condoms; more than he'd ever used in a single night with any woman. And he had a feeling that again tonight he would be using just that many. He needed to take her mind off things for a while and couldn't think of a better way to do it.

He moved and she glanced up. He met her eyes and instantly he felt a surge of heat flare in his stomach, which went straight to his aroused body part like an arrow finding the bull's-eye, making it throb that much more. She put the book aside when he began walking toward her. Halfway there he picked up her scent, a succulent blend of her own body chemistry and her favorite perfume.

When he stopped at the bed she tilted her head back to look up at him, and without saying a single word he lowered his head, captured her lips, and tasted her deeply with a hunger that he felt all the way to his toes. Her initial reaction had been a gasp, then a moan, and without disconnecting their mouths he eased onto the bed with her.

Driven with a need to touch her everywhere, he parted her robe and his hands automatically moved to her breasts, fondling and caressing the hardened nipples of the twin peaks before shifting downward to the swell of her hips. And then his hands glided lower to her stomach, while mating with her mouth in a way that could only be described as blatantly erotic.

Slowly, his hand left her stomach to slide downward to the hot spot between her legs. Once there his fingers gently toiled in her wetness, stroking her there while his lips bathed kisses along the base of her throat and neck.

He pulled back and removed his hand from her to adjust his body so that he was kneeling in front of her. He lowered his gaze to the feminine area exposed for his view and then back up at her eyes. He knew what he wanted to do and decided she should know as well. "I want to taste you, there," he said evocatively.

He looked back down at her and when he met her gaze

again, he added in a deep, husky voice, "Sweetheart, I want to totally devour you."

Totally devour you.

Mackenzie swallowed, not sure what she was supposed to say. No man had ever said such a thing to her . . . had never performed such an act on her. Lawrence was too traditional to ever consider such a thing. But the one thing she had discovered about Luke, especially after last night in the kitchen and later in this very bedroom, he was open-minded about doing almost anything when it came to making love.

He reached out and touched her chin and she met his gaze. From the look in his eyes she figured that somehow he knew. She wasn't sure what might have given her away. It was probably because she had yet to say anything, or it could have been the way her lashes swept up.

"I'm going to make it special. As special as I think you are."

His words held a promise that she knew he was going to fulfill and doubted she could love him any more than she did at that very moment. Her heart was pounding hard in her chest and a heated sensation was rushing through her veins. She wanted him.

"Luke . . ."

He lowered his head and she parted her lips, and then he captured her mouth in his. The soft stroke of his tongue on hers had her groaning deep in her throat, and when she felt his hand go back to her feminine core, touch her the same way he had earlier, she nearly lifted her hips off the bed.

He removed his hands from her long enough to ease the robe from her body and then, in an unexpected move, he shifted her to her stomach. Leaning over, he whispered in her ear, "Close your eyes and just feel."

And she did.

She hadn't known her flesh was so sensitive until she felt his heated tongue trace a path all over it. Starting at her upper back, he ran the tip of his tongue down the back of her neck to her collarbone and then he began tasting her, licking every inch of her skin and sending sensations she had never felt before spreading all through her. By the time he had made it down to the area just above her buttocks, she could barely lie still. It seemed every part of her that his mouth touched was damp and her limbs felt heavy.

"Luke . . ."

She was startled when she felt him place a hickey, branding her as his, right smack on her buttocks. "Now for the other side," he said, slowly flipping her over on her back.

For a moment she felt totally exposed while he slowly raked his gaze over her. "You're beautiful," he whispered hoarsely. And before she could thank him for his compliment, he lowered his mouth to kiss her. The plunge of his tongue into her mouth made heat settle between her legs, and when he pulled back to trail a kiss to her breasts she almost lost her breath.

Without wasting any time, he licked a circle around her nipple, making it wet and then gently blowing it dry. Her body quivered when he took the nipple into his mouth again, sucking on it in a way that jolted sensations through her. After taking time to pleasure the other breast, he then moved his mouth lower to her stomach.

"You have a sexy navel," he whispered, just moments before taking his tongue and tasting the area surrounding it. He eased lower, and when he was there, right up close to her feminine core, she heard him utter the words "Mac's sweetness" before lowering his head to her.

Another quiver, one more intense than before, ran through her the moment his tongue touched her, and she moaned out loud when he slowly but thoroughly tasted her. And then it seemed he pulled her wet and sensitive flesh into his hot mouth and began devouring her with an intensity that set a mirage of sensations ripping through her body. He used his hands to hook her legs over his shoulders to devour her with a hunger that she didn't know could exist until now.

Her breathing became ragged when she felt herself tumbling to a place she wasn't afraid to go, at least not with him. She felt her fingers reach down to grip his shoulders, felt how she lifted her hips off the bed to get even closer to his mouth.

"Luke!"

She felt her world explode, and his tongue, instead of retreating, went in deeper, with a hunger that made her body tremble in pleasure so complete it took her breath away. And while she forced breath back into her lungs, she felt him alternately nip and lick the sensitive skin surrounding her inner thighs.

She felt the mattress shift and knew the exact moment that he had moved away from the bed to take off his clothes and put on a condom. And then he was back, towering over her, and moved his naked body in place over hers, supporting his weight with his hands on both sides of her.

"Did you enjoy that?" he asked, licking his lips as if he were still savoring her flavor.

There was no way she could lie. "Yes."

"I'm glad." He held her gaze for a moment and then said, "And now I want to get inside of you so bad I can't stand it. I want to ride you in a way you've never been ridden before."

The thought of that barely gave her the strength to smile. For the first time in her life she was a woman whose response to a man was totally overwhelming. Needing to experience what he'd just said, the only reply she could make was, "Then go for it, cowboy."

He returned her smile when he settled his hips between her thighs, and before she could draw her next breath, he entered her. And although she knew she was imagining things, he seemed to have gone deeper inside of her than he had the night before. She inwardly shuddered at the thought as sensations began to slowly build back up within her.

And then he began moving, stroking her body intimately with long, deep thrusts and making her call his name over and over as he rode her with unbridled passion and sent electrical surges rippling through her. She was helpless to do anything but buck her hips upward to meet each of his downward thrusts.

When he increased the pace, reality slipped away and the grinding of his body into hers triggered her entrance into ecstasy. She screamed his name when her body broke into tiny fragmented pieces. And then she heard him holler her name the moment he exploded inside of her. She clamped her muscles to hold him in place, refusing to let him go. Needing to milk him for all she could.

Moments later she lay drained and he shifted his body off her and pulled her into his arms. When he felt her shiver he pulled the covers over them. She fought back the tears that threatened. He'd said that he would make it special for her and he had. They were making memories; the kind that would have to sustain her long after he was gone.

Chapter 16

"Ms. Standfield, a Detective Adams is here to see you."

Mackenzie closed the book she was reading upon hearing her secretary's voice. "Thanks, Priscilla. Please send him in."

She was standing by the time the door opened and the tall, middle-aged man walked in. Like most detectives that she'd encountered, he wore a serious expression on his face.

"Ms. Standfield."

"Mr. Adams." She came from around her desk and handshakes were exchanged. She then offered him the chair in front of her desk before returning to her seat.

"I've been assigned to your case, Ms. Standfield, and need to ask you a few questions."

"Sure." She wondered if the discovery that Jake Madaris was her business partner had anything to do with this. Jake's name carried a lot of weight in this part of the country.

"You think the incidents, the ones involving the break-in of your office and the poisoning of the cattle, are related?"

His question had been the same one the sheriff had asked when he'd arrived yesterday. "Yes, but thinking it and proving it are two separate things. I'm an attorney, Mr. Adams, so I know that. The only thing I'm presently certain of is the fact that I'm working on a case that the other party prefers I leave alone. How far they will go to see that happen, I'm not sure."

He nodded. "Let's explore other possibilities."

"All right," she said, although she truly didn't think there were any.

"What about a jealous boyfriend? I understand you presently have someone living with you."

He'd probably heard that from the sheriff, who had been introduced to Luke. "My present houseguest is a friend, and there aren't any jealous boyfriends because I haven't been involved in a serious relationship in a number of years, almost five to be exact."

Surprise shone on his face. "But you have dated on occasion."

"Yes."

"Then there's a possibility someone may have gotten a little carried away with you. You are a beautiful woman."

She accepted his compliment. "Thank you, but I can't see anyone I've dated over the past five years doing that. Most have been business associates or men who knew I was not ready for anything serious."

"Knowing it doesn't mean that someone may have wished otherwise. Could you provide me with their names so I can check them out?"

A part of her hesitated, and then knowing those men had nothing to hide, she said, "Sure."

Maybe when Adams saw he was barking up the wrong tree, he could turn his attention to Whitedyer as the guilty party. She provided him with the names. Seeing there were only three, he lifted his gaze from his notepad.

"Over a five-year period you've only dated three men?"

She shrugged. "Yes. I've been devoting a lot of my time to building up my business." And she had. Ashton had been her first client, and thanks to him others—a lot of them friends of his living in Oklahoma—had sought out her services as well.

"And what about the last guy you were pretty serious about?"

Her thoughts shifted and immediately went to Lawrence. "What about him? It's been over between us for a little more than five years. He's married now and has a family."

"That's nice but I still need information on him."

Adams was certainly covering all the bases, she thought, providing him with information on Lawrence. He then asked her questions about the men who worked for her at the ranch, their comings and goings, and how well she knew them. She watched as he jotted all that information into his little notebook.

"Now about the man you're currently involved with."

At her raised brow, he rephrased the question to say, "Your friend. The one living with you now."

She sighed deeply. She had introduced Luke to the sheriff as a family friend. Evidently, the sheriff hadn't bought her story about Luke being a family friend. Not with the hickey that had been visible on her neck. "His name is Luke Madaris and he's only with me recuperating for an injury he sustained while performing in a rodeo."

"Is he married?"

"No."

"Seriously involved with anyone?"

"From what I understand, he's not."

"Are you sure of that?"

"I believe so, but you can always ask him."

"And I will."

A part of Mackenzie felt annoyed with the questions being asked. "While you are checking out those guys who have no reason to harass me, what will be done about Whitedyer?"

"I have contacted them and they have denied any involvement in either incident."

"They would."

Adams flipped his notepad over. "So, other than the break-in of your office and the incident involving the cattle, can you recall anything you may have dismissed as irrelevant but may now wonder about?"

Mackenzie squinted against the sun coming through the

window as she thought about his question a moment then said, "No, other than the hit-and-run involving my mailbox."

He raised a brow. "What hit-and-run?"

It only took Mackenzie a few moments to explain what had happened, and she was surprised to see how Adams was hanging on to her every word and had reopened his notepad to jot down a few things.

"And at the time you didn't think anything of it?" he asked.

"No."

"Why not?"

"Why would I?", she countered. "My ranch is in an isolated area off the main road and I figured the accident was caused by a bunch of rowdy teens with too much to drink. I've discovered empty beer bottles at the entrance of my ranch before."

"Were there any beer bottles anywhere then?"

She had to think a moment. She and Theo had surveyed the damage. "No."

"Has the mailbox been repaired?"

"No, not yet. A temporary mailbox has been erected but the bricks are still scattered about."

He nodded. "When I stop by your place to visit with Mr. Madaris I think I'll take a look around. And if we find proof Whitedyer is involved in any of these incidents we will make sure they are dealt with to the full extent of the law. Your client has a right to seek legal counsel and you have a right to represent him. Anyone trying to interfere with those rights can find themselves in very serious trouble not only with us but also with the federal government.

"Did you tell that to the people at Whitedyer?"

"Yes."

She didn't say anything for a few moments and then, "So what's next, Mr. Adams?"

"Now I talk to the men who work for you and Luke Madaris, and anyone else I feel I might need to contact. I'm also working with the lab trying to obtain more information about those sets of tire tracks, to determine what type vehicle they belong to, although I believe it was a pickup truck. And the sheriff thinks they were able to get fingerprints off the gate, which might be helpful if there's a match in the database."

Mackenzie nodded. "You will let me know if you find out something?"

For the first time a smile touched Adams's lips, as he came to his feet. "Of course, Ms. Standfield. I will certainly keep you informed."

"How are things going, buddy?"

Luke smiled on hearing the sound of Camden's voice. They talked at least once a week and he was always glad to hear all the rodeo updates his friend provided. It was good to know who he might be competing against for the title.

They had been talking for almost a half hour when Camden said, "Oh, yeah, by the way, Nadine has been asking about you."

Luke rolled his eyes. Camden of all people knew that Nadine Turner was the last woman he wanted to hear about. "Whatever."

"Hey, relax. She might be leaving you alone for a while. Seems she has a new beau. He looks younger than her and she's been parading him around in front of everyone. I guess she's trying to prove she's over you, Luke."

"I'm glad to hear it. Best news I've heard all week."

Deciding he wanted to change the subject, Luke then talked about the upcoming rodeo event that Camden would be competing in in a few weeks. "I'm going to try and make it there that night to see you. I can't be a participant but I can sure as hell be a spectator."

"That will be great. Everyone has been asking about you. They know how lucky you are. Things could have been worse."

Luke knew that was the truth. "Did they ever find out how that bull got out that night?" he asked.

"Not really. Someone was careless and didn't close the pen but nobody wants to own up to it. You can't blame them. Gilmore is still pretty pissed about what happened and is dead serious about letting the person responsible go when he finds out who did it."

"Thanks for meeting with me," Felicia Laverne Madaris said to seven women sitting around the table.

She had called a meeting of what she considered the Madaris Wives, those married to the sons she had birthed, including the one she had lost. It didn't matter one iota that Diane, who had been married to Robert, was no longer a Madaris since marrying a retired senator last year. It was Mama Laverne's opinion that Diane, who had given her a granddaughter that she'd named after her, was still very much in the family.

All the women except for Marilyn and Diamond had been handpicked by her, although at the time none of her sons—or the wives for that matter—had known it. And even if she hadn't had a hand in choosing Marilyn and Diamond, she was very pleased with her two youngest sons' choices.

Dora, who'd been her daughter-in-law the longest, was married to her oldest son Milton. Pearl had been married over fifty-something years to Lee, and Bessie had been married just as long to Nolan. The same thing applied to Carrie and Lucas. Diane was very close to her heart since she'd known Diane all her life. Diane's grandmother had been one of her dearest friends. Robert and Diane had dated most of their lives so a marriage between them had been expected.

Marilyn had been married to Jonathan over forty-six years, was just what he'd needed at the time, although Jonathan had been determined to be difficult. And Diamond, her newest daughter-in-law, had appeared on the scene to make utter nonsense of Jake's proclamation that he would never marry again because he was already married to Whispering Pines. Their marriage had caught her off guard, completely taken her by surprise, because Jake and Diamond had kept it a secret a while before finally telling the family.

"Was there a particular reason you called this meeting, Mama Laverne?" Bessie asked. It was a known fact that she enjoyed her soaps and it was almost time for them to come on the television.

Mama Laverne rested back in her chair. "Yes, there are a couple. First, I want to thank you for all your hard work in the church's clothing drive. It was a huge success. The second thing is that I'm proud to say that with the exception of Jake and Diamond's two, all of my grandchildren are happily married. Now I can channel my focus on my great-grands."

"You mean you're not going to get an early start on Granite and Amethyst?" Diamond asked, grinning.

Mama Laverne chuckled as she shook her head. "Nope. I figure you and Jake can just pick out a couple of those Garwood kids since there's more than enough to go around. Of my great-grands, Slade is out of the way. And I decided to skip over Blade since the boy has issues. I'm concentrating on Luke for now."

Marilyn Madaris smiled. "And you still believe he has an interest in Mackenzie Standfield?"

"It's more than an interest. The boy is smitten. He just doesn't know it. Mackenzie is a lovely girl and he's bound to realize that he cares for her sooner or later, and since she's taking care of him while he recuperates, Carrie and I figure it will be just a matter of time."

Bessie Madaris leaned in close. "But Luke's told the family more than once that he's never giving up the rodeo for any woman," she said.

Mama Laverne smiled. "I know, but I have a feeling that before long, Mackenzie will change the boy's mind."

Diamond, who always found these meetings with her mother-in-law and sisters-in-law enjoyable, as well as informative, couldn't refrain from asking, "After Luke is married off then you'll go back to Blade?"

Mama Laverne sighed deeply. "Like I said, Blade has issues. I think he has more issues than Clayton had in his day. So it really depends on where Blade's mind is after Luke is finished with. Otherwise, I'm going to move on to Lee or Nolan since they both turned thirty this year. It's my hope that I live to see the day Blade settles down, and if the right woman comes along there is no doubt in my mind that he will, regardless of whether he thinks he's ready or not. So for now I'll concentrate on Luke."

Lewis Farley frowned at Detective Adams. "Really, Detective, do you honestly believe someone in our employ is responsible for Mackenzie Standfield's misfortunes?"

Adams leaned back in his chair, the one Farley had finally offered him after he'd been in the man's office for over ten minutes. It was his guess that Farley had initially assumed his visit was some sort of courtesy call and that Whitedyer's gracious contribution to the Police Benevolent Fund last year would come into play. It hadn't and it wouldn't.

"I don't know, Mr. Farley, you tell me."

The man's frown deepened. "I'll tell you the same thing I told the two officers who came a few weeks ago after her office was ransacked. Whitedyer is a highly respected corporation. We fight our battles in the courtroom. We don't have the time or the inclination to scare off those who consider themselves our enemies."

"I'm sure Jacob Madaris will be glad to know that." Adams's gaze was trained expertly on Farley, and although the man tried to downplay the effect, the detective could tell the mention of Madaris's name came as a surprise.

"Jacob Madaris? What does he have to do with any of this?"

Adams couldn't help but smile. "Umm, didn't you know? Jacob Madaris is a business partner of Ms. Standfield's, and those poisoned cattle were actually his."

The sun coming in through the window cast enough light to show how the blood suddenly seemed to drain from Farley's face. He suspected, and with good reason, that Whitedyer Corporation, or any other corporation for that matter, wouldn't want to take on the likes of Madaris. The man had money and he had friends with money. "But since you didn't have anything to do with what happened to those cattle . . . as well as the ransacking of her office . . . you don't have anything to worry about."

Farley looked across the desk at Adams. "That's right, and I'll be the first to assure Mr. Madaris of that. Like I said, I handle our enemies in the courtroom and I'm looking forward to taking on Ms. Standfield, give her a little on-the-job training, so to speak. She needs to see that she has a lot to learn."

Adams was tempted to roll his eyes, but refrained from doing so. Instead he asked, "And where is Henry Whitedyer? The CEO and president of this corporation. I'd like to speak with him."

"Not sure that's possible. He's an extremely busy man."

Now that ticked Adams off. He leaned forward in his chair and fixed his gaze on Farley. "So am I. I suggest as his attorney you advise him to carve out some time for me." He paused and added, "He can do it here or we can request his presence at headquarters."

Farley snorted. "Really, Detective, is that necessary?"

Still holding the man's eyes, he said, "Yes, I think so, and now that you're aware of one of the key players involved, I would suggest that you think the same thing."

Half an hour later Farley stood at the window and glanced out while thinking about the bombshell the detective had dropped. He tamped down the urge to hit something before crossing the room to his desk to pick up the phone. "Camille, come in here for a second."

A few moments later his personal assistant, Camille Yeager, walked in. She was in her late twenties and had begun working for him a year ago. He found her to be very efficient both in the office and, on occasion, in the bedroom. He had to hand it to her that she was pretty bright as well as good-looking. She was definitely someone he enjoyed having around. He could talk to her and usually did, and felt comfortable knowing that whatever pillow talk they shared went no further.

"Yes, Mr. Farley?"

"Did you know Mr. Coroni's attorney had a business on the side and that Jake Madaris was her business partner?"

He saw the surprised look that touched his assistant's face. She didn't have to ask who Jake Madaris was since the man was legendary. And on top of that, he was married to Diamond Swain.

"No, I didn't know that. What should we do now?" Camille asked.

He sighed. "Nothing. But I need you to get Henry Whitedyer on the line."

"Yes, sir."

He watched her leave and leaned back in his chair. His boss wasn't going to like what he had to tell him.

"Mr. Whitedyer is on the line," Camille's voice said over the intercom.

Farley picked up the phone and said, "Henry, this is Lewis. I need to meet with you sometime today. And yes, it is important."

Chapter 17

"So when exactly were you going to tell me that Jake was coming for a visit?"

Instead of answering, Luke pulled Mackenzie back down in the bed with him. "When you got home today, but it kind of slipped my mind."

Now that had been the truth. The moment she had walked in the door, he had been there, waiting, and with a need he'd found almost unbearable. At the time the only thing he'd wanted was her. He had figured anything else could wait. And it had. Here it was close to eight o'clock and they hadn't eaten, although he had cooked dinner. Since the time she had come home she had spent those hours in bed, in his arms with his body intimately connected to hers the majority of the time.

The intensity of his desire for Mac had not come as any surprise. But what had stunned his nervous system, startled him, was the force of hers for him. She had all but removed his clothes before he had removed hers. Even now she was sprawled over him, very much naked. When she had shifted position, just a little, to ask the question about Jake, her breasts had literally swung right to his face. All he would have to do was stick out his tongue to capture a nipple in his mouth, cop a taste.

"If he and Diamond are coming this weekend, there are a million things to do," she said, attempting to lift her body off his.

"And none of them will get done tonight," he said, clamping down on her backside with his hand to keep her in place, and liking the feel of his hand on her bare skin. For some reason he felt possessive, a word he'd never before linked with a woman. "Besides, he didn't say Diamond was coming, so I take it that it's just him. He can stay in the guest room."

She looked down at him, met his gaze. He knew exactly what she was thinking. If Jake stayed in the guest room that meant that Luke would sleep in her bed, which he'd been doing every night for the past week anyway. It would be crystal clear to his uncle that they were lovers. It didn't bother him and he hoped it wouldn't bother her. It was time to find out if it would.

"Will there be a problem for Jake to stay in the guest room while I sleep in here with you?" he asked in a low voice, studying her face. "If you prefer, I can always sleep on the sofa," he offered.

Her gaze held his and finally she shook her head and said, "No. We're grown-ups and consenting adults. What we do is our business."

He couldn't agree more and was glad she had taken that position. "Uncle Jake has never been judgmental and has always been one to let us live our lives without interference." He chuckled. "If anything, he tried to convince our parents to give us breathing space and not try and smother us."

She didn't say anything for a while, and then as if she suddenly thought of something, she looked at him and asked, "Detective Adams. Did he pay you a visit today?"

Luke nodded. "Yes, he came by. It's a good thing because of Alex that I have an idea how a detective, private or otherwise, operates or I would have been somewhat annoyed with his line of questioning. But I was glad to tell him anything he wanted to know, especially if it will move things along in the investigation. I completely understand that he has to check out every single detail. Like he said, Whitedyer Corporation is innocent until proven guilty."

With her being an attorney he knew she was the last person he had to remind, but felt he should to do so any way. "Has anyone from Whitedyer contacted you recently?"

She nodded. "Today, in fact. I gather Adams met with Farley. He wanted me to know that he didn't appreciate me implicating them in any way with anything, especially with the cattle. Adams must have mentioned Jake's involvement."

Luke smiled. "He must have. I made sure I emphasized to Adams more than once that Jake intended to get to the bottom of what happened to those cattle; even if he had to bring in his own investigator."

She lifted a brow. "Would Jake do that?"

"Yes, he would solicit Alex's help in a heartbeat. And everyone knows how thorough Alex is. There won't a single stone left unturned."

Mackenzie thought about what Luke had said as she studied the designs on her bedspread. From the time she first met the Madaris family, she'd always heard about Alex Maxwell's extraordinary skills as a private investigator. A former FBI agent who retained plenty of contacts, he was known to piece together even the most challenging of puzzles. He was also married to Luke's cousin Christy, which meant that Alex was officially a member of the Madaris family.

"Mac."

She switched her gaze to him. "Yes?"

Even before she had answered him she'd known what was on his mind. It was there, blatantly obvious in the dark depths of his eyes, and the knowledge, the deliberate awareness, made her breath catch. And then she watched as his lips, those same lips that had kissed her with passion, tasted her with hunger, and devoured her with reckless abandon, eased into a slow, sexy smile. It was a smile that sent a shiver through her body. It didn't help matters that she was already naked. That state of undress only brought her senses to a whole other level.

"Do I need to tell you what I want?" he asked when he reached out and stroked his hand across her breasts, causing fire to thrum through her.

No, he didn't need to tell her. She saw it in his eyes, felt it from his smile, and recognized it in his touch. The man could be both arrogant and humble most of the time, but when it came to making love to her, he was superiorly passionate all of the time. He had as much stamina as those bulls he rode.

Instead of answering him, she rose up and went straight for his mouth, covering his lips with her own and then kissing him with the same degree of passion that he always kissed her. She pressed her chest against his and knew he could feel the strong beat of her heart; a heart that he wasn't even aware belonged to him.

As he took over control of the kiss, she felt his hand touching her practically everywhere it could reach and sending sensations all through her, especially in the apex of her thighs. And before she could wonder what his next move would be, he shifted their positions at the same moment that he gently gripped her backside with both hands and impelled her on to him, thrust into her, letting his huge erection fill every inch of her. And with it came a need and a hunger that she felt all the way down to her toes.

For a moment he didn't move. It was if he wanted to savor the feel of her body anchored to his, her bare hips and thighs clenching his. She wanted to savor it as well. Relish the moment of having him embedded inside of her so deep.

And then she released his mouth on a silent "oh" when it became clear to her that he wasn't wearing a condom. The head of his staff buried inside of her felt hot and engorged. She was aware of when he realized that fact as well and was about to retreat, and she tightened her thighs on him and whispered, "I'm on the pill, Luke."

He blew breath through his lungs as if she'd thrown him a lifeline with what she'd said. But then he withdrew from inside of her, only to thrust back in a stroke that was long, deep, and heavy.

Over and over he repeated the process, pushing her over the edge, taking her senses with him, and causing her body to purr in sensuous pleasure. Everything about him, about this, was right—perfect and beautiful. When it came to pleasuring her he always took it a notch higher each time.

Tonight was no different. Already waves of desire were taking on a new meaning. She was elated by every movement of his body. Breathlessly she succumbed, and when she heard him call her name, felt the hard bucking of his body, felt that long, final thrust before he exploded, sending his hot release to all parts of her womanly core, she cried out his name, tightened her muscles that clamped him, determined to get all that she could and then some.

She loved him with her mind, body, and soul. For this little while, he was hers and she was his. All was well.

"Glad to see you, Uncle Jake," Luke said, smiling when he was enveloped in a gentle but genuinely affectionate bear hug by the man who had always been there for him.

Jake Madaris released Luke and chuckled. "You knew I would be coming this way sooner or later, if nothing more than to keep Mama off your back."

He then gazed at his nephew from his head to his feet. "Other than the fact you could use a shave, I'd say you look healthy enough."

Luke smiled and decided not to mention to his uncle that Mackenzie liked his "need-a-shave" look. "Come on in. Mac's got the guest room prepared for you."

"I don't want to put her out. I can stay at the hotel."

"You won't be putting her out. She wants you to stay here. Besides, she knows you want to check on the rest of the cattle."

Jake nodded. "Have the police discovered anything new?"

"No, not yet."

Jake shook his head. "Well, I got a call from Henry Whitedyer a few days ago. The man wanted to assure me there's been a mistake and his company has had nothing to do with those two incidents involving Mac, especially the poisoning of my cattle. He feels his company doesn't have to resort to underhanded tactics and behaviors, and when the time comes his attorney will handle Mac in the courtroom."

"Sounds like he's pretty sure of that," Luke said, not liking the man's overstated confidence.

"Evidently. Has Mac heard from Ashton?"

"Yes, he called several times and of course he's ready to come back to Oklahoma if there's a need. But this is something Mac wants to handle on her own. However, I did convince her to talk to Clayton and Syneda. They may be able to shed some light on a few laws that she's not sure about."

Jake nodded. "That's a good idea." He glanced around. "And where is Mac?"

"Riding the land with the men. She does it every Saturday morning. She'll be back soon."

Jake studied Luke's features. "You're dying to get back on a horse, aren't you?"

Luke laughed. "How can you tell?"

"By the deep longing in your voice when you mentioned that Mac was out riding. Has the doctor given you a date when you can return to the circuit?"

Luke shook his head. "I have a follow-up appointment in two weeks and will know something then. My physical therapy ends next week and both my knees and chest are feeling fine."

"And I guess you can't wait to return."

"No, I can't wait." Luke quickly dismissed the fact that what he'd said was a lie. At least partly. Especially when returning to the circuit meant leaving Mac behind. His entire body tightened at the thought of how they shared a bed every night and woke up to each other every morning. At first he'd assumed he was so captivated by her because of his long sexual drought, but now he wasn't so sure what it was. All he knew was that he enjoyed being with her more than he'd ever enjoyed being with any woman. She could raise his temperature from a look, a touch, a plain old sigh.

"Come on, Uncle Jake, let's get you settled in before Mac gets back. I gave her my word that I would take care of you."

Mackenzie took a sip of her coffee while glancing across her desktop to study the man who was quietly going over the livestock breeding records. To say that even in his late forties, Jake Madaris was the epitome of a vividly handsome man would definitely be an accurate assessment. He had to be every bit of six feet seven inches tall and his curly hair was an enticing blend of gray and black. His features were striking, the kind that would immediately reach out and grab any woman's attention. He had dark eyes and skin the color of smooth chestnut and a fierce jawline. It was evident that he kept his muscled body in great shape, and there was something both sexy and charismatic about him. But then she had to admit that although Jake had dark good looks and gentlemanly manners, it was Luke who had captured her heart. Luke who could start her pulse racing whenever he looked at her. And it was Luke who gave her the energy to make love with him all night long if that's what he wanted.

Jake closed the books, glanced over at her and smiled. "Things are as they should be. You've been doing an excellent job."

"Thanks," she said, feeling immediate relief. To be able to do business with Jake was a dream come true for any person. "I just wish I had somehow prevented what happened to those cattle."

Jake waved off her statement. "There was no way you could have foreseen what happened. The only thing we can do is recoup our losses, move on, and take every precaution to prevent a repeat."

"That's what I told her, Uncle Jake," Luke said, coming

into Mackenzie's office. He had been in the kitchen while talking on the phone to his parents. They called each week to make sure he was doing okay and didn't need anything. Luke Jr. and Sarah Madaris were the best parents anyone could have.

"Then I'm going to depend on you to help me convince her," Jake said. "There is no doubt in my mind that the authorities will eventually get those responsible."

Jake pushed aside the report he'd been reading. "Luke gave me a brief overview of what's going on with you and Whitedyer and the case you have against them. In fact, Henry Whitedyer contacted me a few days ago about it."

Mackenzie blinked, surprised. "He did?"

"Yes. He heard of my involvement with the cattle since we're business partners and wanted to assure me that no matter what you assume, Mac, neither he nor his company is in any way responsible for what's been going on. And they are willing to battle it out in court with you and are not using any type of scare tactics."

"And what was your response, Uncle Jake?" Luke wanted to know.

"Mainly that I truly hoped not and that I believed the authorities would find the person or persons responsible. And I did let him know that if it's determined Whitedyer *is* involved, I will make sure his company isn't just rendered some sort of hand-lapping or fine. That I will make it my business to make sure they are punished to the full extent of the law."

Both Luke and Mackenzie knew that Jake's words weren't meant as an idle threat. He had the means and the connections to make sure it happened.

"And I heard that Blade and Slade are sending a mini-crew out here next week to do some work for you," Jake said.

Mackenzie knew that was his way of changing the subject. There was nothing left to be said. "Yes, there's a miniature cabin behind the kitchen that I used pretty much to store junk. I realized what limited space I have when anyone comes visiting and thought it would be nice to turn it into a guest cottage, similar to the ones you have at Whispering Pines. Slade took a look at it when he was here and said he could send out a small work crew and they can have it completed in no time. That means it will be ready for Clayton and Syneda's visit." She smiled. "They've agreed to act as my consultants on the Whitedyer case."

Jake chuckled. "Then you have a winning team, although I don't know how they will pull it off since they practically never agree on anything."

Mackenzie wasn't sure how they did it either, but she was grateful for their willingness to help.

"I would appreciate it if you just hear me out, Madaris," Syneda said to her husband, attempting with an upraised hand to silence him if only for a second. He was notorious for trying to get her to see things his way even when she was adamant about *not* doing so.

"All law students practically cut their teeth on the *Berman* versus *Parker* case of 1954. I, for one, did not agree with the Supreme Court's decision, just as I didn't agree with their decision regarding Kelo of 2005," she proceeded on to say. "The outcome of that one was definitely an unfair infringement on the rights of property owners. I can see the same thing happening with Whitedyer. They want that land for their personal use."

Clayton leaned against the corner of her desk. "And it's within their constitutional rights to do so if it can provide an economic boost to the community. Whitedyer is claiming that it can."

"But that land has been in the Coroni family for years. It's no different than if the government decides to take Whispering Pines away from the Madaris family because Disney wants to build another 'World' out there that will employ a lot of people. At some point the government has to protect its citizens."

Clayton sighed, deciding to stop his wife before she got on a roll. "We can argue back and forth all day but none of it will help Mac. And the example of Whispering Pines isn't a good one because it was given to the Madarises in a Mexican land grant. Thanks to Carlos Antonio Madaris, Whispering Pines will always remain in the Madaris family and is exempt from eminent domain."

Syneda rolled her eyes. Of course she had heard the story many times of how back in the early eighteen hundreds, Carlos—half Mexican and half African American— and his wife of Mexican descent, Christina Marie, settled on the ten thousand acres of land that was known today as Whispering Pines, where Jake made his home. "In order to help Mac we need to find out everything," she said. "If Whitedyer is responsible for what happened to her office and with the cattle then there has to be a reason they're going to such extremes."

She sighed deeply. "Another thing I'm curious about is whether or not what Mac heard is true, whether they intend to do what they claim with the land, or if once they take possession of the land they will pass it on to a third party who has other plans," she said.

"But even if that's the case, will it matter to the courts as long as it boosts the economy?" Clayton asked with a serious expression.

Syneda knew Clayton had asked a good question. The Oklahoma City court system could still try and use the Fifth Amendment to support their stance that it was okay to take private property for private development if it would create jobs.

"I think we should try and find out if what Mac heard is true," Syneda said.

Clayton agreed. "But doing so would be equivalent of finding a needle in a haystack," he said.

Syneda nodded. "Yes, but we both know someone who's capable of doing that very thing."

They smiled and said the name at the same time. "Alex."

Chapter 18

Mackenzie decided to hang back and remain on the porch while Luke walked Jake to the car. Both men were tall and extremely good-looking, and over the past few days she'd gotten the opportunity to see just how alike they were. Both had a love of livestock, specifically horses. They were true horsemen in every sense of the word and had ranching in their blood.

Although Luke was a dedicated cowboy on the rodeo circuit, she'd discovered during his interactions with Jake just how much he knew about ranching. He was as knowledgeable about the cattle industry as Jake was, and it had been rather educational listening to them discuss the ins and outs of cattle and horse breeding.

Jake said something that made Luke throw his head back and laugh. The sound was rich and vibrant just like the man himself. Although she had told Luke that it wouldn't bother her if Jake discovered they were lovers, he'd made the decision to keep things between them private and had slept on the sofa.

But that hadn't stopped the want and desire from appearing in his eyes whenever he looked at her. She wouldn't be surprised if Jake had seen it as well. But it truly wouldn't matter if Luke had tried to hide it. Jake Madaris was a very observant man and there was no way he didn't know there was something going on between them. They might pretend to be just friends but she figured Jake had picked up on the fact there was a lot more to it.

And it hadn't stopped her heart from becoming more Luke's with each passing moment. She'd always figured that when she fell in love, she would fall hard. That was one of the reasons she could now say that Lawrence had swept her off her feet for all the wrong reasons and for a little while she hadn't been immune to his charm.

Things were totally different with Luke. He had a different type of charm than the one Lawrence possessed. Luke had a style that rejected phoniness of any kind. He was who he was and didn't try to be anyone else. He never resorted to sugarcoating his words or making you believe the situation was any different than what was presented. Mackenzie knew that no matter how much he might enjoy her in bed, he wasn't in love with her, and when the time came he would walk out the door and not look back.

On that day her heart would shatter into a million pieces, but she couldn't help but love him anyway. The woman inside of her couldn't resist doing so. It was something she couldn't deny. Being on the rodeo circuit had a grip on him in a way that she never could or ever would. She knew his passion in life. Knew it and accepted it.

As if he'd felt her eyes on him, Luke looked over in her direction and a smile touched his lips. He then held out his hand to her. She inhaled deeply and descended the steps to take it. When she felt her fingers encompassed in the warmth of his, a pulsating sensation flowed through her and she met his gaze, wondering if he'd felt it as well. As far as she was concerned there was no reason for him not to. The sensation had been a poignant one, sharp and hard at the same time.

"Thanks for your hospitality, Mac," Jacob Madaris was saying, drawing her attention to him.

She glanced his way. "You're always welcome here, Jake, and thanks for the vote of confidence with the cattle."

"No problem, and I'm sure that everything will continue to run smoothly."

"So am I."

He then glanced over at Luke. "And if my nephew decides to become a difficult patient—"

"I can handle him," she finished, chuckling.

Jake switched his gaze back to her and lowered his eyes to their joined hands before returning it to her face. He smiled. "Yes, I believe that you can."

Mackenzie stood beside Luke as Jake got into the rental car and drove off. She didn't have to look over at Luke to know his eyes were on her. She could feel his gaze like a soft intimate caress. It seemed the temperature in the hand holding hers went up a notch and she became even more aware of her own passionate nature, the one that was now drawing her toward something that was as elemental as breathing.

"Do you think Jake suspects anything about us?" she heard him ask her.

Without looking at him, she asked, "Would it matter to you if he did?"

He gently turned her to him and she was forced to look up at him, meet his gaze. His voice was low and shackled when he said, "Only as it relates to you."

She knew what he was saying. He didn't want to give anyone, especially any member of his family, the impression that the two of them were a couple with notions of "forever after" on their minds. That would be the expectation his family would have of them.

His dark gaze roamed her face and she felt the heat from the intensity of his close perusal. "I can take care of myself, Luke." She decided not to add, *Somehow I'll deal with the heartbreak because being with you now is what I want. I'll survive any pain.*

Instead of saying those words, she dragged in a deep breath. "Do you want to go inside?"

She didn't have to explain what was behind the invitation or the reason for it. Every day his health improved brought him closer to the day he would be leaving to return to the circuit.

He looked deep into her eyes and she felt it, the tingling sensation that would erupt inside of her whenever he looked at her with such a high degree of desire in his gaze. She felt his heat. It was inflaming every inch of her, burning a path through parts of her body that only came ablaze around him. He was the only man who could evoke such a reaction from her.

"Go on inside," he said, walking her back to the front porch. "I want to let Theo know that we're in for the evening. I'll be back in a minute."

"All right."

When she made it to the door she glanced over her shoulder to see that Luke was still standing there and was looking at her. And pushing his Stetson back with his thumb, he continued to stand there and stare at her, letting his gaze rake over her from head to toe.

She was wearing a skirt and a blouse but from the way his eyes were glued to her she might not have been wearing anything at all. It was as if he had the ability to see right through her clothes. His look was sending those sensations she had felt earlier skittering down her spine, in anticipation of what she knew was to come—release they would be sharing after five whole days of going without. She had gone five years without having a man in her bed and now it was as if Luke had a definite place there. Not a permanent place but a place just the same.

She felt hot and knew that if she continued to stand there, she would burn to a crisp, so she opened the door and went inside.

Luke watched her go before finally turning toward the barn.

It was strange how in that sudden moment of looking at her, his testosterone had plunged into overdrive and he had wanted her to a degree that he found unsettling. He was discovering that with Mac his mind and his body had no restrictions. Sparks would flare, flames would ignite, and his senses would get shot to hell. The only thing that would seem vital to his living or dying was passion, passion she could stir in a way that he found totally compelling. He had told her that he wanted to give her a taste of passion and now it seemed like she'd turned the tables, and without even realizing the extent of her capabilities, she wasn't just giving him a taste of passion, he was getting a whole whopping mouthful.

Thinking of what they'd been sharing over the past weeks and what he'd gone without during the past few days pushed him to move quickly across the yard. It still amazed him how Mac could have a full-time career as an attorney, yet was able to successfully run an operating ranch. One reason was because she had good and dependable men working for her. Theo, Luke had discovered, was as loyal as they came and mainly because of Mac's grandfather. Theo, who was now in his late fifties, had been in his early twenties, down on his luck, hungry, and with no place to stay when he had stumbled onto Mac's grandfather's place. He had been employed with the Standfields ever since.

Luke knew the man was very protective of Mac and he couldn't very well blame him for that. But at the same time Theo knew when to mind his own business and accept the fact that Mac was an adult who was old enough to make her own decisions.

Circling the building and going around back to where he knew Theo and the men were, he glanced over to where Mac's horse was prancing around the locked gate. She definitely was a beauty and he could just imagine the offspring she and Cisco could produce. He wondered if Mac would go along with the idea of Cisco and Princess getting together and decided to bring it up to her.

He smiled. That particular topic of conversation would have to take place later. Once he joined Mac in the house, talking would be the last thing on his mind and he intended to make sure it was the last thing on her mind as well.

* * *

"This had better be good, Clayton."

Clayton rolled his eyes. Alex's tone suggested that he might have interrupted something. If he had then that was too friggin' bad since the man was married to his sister. His *baby* sister. So what if Christy would be celebrating her twenty-sixth birthday soon and that three months ago she had given birth to a beautiful little girl she'd named Alexandria Christina Maxwell. Okay, he would be the first to admit that whenever he saw Christy she looked happy, content, and well loved. That meant Alex must be doing something right. But still, he couldn't overlook the fact that Alex had pulled a fast one on him and his two brothers, Justin and Dex.

"I need your help on something," Clayton said.

There was only a brief pause and then Alex asked, "Something like what?"

"All the information you can find out on the Whitedyer Corporation."

The name drifted off Alex's lips when he repeated it. "Whitedyer Corporation. Anything in particular I need to be looking for?"

"I want to know everything about them. Specifically, who they might be doing business with in private and whether they're desperate enough to keep things hush-hush by trying to harass Mac off the case she's handling against them."

"Luke's Mac?"

Clayton frowned. Was he the only one who hadn't noticed anything going on between those two? "Yes, apparently. Someone ransacked her office a few weeks ago and now they went after Jake's cattle on Mac's land. Six were poisoned."

"Damn."

"If Whitedyer is behind any such foolishness then I want to know why and what they're trying to hide."

"Okay, I'll begin checking them out in the morning."

"Thanks. How're Christy and AC?" "AC" was the nickname the family had given the baby.

"Both are doing fine. They can't be happier," Alex said.

"So you say."

"So I know. My goal in life is to take care of *my* ladies. Their every wish is my command," Alex responded.

Clayton couldn't help but smile. "Whatever. Talk to you later." He then hung up the phone.

"I gather that was Clayton."

Alex glanced up at his wife who was standing beside the bed. "Who else." When the phone had rung she had gotten out of bed to go to the nursery to get their daughter, who had awakened and started crying.

"The next time I see Clayton I'm going to make sure I tell him to table his calls to when AC is awake," she said, handing him their daughter. "He just interrupted 'Mom and Dad' time."

Alex chuckled as he took AC into his arms, instinctively cradling her to his chest. He stared down at the baby he and Christy had made together. She was simply beautiful. She had her mother's reddish-brown hair as well as most of Christy's facial features, with the exception of her nose and ears. Now those were truly his.

Christy got back into the bed and turned slightly toward them. "So, what does Clayton want this time?" The Madaris and Madaris law firm often used Alex's services when they were working on an important case that involved private investigative work.

"The usual but this involves Mac."

Christy lifted a brow. "Luke's Mac."

Alex couldn't help but grin. "I wonder if Luke knows yet that she's his."

Christy shrugged as she took AC from out of her father's arms. "Probably not. You know how slow you men are."

Alex knew she was hinting at how slow he'd been back in the day. That was then. This was now. He looked over at his daughter, who was wide awake. "How long do you think it will be before she drifts back to sleep?"

"Hard to tell. Why? You got something to do?"

He smiled. "Umm, when it comes to you, sweetheart, I always have something to do."

He reached up and caught a flaming red lock of hair to twirl around his finger. Mindful of his child in his wife's arms, he leaned over and placed a kiss on the corner of her mouth and could vividly recall the first time he had ever kissed her. "I thought we could go ahead and get started on AC's brother," he said in a husky tone.

He heard Christy draw in a deep breath before saying, "I thought we had agreed to wait until Alexandria was at least two."

"We are, but practice makes perfect. I figured we should get in as many practice sessions as we can so when the time comes it will be a piece of cake."

"A piece of cake?"

He grinned. "As sweet as it can get."

Mackenzie stood at her bedroom window and looked out at the lake. With Jake's visit she had put aside her research. And now Clayton and Syneda had suggested that she let them handle that end of things for her. If there was misuse of eminent domain in the Whitedyer case they were willing to help her find it. She had been more than appreciative of their offer. Now she could concentrate on what courtroom strategies to use and perfect them. For Farley this would be a performance in front of the judge and jury. He enjoyed being on stage and in that regard he reminded her so much of Lawrence. But where Lawrence had physical beauty to captivate his audience, she'd found out that Farley was big on dramatics. She'd heard the man could be a complete bully in the courtroom. He saw her as an inexperienced attorney and he was so darn sure of himself that he had told her more than once to back off or she would get eaten by a shark. But she was committed, no matter what, to providing Mr. Coroni with the best legal counsel possible.

Her stomach suddenly clenched at the same moment that she heard booted footsteps. Without turning around she knew that Luke had come inside the house. Her heart rate increased with every step he took down the hallway, moving toward her bedroom.

She became caught up in what she knew would happen the moment he set foot in her bedroom. She wished there was a way to explain why a woman who had gone without passion for so long could suddenly be swept away to the point it was almost blinding. Even now, if she wanted to, she could close her eyes and recall every vivid detail of the lovemaking sessions they had shared. She doubted the memories would ever be eradicated from her mind. They were probably singed there forever.

She swallowed. Her stomach clenched tighter the moment she knew he had walked into the room. She tried to force her heartbeat to slow, but it was useless. A need gnawed at her; made her appreciation of the passion he had introduced her to that much stronger.

She could hear his footsteps coming toward her. And then he was there. The heat of his broad chest was pressed against her back. His aroused body part, thick and hard, was bearing down on her bottom. Without saying a single word, his hands reached out and wrapped around her waist and pulled her closer to him.

"We're alone again," he said, leaning down and whispering the words close to her ear. His warm lips moved to place a kiss on her throat. "I missed this," he said, moving to place another kiss close to her ear. "I've been craving you for five whole days. If Uncle Jake had taken you up on your offer to stay another day I probably would have died."

His words stirred something elemental within her. Did he know what he was saying? If he couldn't do without her for five days then how was he going to handle the rest of his life? She knew the answer to that. Once he got back on the rodeo circuit, she and any other leisure pastime would be forgotten.

He shifted his stance and all thoughts fled from her mind. The only thing she could think about was the liquid fire her body seemed to have suddenly turned into. His hands had dropped from her waist and were moving possessively all over her body. And when he cupped her breasts through the material of her blouse, she felt weak and instinctively leaned back against him.

She shuddered as he began unbuttoning her blouse.

"Do you know what I love most about your breasts?" he asked as his hand slid into the opening of her blouse, while his lips branded her throat.

"No," was her response in a low voice, while shivers raced through her.

"The way your nipples fit around my tongue. The way they taste when they are in my mouth."

His words, whispered in a hot rush of breath close to her ear, increased the heat she felt between her legs. In response she pressed her thighs together.

He felt the shifting of her body and knew what she'd done and said, "No, I want your legs open." He then leaned forward and closed the window blinds. "And now we have all the privacy we need."

She had a feeling it would be a while before they made it over to the bed, which was fine with her, and doubted she could get her legs to take very many steps anyway. His hand then returned to her chest to remove her blouse and bra and toss them aside. He opened the zipper of her skirt with a flick of his wrist, and a slight tug made the garment fall in a heap at her feet, leaving her clad in her panties.

He still stood behind her as he said, "Now I want you to lean forward and brace your hands on the windowsill."

She was tempted to look over her shoulder at him but refrained. Instead she did what he asked.

"That's right," he said, pressing his body closer to her bowed one, sandwiching her between the hardness of his body and the windowsill. "Now we're going to mate."

Her pulse leaped at his words, her breath caught in her throat. Before she could sink down to the floor from weakened knees, he leaned over and captured her lips while his hands kneaded her breasts. She tilted her head back to let him have his way with her mouth, and he slid his tongue intimately back and forth between her lips before staking a claim when she opened her lips on a breathless sigh. He kissed her with a hunger that she could feel all the way to her bare feet and she couldn't do anything but kiss him back with that same greediness, that same desperation, entwining her tongue with his, dueling not for control but for self-preservation.

And then his hands moved from her breasts to rest upon her hips, to ease her panties down her legs. He paused a moment and from the sounds behind her Mackenzie knew he was removing his own clothes. And then moments later he returned to her, resting his hard engorged erection against her backside, skin to skin, flesh to flesh.

He leaned toward her back and with his mouth he branded her in the center of her back and vamped her brain in the process. At the moment she couldn't think. She didn't want to think. She could barely breathe. All she wanted to do was satisfy the driving need that was racing through her, bombarding her senses, rushing through her veins.

"Hold tight."

Those words were probably the last she remembered before she felt his knee nudge her thighs apart, sweeping his hand between them. The moment his fingers touched her womanly core she moaned out his name. Heat stirred everywhere he made contact. How had she missed such an intimate touch as this? The provocative caress of his hand expertly stroking her sent sharp sensations plummeting through her. There was something about his touch—the way he fondled her was a skill he had cultivated into an art form.

She gripped the windowsill tighter as currents swept through her, amazed at how the curve of her bottom seemed to fit perfectly to the front of him. And when he clutched her hips tightly she felt it the moment he placed the head of his erection, there, right there, at her womanly core.

And then he eased inside of her, filling her in a way that only he could do, going deep, all the way to the hilt, then withdrawing. Over and over he repeated the process, thrusting back and forth inside of her in long, sinuous strokes. Again and again. Whatever was driving him was also driving her. It was as if he wanted to lose himself in her and she wanted him to be lost inside of her.

Her body began to quiver when she felt an eruption about to take place inside of her. Sensations caused heat to flare within her, starting at the base of her toes and moving quickly up her spine. Her moans became sobs and her inner muscles clenched him in a way that only made him increase his thrusts.

"Luke!"

She was suddenly swept away on a wave that had the force to push her to the stars, and she went there, taking him with her when she heard his guttural moan just seconds before he filled her body with his hot release.

She hadn't been aware her body was capable of getting in a bowed position, hadn't been aware that a joining so forceful could end up being so compelling, and could leave her so complete yet utterly drained. She had wanted him. She had needed him.

And for all intents and purposes, she had gotten him.

The ruggedly built man regarded the man standing beside him at the bar with uncertainty in his gaze. "And you're sure that's what the boss wants us to do?"

"Yes, for now. I know you were beginning to have fun but we have to pull back for a while. Neither of us wants to do any jailtime and so far no one has gotten hurt. All we did was deliver several warnings."

"And if the little lady doesn't heed our warnings?"

"Then we might have to take more drastic actions but that will be for the boss to decide."

Chapter 19

"So, Mac, how was your weekend?"

Mackenzie glanced across the conference table and caught both Sam's and Peyton's curious gazes and tried to ignore them. She was very much aware of what had prompted Sam's question. It was the hickey Luke had placed on the side of her neck. She had tried covering it up with a scarf but it hadn't worked.

Knowing they were waiting for an answer, she pushed away from the table to lean back in her chair and said, "My weekend was just fine, Sam, what about yours?"

Sam chuckled. "Evidently not as good as yours."

Mackenzie couldn't help but smile. "Well, what can I say?" She decided not to divulge any details although she was sure her two best friends were ready to hang on her every word. Instead she decided to change the subject. "Thanks for handling things when I was out of the office while Jake Madaris was in town last week."

Peyton's features then turned serious. "You don't have to thank us. Have the police found anything yet?"

Mackenzie shook her head disappointedly. "No, although they were able to tell from the tire tracks that a pickup truck was on my property around the same time the cattle were poisoned. And they know what kind of poison was used and are trying to track the purchase of it to a nearby hardware store."

Sam nodded. "I'm sure Mr. Madaris was upset about his cattle?"

"Yes, but not as much as he could have been. He's putting his faith in the authorities to find the person or persons responsible."

"And you still think Whitedyer is involved?" Peyton asked.

Mackenzie sighed deeply. "I can't think of anyone else that it could possibly be. Besides, I wouldn't put anything past Farley. One minute he's sending subtle hints that I should get off the case and then the next he's letting me know how anxious he is to humiliate me in the courtroom."

"He's probably trying to throw you off balance," Peyton responded.

Mackenzie couldn't help but agree. She knew she had to stay focused now, more so than ever. "One good thing is that Luke's cousin and his wife, who are well-known attorneys in Texas, are looking into several eminent-domain cases for me. Since we know Farley is going to use the argument that taking Mr. Coroni's land will benefit the economy, I need to come up with something to counterattack that claim."

Sam leaned back in her chair. "What about all those layoffs Whitedyer did earlier this year?"

"Yes, but they have promised to return those employees to their jobs if they can get Coroni land in order to expand. If you saw the newspaper this morning then you know that all the public statements coming from Whitedyer are designed to make us look like the bad guy and to garner public sympathy and support. Times are bad and people want to work. I can understand that. But at the same time a man's rights are being taken away. He's being forced to give up the only home he has known. He has offered Whitedyer the use of some of his land but they want all or nothing. That type of greed is totally incomprehensible to me."

No one said anything for a while and then Sam asked, "And how is Mr. Coroni doing?"

Mackenzie smiled sadly. "He came home from the hospital last week and is doing okay. Of course he's worried by what he's seen on the television and read in the papers. If Whitedyer is trying to make us look bad then of course they are trying to make him look even worse. He's had to get his phone number changed. People were calling, angry and upset."

Peyton sighed. "When will it all end?"

Mackenzie glanced over the table and met Sam's and Peyton's gazes. "How about in two weeks? I got a call this morning. The judge has set a date. We'll be in court two weeks from today."

"So, there you have it, Luke, I think it will be a wonderful way to ease you back onto the rodeo circuit, and the guys are looking forward to seeing you again."

Before Luke could respond, Cam then added, "Besides, Cisco is getting restless and this will be a good way for you to give him a good workout."

Luke thought about what Cam had suggested. Both of them occasionally participated in the Bill Pickett International rodeo where they had both gotten their start. Pickett, a legendary cowboy and rodeo star of African-American and Indian descent, was the inspiration that gave birth to America's only touring black rodeo.

Luke sighed deeply. Cam had suggested that once he was given the okay from the doctor he could ease back into rodeo by participating in the Glenn Turman Relay Race that was presented by the Bill Pickett Memorial Scholarship Fund. Part of the profits from the rodeo went to the scholarship fund, which was set up for students who either competed in the rodeo or who were working toward a degree in equine or animal science.

Like Cam, he always enjoyed participating in the relay race and it was a good way to give Cisco the workout he needed while contributing to a worthy cause. So why was he hesitating about doing it? A name quickly came to mind.

Mac.

Agreeing to participate meant he would need to head out to Los Angeles where the event would be held next week. Once he left the ranch to return to the world of rodeo, he would have no reason to return here. No reason to seek Mac out ever again. They both understood what it would mean the day he left, and as much as he wanted to return to the circuit he didn't look forward to leaving.

"Luke?"

He shifted uncomfortably in the chair. His body, his mind, and every part of him had gotten used to being here with her. "Yes?"

"Can we count you in, man?"

"Yes, go ahead," he agreed tautly. "I'll know for certain after my visit to the doctor on Thursday."

"All right, I'll check back with you on Friday and if everything is on go then I can drive over from Missouri to pick you up Saturday morning."

"Make it Saturday evening."

There was a pause. "Oh, okay. Sure. Saturday evening it is."

A half hour later and Luke was still pacing the confines of Mac's living room. Why was the thought of leaving Mac behind so complicated? He was a loner. He liked his space. He didn't have claims on any woman and no woman had a claim on him. The only difference between him and Blade was that Blade loved a lot of women, where he was content to have one on a need-be basis. When had that changed?

When had the thought of kissing a woman started bringing instant memories of Mac to his mind? Memories of his mouth on hers. In hers. Devouring her in deep heated kisses. The kind where she would automatically melt into him, wrap her arms around his neck, and be submerged in the kiss with as much hunger as he had.

And heaven forbid, he didn't want to think about how it felt to wake up with her in the morning; to find their bodies in some cases still entwined; her hair in a tumble of sexiness over her face. Then there was the lovemaking itself, the kind that left him breathless, depleted, drained, but so utterly fulfilled and satisfied he hadn't thought it was possible. No other woman had the ability to make him feel that way. No other woman.

And that, he admitted, was the crux of his problem and was probably a good reason why it was time to leave. Around Mac he felt things he shouldn't. Things that he didn't want to feel. He knew his life's calling and at the present time it didn't belong to a woman. His life belonged on the rodeo circuit. That's where he wanted to be and that's where he would be headed after this week. He had enjoyed his time here with Mac but now he had to move on.

Opening the front door, he stepped out on the porch and glanced around. This place had started growing on him and that wasn't good. He enjoyed being here too much. He hadn't encountered the restlessness he'd assumed he would feel. Some days he would actually wake up with a strange feeling that this was where he belonged. But he would immediately quash such nonsense.

And then there was that business with Mac and White-dyer. The authorities still didn't have any leads regarding either incident and Luke was bothered by the idea there could be another scare tactic planned. There was no way he could eliminate the threat but he intended to do whatever he could to make sure Mac was protected after he left. He would talk to Jake and ask that his men hang around for a while and watch the place, protecting Mac after he was gone.

Luke leaned against the rail and sighed deeply. At dinner tonight he would tell Mac there was a chance he would be leaving soon.

Sheik Rasheed Valdemon glanced over at his good friend Jake Madaris, remembering just how their friendship had begun several years ago. It was a solid friendship, one that had grown stronger over the years. Jake was a man of his word. He was a man that Rasheed knew he could trust. A couple of years ago when Jake's niece had been in a dangerous situation, Rasheed had managed to rescue her from the clutches of madmen, something that had earned him the never-ending appreciation of the Madaris family. They had shown their appreciation by making him an honorary member of the Madaris family. So now, on occasion, while traveling extensively in the United States, and while conducting certain types of business on American soil, he used the name Rasheed Madaris with their blessing.

Whispering Pines was a long way from Rasheed's homeland in the Middle East, but when he had been confronted with a matter that needed his undivided attention, the Whispering Pines Ranch was the first place he had thought about to get the solitude that he needed.

"Thanks for allowing me to be a visitor here, Jake."

Jake looked over at Rasheed. "I've told you a number of times that you'll always be welcome at Whispering Pines. Diamond and I always look forward to your visits. Besides, everyone considers you part of our family."

Jake paused and then said, "I don't want to pry, Rasheed, but you seemed deeply troubled about something. Is it about your homeland? Is there anything I can do?"

Rasheed could only give Jake an appreciative smile. Jake was just that type of friend. He knew if he ever needed anything that Jake would be there to make it happen. Besides Jake, he had made a number of friends that were either in or connected to the Madaris family. But this issue that concerned him was one that he alone could deal with, and whether he liked it or not, he agreed with his father that it was time.

"Thanks for the offer, Jake, and to answer your questions, in a way it does deal with my homeland but there is nothing that you can do. I can't even look at it as a sacrifice for my people like I did when I was much younger. Now at the age of thirty-eight, it is my duty."

Jake lifted a brow. "What is your duty?"

Rasheed met his curious gaze. "Marriage. And before you ask, the answer is no. She is not anyone that you know. In fact, she isn't anyone that I know. Our marriage was arranged years ago."

Jake took a sip of his wine and decided to wait. It was up to Rasheed to tell him any more than that. He was aware that in Rasheed's country arranged marriages were the norm. And with his wealth Rasheed would certainly be a good catch. And according to the females in the Madaris family, Rasheed was also an extremely handsome man. He was tall with piercing dark eyes, brown skin, and straight black hair that flowed loosely around his shoulders.

"It was decided that I would marry her before she was even born," Rasheed said, breaking into Jake's thoughts. "I've never met her and she has never met me."

"But she is aware of the marriage," Jake was curious enough to ask.

Rasheed smiled faintly. "Yes, but I'm sure growing up she figured by the time she had to marry me, I would have died off or something."

At Jake's raised brow, he added, "There's a fifteen-year difference in our ages. Presently, she is in this country attending college. She will graduate next year from Harvard in June, and then she is expected to return to the Middle East where the two of us will officially meet and plan our wedding."

Rasheed then sighed deeply. "I've been single a long time, my friend. I'm set in my ways. I enjoy women but—"

"You're not ready to settle down," Jake finished for him.

Rasheed nodded. "No, I'm not ready to settle down. And I have another concern."

"What?"

"She's young. Probably inexperienced and not anything I'm used to in a woman. Chances are she doesn't possess any of the skills and aptitudes that I expect in a mistress."

Jake chuckled. "But she won't be a mistress, Rasheed."

"True. And that, too, will be different. I'm used to lovers who are here today and gone tomorrow. All my prior relationships have been short and meaningless. As a marriage this one will have to be different."

Jake didn't say anything for a moment and then, "Would it help any if I told you that at one time I felt the same way? That I wasn't interested in having a wife, but since marrying Diamond I can't imagine life without her?"

Rasheed smiled before shaking his head. "I know that you love Diamond, Jake. But then you selected her as your partner in life. She was not selected for you."

Jake knew that to be true. "Well, I wish you the best in whatever you decide to do."

Rasheed sat back in his chair. "I really don't have a choice in the matter. I just need time to get prepared and hope that when the day comes I will be."

Roger Coroni's mouth tightened into a frown. "Why can't those people just accept my decision not to sell my land and leave me alone?"

Mackenzie could only sympathize with what he was saying. She had taken time to come visit with him during her lunch hour to find him sitting on the porch in a rocking chair looking tired and despondent. "I understand how you feel, Mr. Coroni, and I'm going to do everything I can to make sure that you keep it. Has anyone at Whitedyer tried contacting you?"

"No, but I get irate calls. People are blaming me for not having jobs and that's not fair."

Mackenzie nodded. "You're right, it's not fair, but hopefully things will be over soon. I got a call this morning. The judge has set a date and time for the hearing. It's going to be two weeks from now."

He raised a surprised brow. "That soon?"

"Yes." She waited for Mr. Coroni to say something, not sure what he was thinking. And then he asked her, "How good are our chances?"

She didn't want to dampen his spirits nor did she want to give him false hope. "I honestly don't know. The most recent eminent domain cases that went all the way to the Supreme Court were ruled in favor of the private developer or corporation. But that doesn't mean it will go that way again."

"I hope that you're right, Ms. Standfield. I was born on

this property and so were my daddy and his daddy before
him and his daddy before that. This land has been in the
Coroni family for generations and I can't see myself losing
it to a bunch of stuffed shirts who want to use it for their
personal gain. What about the blood, sweat, and tears my
family endured to cultivate this land, hold on to it? That
has to stand for something."

Mackenzie heard the frustration in his voice and the
traces of anger as well. "Yes, Mr. Coroni, it does stand for
something, and as your attorney it will be my job to convince a judge and jury of that."

She knew that Mr. Coroni had sought out several law
firms before deciding on Standfield, De Meglio, and Mahoney. Everyone else, foreseeing the case turning into a
three-ring circus because of who they'd be up against,
had backed away saying thanks but no thanks. How could
you fight a major corporation that had in their arsenal
promises of jobs—jobs people needed to make their lives
go a little easier?

A few hours later when Mackenzie pulled into the yard
of her ranch home that same question was on her mind.
That answer, whatever it was, would be the key to winning
the case. And if her day could have gotten any worse, she
had returned to the office after meeting with Mr. Coroni to
find the post office had delivered a letter of condemnation
for Mr. Coroni's property. By exercising their condemnation powers the city was officially letting her know they
were siding with Whitedyer. Not that she had been surprised.

Before leaving the office she had talked to Syneda and
she'd mentioned that Clayton had called Alex Maxwell
and he had agreed to try to dig up information on a possible third-party involvement. But Mackenzie knew that as
good a private investigator as Alex was, she couldn't bank
on him finding anything that might help her client. Today
had certainly not been a good day for her.

The moment she walked into the house she could smell

the casserole cooking in the oven. She was getting used to coming home and getting fed, pampered, and loved. Okay, it was probably wishful thinking with the "love" part, but a girl had to have some kind of hope. Right?

"Luke, I'm home!" she called out after placing her briefcase on the table.

The moment she said his name he strolled out of wherever he'd been and crossed the living room to where she stood. He placed his arms at her waist and pulled her closer to him. "You were missed today."

Likewise, she settled into the cradle of his frame while placing her arms around his neck. "You were missed today, too," she said, meaning every word. "I need a kiss real bad, Luke."

The intensity of his gaze made heat settle low in her stomach. And when he shifted his eyes to her lips, she felt more than heat. She felt a rumbling in her stomach that had nothing to do with a missed meal. And when he bent his head and lowered his mouth to hers, she was more than ready to receive him.

And receive him she did, on a breathless sigh, which only gave him the opportunity to deepen the kiss, take it to another level and then some. She gripped his shoulders thinking he had introduced her to a different form of kissing. He mated with her mouth, taking the edge off her day and at the same time clearing her mind. All she could do was return the kiss as unabashedly as he gave it.

When he released her mouth sometime later, her body quivered at the loss. Before she could say anything—not sure at that point what it would be—he swooped back down to her mouth for a quick lick, brushing against her lips with his tongue.

Satisfied, he gave her a smile; the same one that had endeared him to her for life. "So," she asked when she was able to pull air through her lungs, "what's cooking?"

His smile widened in a way that made a dimple appear in his cheek. "Another boring casserole."

She chuckled. "Trust me. Your casseroles are anything but boring. In fact, I can't think of a single boring thing about you, Luke Madaris."

"Prove it."

No problem, she thought, and immediately pulled his mouth down to hers. They stood there and for the next few moments by silent mutual assent they made time for a playful interlude. As if he sensed her body's stress and had somehow detected her inner frustrations from the day, with deliberate precision and a meticulousness that had her moaning, he used his tongue to stroke away any tension and anxiety. By the time he had finished, she was panting, barely able to stand on her feet.

"Now for your bath," he whispered close to her ear.

"My bath?" she asked, trying to regain the senses she always lost during the kiss.

"Yes, I already ran your bathwater. All you have to do is take off your clothes and get in the tub and play in the bubbles."

Mac thought that sounded heavenly. She removed her hands from around his neck to slide down to his chest, then lower to cup him through the material of his jeans. She felt the way his body responded and when she looked into his eyes, she saw heavy desire staring back at her. "And will you get into the tub with me?" she leaned close to ask in a seductive tone.

"Tempting, sweetheart, but no," he said, taking a step back. "I'm going to get dinner ready and placed on the table."

Suddenly, an uncomfortable feeling settled in her stomach. It was as if he were determined to stay in control tonight. Why? "Is anything wrong, Luke?"

He didn't immediately answer. Instead he met her gaze and she couldn't read anything in his eyes. But that funny feeling wouldn't go away.

"No, there's nothing wrong," he finally said. "But we need to talk and we'll do so over dinner."

Mackenzie wondered what they had to talk about. What

did he want to say to her that required him to deny them both pleasure right now.

"Mac?"

She blinked and then realized she'd just been standing there. "Yes?"

"Your water is getting cold. We'll talk over dinner," he murmured in a low tone.

She felt her throat tighten but got out the words anyway. "All right, I'll be back in a minute."

And then she was rushing off toward the bathroom. She had a strong feeling that her bad day was about to get worse.

Chapter 20

As usual the casserole Luke had cooked was excellent. However, it could have been topped with vanilla ice cream and garnished with glazed walnuts and Mackenzie would still have had a hard time forcing it down her throat.

She had a feeling about what Luke was going to say, and at the moment she didn't want to hear it. Just as well, since it seemed he wasn't in a talkative mood either. It reminded her of the old days when he'd first arrived and they sat across from each other at the kitchen table and barely exchanged a single word. But that was before the time in the kitchen when he had taken her—or she had taken him—in that very chair he was sitting in. And it was before all those times, too numerous to count and too precious to forget, when he would make love to her until she moaned and groaned while teetering on the edge of pleasure and then plunging her there with a force that could rob her of her senses in one climactic scream.

She always found it utterly amazing how her body would ripple in anticipation even before he touched her. Just knowing what was to come kept her cloaked in sensual awareness, made her body want him even when it should have had enough. And that was one of the problems. With Luke there was never enough. She had an unquenchable hunger, a desire that kept going and going. And all it took was a look from him. A smile. A touch.

She would become all hot and bothered, all hungry and greedy, so quintessentially needy. So—

"I take it you had a bad day."

His words made her glance up and she wished she hadn't. For some reason her gaze went straight to his lips. Lips that liked kissing her, tasting her, and a tongue that could send her over the edge with a skill that he ought to patent. And just knowing that skillful tongue was behind such beautiful lips had her senses purring, heat moving low to settle in one particular part of her body.

"Mac?"

She blinked and her gaze snapped to his eyes. "Yes?"

"Did you have a bad day?"

She shrugged as she tried to continue eating her food. "It hasn't been the best. First thing this morning I got a call saying that the judge has set a date for our hearing against Whitedyer. Then I visited Mr. Coroni and found out that he's really nervous about what's going to happen and there was no way I could assure him that he had no reason to be nervous. Then when I got back to my office I saw that the city had sent a letter of condemnation on his property."

Luke arched a brow. "A condemnation letter?"

"Yes, it's standard procedure in an eminent domain case so I really should not have been surprised. A government body, in this case our city, supposedly acting in the public's best interest, orders the company to condemn the property. Usually that's done before attorneys can formulate a case for their plaintiffs. But in this case, I was able to represent Mr. Coroni based on the support he was receiving. So in a way, although he is the plaintiff, I'm representing a group that was organized to support him. The letter was annoying because it ordered him to move off the property while we're still in litigation. It's as if they assume they're going to win."

Luke didn't say anything. But she could tell by the way his hand tightened around his fork that what she'd said had angered him. "Where is he supposed to go?"

"Nowhere if I have anything to do with it. I've filed an

injunction to block the condemnation and I'm hoping
Judge Ivory will approve it. He's up for reelection next
year and now he's between a rock and a hard place. Some
citizens support Whitedyer but others do not."

"So what's next?" Luke asked.

"Now through me they will make him an offer, which
they've done once before and he turned them down. Last
time they offered him two million dollars."

Luke let out a whistle. "And he turned it down?"

Mackenzie nodded. "Yes. I suspect they will make
him another offer before the date of the hearing to avoid
going to court. If they want the land bad enough they
might double it."

"And you don't think he'll take it?"

She shook her head. "For him it's not about the money.
It's about keeping something that he feels belongs to him."

A few moments passed and they were quiet again. Deciding it was time to change the subject and finally find
out what he wanted to talk to her about, she placed her
fork down and said, "Okay, Luke, what is it? What do you
want to talk to me about?"

He stared at her for a moment before placing his own
fork down. "I got a call from Cam today."

She nodded. "And?"

"A rodeo, the first outfit that we toured with, the Bill
Picket International rodeo, will be in Los Angeles next
week. It will be too soon for me to complete except for
maybe one event. Depending on what the doctor says on
Thursday, of course."

She felt her lungs beginning to burn and swallowed
deeply. "And which event is that?"

"The relay race. It will be just what I need to ease back
into things. I'll be riding Cisco and will know how much
I can handle."

She wanted to give him a reassuring smile but knew if
she tried doing so she would probably fail miserably. "So
when are you leaving?"

"Saturday afternoon. And again that depends on

whether the doctor says I'm good to go. He said four to six weeks recuperation time and it's been four weeks."

She nodded again and resumed eating her food. There was no doubt in her mind the doctor would say he would be good to go, just like there was no doubt in her mind that he would be going. But why was hearing that he was leaving bothering her when she'd known that he would? Why did the thought of not waking up beside him any longer send a lonely chill down her spine? There would be no more casseroles waiting for her when she walked through the door. No more hot and torrid kisses to greet her whenever she'd had a bad day, and no more of Luke's lovemaking putting her to sleep each night.

"Mac?"

She forced her head up and met his gaze. She loved him and wondered if he saw the truth in her eyes. Probably not. "Yes?"

"We knew I would be leaving one day and—"

"Hey, no sweat," she said, deciding to stop whatever he was about to say. "It was enjoyable while it lasted but we both knew it wasn't forever, Luke. I'm fine," she lied. But then truthfully, she added, "And I'm going to miss you."

She watched Luke blow out a frustrated breath before slowly pushing away from the table. And then he was there, standing beside her and offering her his hand. "And I'm going to miss you too."

She looked up into his eyes as she placed her hand in his. He then gently assisted her to her feet. The moment she stood he was pulling her into his arms and taking her mouth like he needed this kiss as much as she did. He needed to taste her passion, feed on it, feed off it, and do what she planned to do, store it inside of her when they were no longer together. She would keep busy. She certainly had plenty to do. Farley would make sure of that. She would have to be on her toes, although she'd rather be on her back in bed somewhere with Luke. But that wouldn't be happening. When he left on Saturday he wouldn't be coming back.

She plastered her body against his, needing to feed off

his strength. Okay, he was leaving but she would make sure he missed her when he did go. This would be an affair he would remember.

And so she returned his kiss with a force she hoped would jar his senses, ram his nerves. She felt him quiver and deliberately let her hips settle in the alcove of his thighs. And she knew that tonight and those remaining nights until he left would belong only to them.

"So, did you find out anything?" Clayton asked Alex the moment he walked into his office and sat down in the chair across from his desk.

Alex rubbed his hand down his face. "Not sure, so you might want to grab Syneda so I can tell you both at the same time."

It took Clayton less than a minute to summon his wife. She swept into the room with her mass of golden-bronze hair flying around her shoulders. She smiled at Alex. "How are you holding up, Dad?"

Alex grinned as he stood and offered her his seat but she waved to decline. "I'm holding up just fine," he said, sitting back down. "Had I known fatherhood was so much fun, I would have gotten Christy pregnant a long time ago."

Clayton frowned. "No, you would not have," he said with an edge in his voice.

Syneda rolled her eyes. "I'm sure Alex meant after they were married, Clayton, so please stop looking like you want to hurt somebody. You're reminding me of Dex." She smiled over at Alex. "So what have you found?"

"Nothing, which has me suspicious?"

Syneda raised an arched brow. "Why would that have you suspicious?"

"Because in my line of work I've discovered if anything is too good to be true, usually it isn't. Then on the drive over here while I was talking to Christy on the mobile phone, the reporter in her asked a lot of questions; especially after I told her what happened to Mac's office and Jake's cows."

"What kind of questions did she ask?" Clayton said, knowing how inquisitive his baby sister could be.

He moved from behind his desk and sat on the edge, freeing his chair for his wife. It was the gentlemanly thing to do. Besides, as long as she was standing, his attention would be on her legs and not what Alex was saying.

When Syneda took her seat, Alex continued. "If the intent of those two incidents was to scare Mac off the case, then why not go to the source, which is Mr. Coroni? He's an old man, so why not go about scaring him instead of Mac? After all he's the one holding back, the one who owns the land with no intention to ever sell. Mac is merely representing him or, in this case, the group of people banded together to support him."

Syneda and Clayton exchanged glances. Then Syneda spoke. "Umm, Christy does have a good point. But I think the reason has something to do with Whitedyer's attorney. At first he threw subtle hints that it would be in Mac's best interest to get off the case."

"Yes," Alex agreed. "But from what I was able to dig up on Lewis Farley, he is the kind of attorney who likes the attention to be on him in the courtroom. I think the first time he saw Mac he figured she might be a liability, since more than likely the focus would shift off him onto her."

"Especially if there were any male jurors," Syneda said, smiling, shaking her head slowly as she followed Alex's train of thought. She not only followed what he was insinuating but totally agreed with it. She couldn't help but remember the night of the auction five years ago and how the moment Mackenzie had come forward to bid on Ashton, the entire room got silent, and the eyes of most of the men there that night, including Clayton's, had nearly popped out of their sockets. Mac was a very beautiful woman.

"Farley is just that much of a jerk?" Clayton asked.

"Seems that way. I was able to get the videotapes of a few courtroom cases he was involved with," Alex said. "The man is the drama king."

Syneda shook her head. She knew a few such attorneys

who made it their business to use the courtroom as their showroom. Instead of simply presenting their case, they spent their time delivering a performance they felt worthy of an Oscar. "Okay, there's nothing we can do about Farley but make sure Mac is well prepared," she said. "However, I'm still curious as to why no one has bothered to harass Mr. Coroni. And I'm even more curious to find out what happens to the land when he dies. He's in his late seventies, was recently hospitalized for health reasons, and according to the report Mac faxed me, he has no living relatives."

"Umm, that's very interesting," Alex said, getting to his feet and heading for the door. "I think I need to check out a few more things."

"The hunk is actually leaving?" Sam asked, slipping into the chair across from Mackenzie's desk.

Mackenzie tried to fight the tightening she felt in her chest. Yesterday the doctor had given Luke his approval for him to participate in the relay race, but he had stressed it would be another month or so before he could actually take on the full activities of a bull rider.

Luke was still anticipating being ready for the Reno rodeo in September. If he followed the doctor's orders and didn't overexert himself, he would be ready to participate by then. "Yes, he's leaving, but I knew he would. There was never a time that I thought he would stay. I told you that."

"Yes, but I was hoping. The two of you had gotten so close. Darn it. I'm going to miss teasing you about all those hickeys on your neck."

Mackenzie didn't say anything. If only Sam knew about the marks that Luke had left in places no one could see. To say the man liked branding her was an understatement. But then again, she had to admit she enjoyed waking up each day wearing his brand.

"What are you going to do with yourself once he's gone?" Sam asked, reclaiming her attention.

"The same thing I did before he got here. Stay busy.

The Whitedyer case assures me of that. I need to have all my wits about me when I face off with Farley."

"And Mr. Coroni hasn't changed his mind about the offer the city and Whitedyer are making him? That's a lot of money he's turning down. And each offer gets substantially higher."

"I know and I can see them making yet another one before the hearing next week. Heck, it wouldn't surprise me if they pulled out a check at the hearing and made a final offer, although doing so would steal some of Farley's fire, since he's looking forward to humiliating me in the courtroom. The city and Whitedyer are desperate. Look what they stand to gain if a settlement is reached out of court and Mr. Coroni accepts what they're offering."

Mackenzie shook her head. "And the sad thing about is that I think there was a slim chance Mr. Coroni might have accepted their offer at one time, but then Farley had to go and make him mad."

"With Farley, that was easy to do. The man is a jerk fifty times over."

Mackenzie smiled. There was no way she was not going to agree with Sam. She pulled her purse from the drawer. "I'm checking out early today. Luke and I are going into town to celebrate the good news he got from the doctor yesterday and his last night here in Oklahoma City."

Sam's face brightened. "So the two of you are going on a date?"

Mackenzie shook her head. "No, it's not a date. We're just doing dinner, and he wanted to drop by the mall to pick up a couple of pairs of jeans and a few more shirts."

Sam stood. "Whatever, but it sounds like a date to me."

Mackenzie shook her head as she pushed away from her desk and got to her feet. "Trust me, it won't be a date."

It ended up being a date. Their first.

After enjoying dinner at a nice seafood restaurant and a trip to the mall, they decided since it was a Friday night and downtown Oklahoma City was in full swing, they would spend the rest of the evening visiting some of the popular Bricktown nightclubs. At City Walk they were able to grab a table in the back where they talked while enjoying a glass of wine and listening to live music. They even got on the dance floor a few times. It was after midnight when they drove into Mackenzie's driveway.

She knew it was utter nonsense to dwell on the fact that tonight was their last night together, but as they walked side by side up the walk to her front door, she couldn't help it. She loved him.

He glanced over at her when they reached the door. "You okay?" he asked softly.

She inhaled deeply. Despite her outward display of calmness he'd still managed to pick up on her tension. "Yes, why do you ask?"

"Because you've gotten quiet on me."

She searched his eyes and as usual was touched by his concern. "I was just thinking."

"About Mr. Coroni?"

Her lips quirked. This was their last night together. How on earth could he think that her mind would be focused on anybody but him? "No, it wasn't about Mr. Coroni," she replied honestly.

It was then that he looked at her again, his gaze sharpening. Moments later he slowly drew in a deep breath and let it out. "I hope I've shown you this week how much I'm going to miss you," he said in a low, husky voice.

Yes, he had. It had been special to know she had been wanted that much. But then she in turn had shown him just how much he would be missed as well. No limitations had been placed on their lovemaking. It was as if they'd been trying to stock up on what they both would be going without for a while. And she knew that tonight, their last time together, would be no different. In less than twenty-four hours he would be returning to his world and would leave her in hers.

"Mac?"

She glanced up at him. "Yes, I know you're going to miss me and I hope you know that I'll miss you as well."

He nodded. "Yes."

There was no reason to ask if he would return on occasion to see her because she knew that he wouldn't. Luke was a loner and he'd told her a number of times he wasn't into long-term relationships, and he definitely wasn't the marrying kind.

There was nothing else to say. They had enjoyed the weeks they had spent together and it was time to move on. But she had fallen in love with him because he represented everything she'd ever wanted in a man. His physical attributes, although they rated high, were of minor importance compared to the kindness he showed, not only to her but to Theo and her men. They all liked him, respected him. Even Sam and Peyton liked him.

He wasn't quick to fly off the handle like Lawrence had been, and he didn't mind pampering her, something Lawrence never considered doing. Although he was a rough-and-tough cowboy, there was a gentleness to Luke, an ingrained depth of compassion that she always found touching. And she knew he was loyal to a fault to those he loved, and Luke loved his family. Luke also loved the rodeo. She knew that right now it was a love she couldn't even try and compete against. And she wouldn't. Not now. Not ever.

She stood back while he opened the door and the moment she took a few steps inside a thrumming heat moved through her. It was so intense she couldn't do anything but pause a moment and draw in a deep breath. She glanced over her shoulder to see Luke closing the door behind them, and she turned to him, retraced the steps separating them.

She could tell from the look in his eyes that he knew without her saying a word what she was thinking. There was nothing left to be said. They had run out of words and were quickly running out of time. She felt so much

love for him at that moment that the intensity of her emotions overwhelmed her, nearly short-circuited her mind
and caused warmth to seep directly into her bones.

He reached out for her and she all but tumbled into his
arms, seeking and needing that gratification she always
found in his embrace. Reaching up, she wrapped her arms
around his neck, stared up into his handsome, picture-
perfect face. Then stretching up on tiptoes, she brought
her mouth to his.

The moment their lips touched, he took over the kiss.
It wasn't surprising, nor was it disappointing. It was just
what she wanted and she returned the kiss with a hunger
to match his. Her heart raced, and when he locked his
arms around her waist to hold her tight against him, she
told him with her lips, her tongue, as much of her mouth
as she could, just what his kiss was doing to her. What his
touch was doing to her.

Their tongues mated as intimately as tongues could
mate and as greedily. He was doing more than tasting her
passion, he was provoking it. Taking it to another level.
One that would require a high degree of sensual interven-
tion. She had never wanted or needed a man the way she
needed him. Right now. This very second.

He pulled back from the kiss and whispered hotly
against her lips. "The bedroom."

She shook her head. "No, right here," she responded in
an anxious tone.

Not giving him a chance to say anything, she tossed her
shoulder bag aside and eased down to the floor, pulling him
with her onto the Oriental rug. When he was on his knees
before her, she whispered, "I need you now, Luke."

The passion she saw in his eyes made her pulse race,
made her heart throb in her chest, and as she watched him
tear off his shirt, popping buttons in the process, she knew
this joining would match the intensity of her feelings.

After he had removed his shirt he went for hers, strip-
ping it off but being more careful with her buttons. Her
bra was next and with expert hands he undid the front

clasp, freeing her twin mounds. He bent his head and his mouth was there, greedy, hungry, and she shuddered at the feel of his lips on her breasts; his tongue stroking, caressing, licking her with a vivacity that left her breathless.

He pulled back and pushed up her skirt, inserted his hand between her thighs, caught hold of her panties and tugged them down and off her. Then he went back to the skirt, slid down the zipper, and removed the skirt from her as well. With her completely naked, he took a second to lean back on his haunches and study her, let his gaze take his fill of her before reaching out and sliding his hand up her legs, past her knees, to the area between her thighs. The area he had branded as his weeks ago. The part of her she had decided would always belong to him.

And then his hands tightened on her hips, gripped them in a way that brought heat there and made sensations flow through her, so that she would be fully aware of what he was about to do. He moved closer, eased down, tilted up her hips and brought his face down to her, right there to her center.

The moment his tongue slid inside of her she shuddered into spasms that seemed endless. Unbearable. Yet needed. Started a spark that ignited into a raging inferno within her. He deepened the kiss while holding her hips firmly in place, locking his mouth on her, not intending for her to go anywhere. Her lungs hurt when she tried withholding a scream, but it was useless and when he thrust his tongue deeper still, she could no longer fight the sensations that ripped through her and was forced to let it go.

She screamed.

Sensations washed over her, through her, and he didn't let up. Her body was throbbing; her mind spun and every part of her felt sensitive to a degree that stunned her. While she lay there, trying to force air back through her lungs, he pulled back and then stood to remove the rest of his clothes.

And then he rejoined her, straddled her body; and she gazed up into his eyes, locked with them, just seconds before he pressed his arousal down and then in, entering her and going deep and thrusting hard. He withdrew and thrust deep again, repeating the process over and over.

She inhaled sharply when sensations returned, crashing down on her, engulfing her with every stroke he made into her. And then he groaned out her name and pushed her over the edge with him as she became enmeshed in sensations so keen, they almost sliced through her, made her body feel as if it were being swept away on a tide of concentrated sensations that led out to an open sea of intense sexual bliss. It was there that she drowned in pleasure, convulsed in ecstasy.

And then she called his name, fought back the urge to whisper that she loved him, as she plunged into what seemed like an abyss of total fulfillment and unending passion.

"Take care of yourself, Luke."

Mackenzie's statement, spoken in a quiet tone of voice, had Luke studying the depths of her eyes. Cam had arrived and it was time for him to go. But for some reason he didn't want to leave her just yet. What they had shared last night and through most of the day had blown him away. Emotions he didn't want to deal with were trying to overtake his common sense.

He forced himself to glance around. He would have fond memories of this kitchen, the first place they had made love when making it to the bedroom hadn't been an option. And he would miss his early morning coffee chats with Theo and the guys. But most of all, he would miss the time he had spent with Mac.

In the month he had been here, she had done something no other woman had done. She had gotten under his skin. And he of all people knew that that wasn't good. They needed distance between them now. Once he was on the rodeo circuit again he would get himself together, screw his head back on straight, and appreciate the time they spent together. And he would accept that she was not in his future. No woman was.

Sighing deeply, he finally responded by saying, "You take care of yourself as well. And I hope things go in your favor regarding the Whitedyer Corporation." He smiled. "I have a feeling that Farley guy won't be ready for you."

"Thanks for the vote of confidence. It means a lot." She paused and then asked, "Will you be attending Quantum's graduation celebration in a few weeks?"

He paused for a second and then shook his head and said, "No, I've already told the family I'm going to be busy that weekend and won't be able to make it"

She nodded slowly. "Oh, I see"

He doubted she did, because if she was *that* intuitive then she would know he had decided not to go because he knew she would be there and he needed a clean break from her. He didn't want to run into her anytime soon at a Madaris family gathering.

He took a step back. "I need to go. Cam is waiting."

"All right."

He wanted to reach out and take her into his arms and kiss her one last time, but he knew that once more wouldn't be enough. And it was a risk he didn't want to take. "You take care."

"I will and you do the same. And remember what the doctor said. Don't overdo anything."

A smile tugged at his lips. He couldn't help remembering how he nearly overexerted himself last night and today while in bed with her, but he definitely didn't have any complaints. "I won't."

He was about to turn around to leave, but couldn't make himself do so, he was so damn tempted to taste her mouth one last time. Evidently she knew what he was thinking and took the matter out of his hands by reaching out and wrapping her arms around his neck and leaning in closer to kiss him.

He returned her kiss, sinking into her mouth with an urgency that he felt in all parts of his body. There was no doubt in his mind that he would miss her. And moments later when she pulled back he knew he had to leave now or no telling what he would be tempted to do next.

"See you," he said softly, reaching out and rubbing her cheek with the tip of his thumb, needing to touch her one last time.

And then he turned and walked out the door, forcing himself to move by placing one foot in front of the other, trying to ignore the pang of regret that was trying to consume him. Fighting the urge to look back.

His bags were already in the car so he opened the door and slid inside. Cam glanced over at him and didn't say anything for a moment and then looked over at him and asked, "You sure about this?"

He frowned, wondering what Cam was getting at and why. But then he had an idea. Cam knew him. The two of them were thick as thieves so Cam probably guessed what he was feeling. Just what he was fighting. Otherwise he wouldn't have asked. And the pitiful truth was that, no, he wasn't sure about it. Hell, at the moment he wasn't sure of anything. But he didn't want to dwell on that. So he responded by saying, "Let's get out of here."

Cam started the ignition and Luke was tempted to look back when the car began moving down the long driveway. But he didn't.

Chapter 21

The following week was the hardest for Mackenzie. She buried herself in work so deep, she didn't have time to dwell on how much she missed Luke. But at night in her lonely bed she had dwelled on it. She had missed him. And took each day, each night, one moment at a time.

The judge had agreed to let Mr. Coroni remain in the house until after the hearing was over and she was grateful for that. But she knew the Whitedyer Corporation wasn't happy about it. During a hearing in the judge's chambers, both sides were set to deliver oral arguments, after which the judge would offer a recommendation.

Mackenzie wasn't sure how that would go in light of the official notice she had received that morning Whitedyer, along with the city, had put together a comprehensive redevelopment plan. In addition to Whitedyer's utilizing some of the acres for expansion of their company, they had also come up with a proposal where the remaining acreage would be further utilized to relieve economic stress with the construction of a conference center and city park.

On top of that, they had increased their settlement offer to Mr Coroni by another million dollars. What Whitedyer had done was maneuver things in such a way that if the case were ever appealed to a higher court, a decision of any kind would lean in Whitedyer's favor because they could easily prove they had been more than fair and gracious in their dealings with Mr. Coroni. That was a smart move on their part and she could just imagine the smile Lewis Farley was sporting about now.

But still, although things didn't look good on her end, she refused to give up or persuade Mr. Coroni to give in. And after going over all the documentation she had, all the notes she had taken, and all the case studies that she had reviewed, she felt there was something she was missing; some vital piece of information she had overlooked or should be aware of.

The intercom on her desk interrupted her thoughts. "Yes, Priscilla?"

"Mr. and Mrs. Madaris are here to see you."

A surprised smile touched Mackenzie's lips and she literally sighed in relief. She hadn't expected Clayton and Syneda to arrive until later in the week. It had been their plan to spend time at her place to go over every detail of prior eminent domain cases they had reviewed so she could be prepared. The thought that the two of them would give up their time to help her meant a lot. "Please send them in."

She stood and watched the two enter her office, a power couple if ever there was one. Before marrying, they had been successful attorneys in their own right, and since forming the partnership of Madaris and Madaris they were even more so.

Mackenzie could vividly recall the first time she had seen them and had immediately thought they definitely belonged together. Clayton was such a handsome man and Syneda was truly a beautiful woman. And although their disagreements could rattle some of their family, the attorney in her always enjoyed listening to them offer different viewpoints.

She couldn't help but wonder about their position on the Whitedyer case and was eager to hear what they had to say after she filled them in on the latest developments. Standing, she moved around her desk to embrace the couple.

"This is a wonderful surprise. I wasn't expecting you until later in the week," she said, smiling.

"We thought it best to come now," Syneda was saying. Although she was smiling, Mackenzie picked up her serious tone.

"Alex is parking the car and will be joining us," Syneda added

"Alex?" Mackenzie's gaze shifted between Syneda and Clayton. "Does that mean he's found something?"

It was Clayton who responded. "Alex can always be depended on to find *something* But how you'll want to handle what he's discovered is another matter."

Mackenzie lifted a brow. But before she could ask anything further, Priscilla escorted the very handsome Alex Maxwell into her office.

Once everyone was seated Mackenzie sank back into the chair behind her desk and glanced over at Alex. "So, what did you find out?"

"More than I really wanted to," Alex said, shifting in his chair. "There were some things that concerned me about this whole case, things Christy brought up. First, why were you the one being harassed not Mr. Coroni, and then, since he is an elderly man, who would be inheriting all that property upon his death."

Mackenzie nodded. "I wondered about that too, but figured the culprit couldn't do anything to Mr. Coroni because he was confined in the hospital at the time of both incidents. And as for who will be inheriting the property upon his death, it will be the petitioners—his supporters who founded the Coroni Foundation—so they can continue the fight after his death if need be. It's the Coroni Foundation that hired me to represent him."

"But you've never seen a copy of his will, right?" Syneda asked

"Right. I'm not Mr. Coroni's personal attorney so I had no reason to be privy to that," Mackenzie responded.

"The reason that Mr. Coroni came to me instead of using Lamar Perkins, his personal attorney, was because of a conflict of interest. Lamar Perkins's stepmother is on the city council."

"That definitely would have been a conflict of interest," Alex said, nodding.

"And the reason Mr. Coroni wasn't included in the harassment makes sense, but can we be absolutely sure that his will says what everyone assumes it does?" Clayton asked.

"I believe the Coroni foundation would have made absolutely sure and might even have a copy of it," Mackenzie said. "Besides, why would Mr. Coroni lie about something like that?"

"He's not lying if he doesn't know any differently. What if his attorney made changes without him knowing it? Have you ever met Lamar Perkins?" Clayton wanted to know.

"Yes," Mackenzie answered. "The local attorneys get together quarterly as part of a networking group here in town. It's my understanding that Lamar moved to town a year or so before I did to be close to his dad. His parents divorced when he was young and he never established a relationship with his father. His dad died a few months after he moved here but he has a close relationship with his stepmother. Lamar is in his middle thirties and is quite popular with the single ladies around town."

Alex sighed deeply and then he said, "Through my investigation, I've verified all that you've said. However, there are some things that have thrown a monkey wrench into this case."

"More like a crowbar," Syneda said, shaking her head.

Alex chuckled. "Be that as it may, I have reason to believe that Lamar Perkins might be up to no good."

Mackenzie regarded him curiously. "And why would you say that?"

"For two reasons actually," Alex said. "First of all, I had someone check, and I learned that the will the foun-

dation has in their possession isn't the most recent one that
was drawn up by Mr. Coroni. And the next is because
Lamar Perkins is having a secret affair with someone who
works at Whitedyer. Not only does she work there but she
is someone close to the Coroni negotiations."

Mackenzie would pace the floor for a moment, then pause,
glance down at the documents in her hand and then
pace again. The three people sitting in her office knew
what had been revealed in the papers she'd just read was
reason enough to make a person pace . . . among other
things.

Standing to stretch his muscles, Clayton felt it was
time to ask, "So, Mac, what do you plan to do?"

She stopped pacing and glanced over at Clayton,
Syneda, and Alex. She then glanced at the clock on the
wall. Had two hours passed already? She met Clayton's
gaze and shrugged. "I honestly don't know."

"Keep in mind that technically, no laws have been broken," Syneda said.

"Yes, but . . ." Mackenzie didn't finish what she was
about to say, she just shook her head. Taking a deep sigh
she moved back across the room to sit at her desk. "But if
we can prove an affair is going on then that means there's
a chance Lamar Perkins has been privy to information
that he shouldn't know about."

"True," Clayton agreed. "Syneda, Alex, and I discussed
everything in detail yesterday after Alex dropped the report by the office. I think Perkins has been counseling
Coroni on how to handle Whitedyer based on information
he's being fed from this woman who works for Whitedyer.
Coroni has turned down three offers, yet Whitedyer returns
to the table with another one and each offer increases substantially. And now, according to you, their most recent offer more than triples the first."

"And Perkins may have convinced Coroni that since
there's a good chance if the case goes to court, he will lose
anyway, he should hold out until the last and get as much

money out of Whitedyer as he can. Chances are that's what the old man is doing since he trusts Perkins," Syneda added.

Mackenzie nodded. "But how does that benefit Perkins?"

Alex dragged in a deep breath. "It doesn't unless Perkins has convinced Coroni that he deserves a share of the proceeds . . . or unless Perkins has made himself the sole beneficiary in the will and hopes Mr. Coroni's days are numbered, either for health reasons or because Perkins is working behind the scenes to assure Coroni meets with an untimely death."

At Mackenzie's shocked look, Alex added, "Trust me, four million dollars is a lot of money. People have killed for a lot less."

"Yes, but won't that swing suspicions toward Lamar since he'll be the one to gain substantially if something were to happen to Mr. Coroni?"

"Not necessarily," Clayton said. "Especially if it's arranged to look like Coroni died of natural causes, and there are ways to achieve that, especially for someone his age who has medical problems. Like Syneda said, so far no laws have been broken even if Coroni takes the money by settling out of court, which we can all bank on him doing. But I think we should talk with the person who's handling the police investigation of the incidents involving you and let them take over from there."

Mackenzie nodded. "Detective Adams is handling the case and he's pretty sharp."

"In that case he probably won't mind us giving him a heads-up regarding what we've discovered."

Mackenzie reached for her phone. "I'll give him a call right now to see if he can meet with us later this evening."

"Glad to see you back, Luke."

"Thanks, Jim. Glad to be back," he responded, knowing it was a lie. It had been a week and he had yet to get back into the swing of things and that wasn't good. Even Cisco had picked up on it. They had won the relay race but barely.

An hour or so later he was back at the hotel. Cam and the others had decided to hit the town to celebrate but he hadn't been interested. Nadine had tried getting his attention after the show but he had quickly gone the other way. She was definitely someone he hadn't wanted to see and it ticked him off that the woman still thought he was interested in her when he'd done everything to show that he was not.

After his shower he got a beer from the six-pack Cam had on ice before collapsing down on the bed and checking to see what was on the television. Grabbing the remote he, began switching channels when he couldn't find anything that held his interest, trying hard not to let his mind dwell on one particular person. But he couldn't help it.

As much as he tried he couldn't think of anything else and it had been that way for a while. And it was worse at night when he couldn't get to sleep for images of her flashing through his mind. Vivid images. Heated images. He wondered what she was doing. Was she nervous about the hearing that would be coming up soon? Had Clayton and Syneda been able to help her out any?

He reached for his cell phone and then drew his hand back. The last thing he needed was to hear her voice. The way his mind had been playing tricks on him, he thought he heard it sometimes anyway. The only connection he had with her was through Theo. He called the man practically every day to make sure all the men at the ranch were keeping an eye on things. It was important to him that Mac be safe.

He rubbed his face in frustration. Hell, if he'd known it would be this hard to sever their relationship he would never have touched her. No, that was a lie, and he knew it. There was no way he could not have touched Mac.

Closing his eyes, he dragged the details of that night

from his memory. He'd thought then, just like he thought now, that she was the most beautiful woman he had ever seen.

He inwardly sighed and opened his eyes. It was time for him to move on and try to put her out of his mind. It wouldn't be easy but he was determined to do it.

"So, Detective Adams, what do you think?"

The man glanced around at the faces of the four people who had requested a meeting with him, before turning to Mackenzie to answer her question. "As Ms. Madaris said, aside from ethical issues, no actual laws have been broken. However, due to the amount of money involved, I agree with Mr. Maxwell that I need to be on my guard and make sure nothing happens to Mr. Coroni. He's already proven part of your theory is correct by deciding to settle out of court."

No one was surprised when, prior to leaving her office, Mackenzie received a call from Mr. Coroni saying he couldn't take any more pressure and would accept Whitedyer's latest offer. "But how can you make sure nothing happens to him once he gets the money?" she couldn't help but ask.

"We can't. I'm banking on the idea that if Perkins is thinking about something so devious, he'll let things ride for a while and do nothing. But before I assume anything, I would like to know who is the beneficiary of Coroni's will in case we're barking up the wrong tree. Unfortunately, I don't even have a reason to pay Perkins a visit, at least not one that wouldn't raise his suspicions. But I will visit Mr. Coroni under the pretext that I'm still investigating those incidents involving you, and wanted to make sure he hadn't been the victim of similar threats himself. Then, as subtly as I can, I'm going to plant the seed in his mind that maybe he needs to watch his back. I'm hoping he gets my hint. In the meantime I'll keep a close eye on Perkins's girlfriend, Camille Yeager, who happens to be Lewis Farley's assistant. She might be the greedier one in all this I have reason to believe she's been sharing Farley's bed as well and that might be where she's gotten her information to share with Perkins. Farley is such an egomaniac that if he ever discovers she's betrayed him, all hell is going to break loose."

"And there's no way that we can expose her?" Mackenzie asked.

"No, because legally she hasn't broken any laws. And although we can only guess at what information she might have passed on to Perkins, we don't have any proof that she actually told him anything."

Mackenzie paused and considered everything that had been said. "It's really kind of frustrating to have all this information and not be able to do anything with it."

Alex regarded her with understanding. "Yes, and now since Coroni has decided to settle out of court that technically ends your involvement in the matter, Mac, as well as that of the foundation, and I'm sure they aren't going to be happy with Coroni's decision. They were depending on him to stick it out and they expected a long court battle. Technically, he used them."

Mackenzie noted that everyone was nodding. Yes, Mr. Coroni had used the foundation but he had also used her firm. "In all fairness to Mr. Coroni, I think in the beginning he wanted to hold on to his land but somehow Perkins convinced him that he didn't have a snowball's chance in hell of winning so he gave in."

"That might be true," Clayton was saying. "But come next week the man is going to be four times richer than he would have been had he not listened to Perkins. For all we know, all three of them, Perkins, Coroni, and Yeager, might be in this thing together."

Syneda shook her head. "And if that's the case then there's still nothing we can do because everyone is happy. They're getting the amount of money they were aiming for and Whitedyer gets the land it needs to expand their operation. The only one left holding the bag is the group that supported Coroni in the cause, the foundation," she said.

Syneda chuckled as she added, "However, I think Farley might be a tad unhappy since he was looking forward to facing off with you in the courtroom, Mac."

Mackenzie rolled her eyes and heaved a disgusted sigh. "Lewis Farley is the last person on my mind right now. As the foundation's attorney I'm going to try and convince Mr. Coroni that the least he can do is pay their legal fees out of the proceeds. And I also intend to work on his conscience a little bit."

Clayton chuckled. "For some reason I still think there's a lot more to this than what we know."

Alex nodded, glanced around the room at everyone, and said, "I agree and I plan to dig a little further."

Chapter 22

Luke held the phone from his ear a minute and released a deep sigh before putting it back in place. His great grandmother had heard he wouldn't be coming home to QT's graduation celebration and was giving him one blistering scolding.

"Yes, Mama Laverne, I hear what you're saying but I just got back," he injected the moment he was able to get in a word. "And if I want to be in shape for the rodeo in Reno next month I'm going to have to get a lot of practice time. QT knows how proud I am of him and that I'd be there if I could."

A moment passed and he stood there in his kitchen holding the phone while she gave her spiel of how her days were numbered and it was the duty of her grands and great-grands to make sure they availed themselves of every golden opportunity to be with her while they could.

"I'm coming home in a few weeks, I promise," he said, hating that what she was saying was getting to him when he knew she'd probably be around well into the hundreds. But still, she knew how to play him like a fine-tuned guitar, because no matter what, he loved the old gal. She had a phenomenal strength and a firm dedication to her family. And like him, she could be stubborn when it suited her and this was one of those times. She just wouldn't let up. She was digging into him big-time.

Knowing he had to get off the phone before she had him agreeing to catch the next flight out to Houston, he took his finger and began tapping the receiver of the phone. "Oh, what's that noise? Sounds like we're getting a bad connection. I better go. And don't forget, you'll see me in a couple of weeks. Love you. Goodbye."

He then hung up the phone and heaved a deep breath. Boy, she had been on a roll and he couldn't help but wonder what that was about. Knowing no one, not even her six living sons, had ever possessed the ability to figure her out, he decided to let it go.

He glanced around the room, glad to be back at his place for a spell. The next rodeo would be the one in Reno, and as he'd told his great-grandmother he needed plenty of practice time. This little condo here in Abilene was ideal. He also owned a condo in Houston, the one he considered his primary residence although he was seldom there. A few years ago Uncle Jake and his three older cousins, Justin, Dex, and Clayton, had gotten together in a business venture to put up the fifteen-story Madaris Building, which included not only the building but also an entire business park comprising numerous shops, restaurants, banks, boutiques, professional offices, and a movie theater. Keeping it all in the family, they had hired Slade and Blade's company to handle the project, all the way from the design to the construction. The result had been breathtaking and he had been one of the first to invest by purchasing one of the condos that overlooked the office park.

Thinking about his condo in Houston made him miss being home. There was nothing to beat a family gathering of Madarises. It would be good to see everyone and show them that he was doing fine and was all in one piece. But now was not the time, especially since Mac would be attending the event.

He had talked to Clayton a few days ago and he'd told him the outcome of the Whitedyer case and how the old man had cunningly settled out of court. A part of Luke got pissed that anyone could be so devious, and he thought of all the hard work Mac had put into the case, doing what she could to make sure the old coot didn't lose his home when he had every intention of settling out of court anyway, as soon as the right price came along. "Damn."

He glanced at clock on his stove. It was still early and he was hungry. He decided to drive into town for a pizza. Getting back on a bull would be hard work and he needed to make sure he had strength to endure.

Blade reached over to the nightstand and picked up his cell phone, careful not to wake up the woman whose bed he was in, Tina or Nina, hell, he wasn't sure at the moment. He only recalled that she could work her body like nobody else.

He clicked on his phone. "Yes," he answered in a low voice.

"Blade, this is your great-grandmother. I need you to get Luke home."

Blade raised a concerned brow and quickly sat up in bed. His heart began racing. "Why? What's wrong? What's happened?"

"Nothing has happened. I just need him here on Saturday for QT's party. I talked to him yesterday and he said he won't be making it."

Blade inhaled deeply to calm down once he realized there was no emergency. "And he has a good reason for not coming. He has a rodeo he's training for and—"

"I don't care about his rodeo. I need to see him, to make sure he's okay. Either he comes here or I'm going there and I want you to be my escort when I do."

"What!"

He glanced over at the woman, Tina or Nina, who had opened her eyes and was glaring at him. Evidently, she wasn't a morning person. That was understandable since it was barely the crack of dawn. What was his great-grandmother doing up so early anyway?

He held his hand over his cell phone and said in a low

tone, "Sorry," to the woman in bed. "This is a business call that I need to take in private," he added, before easing his naked body out of bed and making it to Tina's or Nina's bathroom, closing the door behind him and frowning deeply as he leaned back against it.

"Didn't Luke tell you that he's okay?" Blade asked. Jeeze, he could just imagine taking his great-grandmother to visit Luke. *Luke would kill me.* According to Luke the last time she visited she had done a little bit of house-cleaning and had thrown out all his *Playboy* magazines . . . among other things. And she wanted *him* to take her? Heaven help him.

He cleared his throat. "Mama Laverne, there's no need for you to go all the way to Abilene to check on Luke. He might not be coming home this weekend but I'm sure he'll be here in a few weeks."

"No, I want to see him this weekend. You, Luke, and Slade are as tight as some of those jeans you like seeing your girlfriends wear, so I'm sure one of you can convince Luke of the wisdom of letting me see for myself that he's all right. Otherwise, you and I will pay him a visit. Just clear your calendar because we'll be gone for a week. Goodbye."

She then hung up the phone. He was left scowling and wondering, among other things, how she knew that he liked seeing women in tight jeans.

Mackenzie smiled when she glanced across the kitchen table at the man who had surprised her and shown up for breakfast. There was no doubt about it, her cousin Ashton Sinclair was an extremely handsome man. All the women in Oklahoma thought so, and had for years, but not a single one of them had managed to grab his interest because the military had been his first love. Now he was Colonel Ashton Sinclair of the United States Marines and had been for years. Like her he was half African American and half Native American, with nut-brown skin, dark eyes, high chiseled cheekbones, and coal-black hair that flowed freely around his shoulders. He was also tall, probably about six-four or more

And he was happily married to Netherland, the woman he had picked out as his mate for life, and the two of them had triplets, three adorable yet rambunctious four-year-old sons. Identical and the spitting image of their father. There was no doubt in her mind that Hunter, Brody, and Wolf Sinclair would all be heartbreakers one day.

Ashton would always have a special place in her heart, because when she hadn't been able to take living in Boston with her aunt any longer, he had been the one she could always depend on to keep her world sane. He had been the one who'd footed her college bill until she'd managed to acquire a scholarship for law school, and when she returned to Oklahoma after her breakup with Lawrence, Ashton had been Standfield, De Meglio, and Mahoney's first client. That was when Mackenzie had acted as his legal representative at the Bachelors Auction. That was also the night she'd met Luke.

She tried not to think about the latter as she took a sip of coffee and watched Ashton eat the breakfast she had prepared. He was hungry and that was good. And his sons whenever they came to visit always had a hearty appetite just like their father.

"Are Nettie and the boys doing okay?" she decided to ask when he placed his fork down to take a sip of his coffee.

He smiled at the mention of his family. "Yes, everyone is doing fine. They were going to come with me, but I told them I was just going to fly in to check on things at the house and fly back out. The boys had a birthday party to go to, Trask and Felicia's daughter, and Netherland is helping out with the food for QT's party that's being held at Whispering Pines this weekend. You are coming, aren't you?"

She returned his smile. "Yes, I'm coming. I got a call

from Syneda two days ago to confirm that I would be there."

He nodded. "I had a chance to talk to Clayton and Syneda earlier this week and they told me how that case you were working on turned out. It never ceases to amaze me what some people will do for money."

She couldn't help but agree. "Yes, and the sad thing is that I can't divulge information to my client or anyone based on speculation. Mr. Coroni did agree to pay the foundation's legal expenses, which was better than nothing, but he still walked away with a lot of money. But then if Whitedyer thought that land was worth that much then who am I to argue."

Ashton leaned back in his chair and took another sip. "Umm, makes you wonder why they would think it was worth that much."

Mackenzie raised a brow. "They got Alex wondering the same thing."

Ashton chuckled. "Hey, if Alex is wondering about it then that's a good thing. He likes solving puzzles and there is no doubt in my mind that he will solve this one. I take it the authorities never found out who messed up your office or poisoned Jake's cows."

She shook her head. "That's another mystery to be solved but there's no doubt in my mind that with both Coroni and Whitedyer happy, I will be left alone."

"Speaking of alone, what happened to your houseguest?"

She shrugged. "Luke got better and moved on. He was in a relay race a few weeks ago out in L.A., and now I assume he's somewhere practicing for the big rodeo out in Reno next month."

"I wonder if he'll be at QT's graduation party this weekend."

"No, he won't be there."

At the lifting of Ashton's brows she quickly said, "He told me before he left that he wouldn't be coming. And I have no reason to think he'll change his mind."

And for her sake, that would be the best. Seeing him again and remembering all they had shared and knowing there was no future for them would be hard. She had even thought about not going this weekend on the off chance he had changed his mind, but when she'd spoken to Syneda, she had mentioned the family was a little disappointed that he wouldn't be coming due to all the practice time he needed to get in. She wondered if that was the real reason. But then he'd told her himself that he wouldn't be coming the day he'd left here.

"Sir Drake and Trevor told me to tell you hello," Ashton said, breaking into her thoughts

A smile touched her lips at the mention of Ashton's two closest friends. "And how is everyone?"

"They're all fine. Devin is walking now."

Mackenzie couldn't help but smile and shake her head. She could just imagine Sir Drake's wife, Tori, trying to keep up with ten-month-old Devin as well as Devin's older brother, three-year-old Deke. Like Sir Drake, Tori was a former marine and CIA agent. "I can imagine how active Deke and Devin are."

"With three busy beavers of my own, I can just imagine as well. Drake and Tori mentioned they're going to try for a girl next year. Now that's really scary."

She lifted a curious brow. "What?"

"The thought of Sir Drake with a daughter. Can you imagine such a thing?"

Mackenzie couldn't help but laugh. "Now that you mention it, no, I can't."

"So, Luke, what have you been up to?" Blade asked after Luke had placed him on a speaker phone so he could freely move around the kitchen.

Luke, who'd just finished taking a shower, had grabbed a beer out of the refrigerator and was leaning against the kitchen counter. "Nothing much. Spending most of my time trying to get back in shape so I'll be ready for Reno next month. How're things going with you?"

"Fine. I just thought I'd check with you one final time on that subject I brought up last month in Oklahoma."

Luke pulled out a chair at the kitchen table and sat down. He then twisted the top off the bottle and took a pull, licked his lips, and asked, "What subject was that?"

"Mac."

The beer bottle froze in midair just inches from Luke's lips. He frowned and set the bottle down on the table with a loud thump. "What about Mac?"

"I told you that Wyatt and Tanner are interested in her and—"

"And I told you to keep your damn horny friends away from her, Blade."

"Luke, be reasonable. You admitted yourself that there's nothing going on between you and Mac, that the two of you are only friends. And I assume that's still the case. If it's not then let me know and—"

"Nothing changed," he growled. "But that doesn't mean I want them hitting on her."

"Well, Luke, I don't know what to tell you. Mac's a grown woman and is free to do what she wants and old enough to look out for herself. The only thing I do know is that Wyatt and Tanner will be attending QT's party this weekend, and I know Mac's going to be here. They've stated more than once that they're attracted to her so chances are they will hit on her."

Luke nearly knocked over the chair in his haste to stand up. "Over my dead body!" he yelled, and the pitch of his voice was coming through loud and clear on the speaker phone.

"Luke, calm down or it *will* be over your dead body because you're liable to burst a blood vessel. I'll talk to Wyatt and Tanner and do my best to make them see reason, but keep in mind that those guys have had the hots for Mac for a long time. Surely you can understand why. She's a looker."

"I'm going to ignore you said that, Blade," Luke said,

taking another pull of his beer, this time emptying the bottle. He wiped his lips with the back of his hand before moving across the room to sling open the refrigerator to grab another bottle.

"Why are you ignoring it when it's true? All I did was give her a compliment. Mac is a beautiful woman, both inside and out, and if you haven't noticed by now, well, you should move aside for some other man who can and will appreciate her."

Luke slammed the refrigerator shut and then screwed the top off the beer bottle before taking a long, deep pull as if would somehow soothe his anger. It didn't. "I meant what I said, Blade," he said in a voice laced with steel. "You keep those two away from her."

"I'll try. But then what about QT's friends that are flying in for the party, not to mention Nettie's brothers, those Kallorens? What am I supposed to do about them after they take a look at Mac? I can't keep them away from her for no reason. Besides, I understand there are a number of single women attending. I got to spend time handling my own business."

Luke crossed the room and took Blade off speaker. "Damn your business. You just better keep Wyatt and Tanner away from Mac."

"I can't make you any promises, Luke."

Seeing red, Luke slammed down the phone, ending the call.

Blade hung up the phone and glanced across the room at Slade. "He's pretty damn mad."

A smile touched Slade's lips. "I heard all the way through the phone. So you think he'll come now?"

Blade chuckled. "Hell, I'm willing to bet any amount of money wild horses won't be able to keep him away."

Pulling in a deep breath, Luke left the kitchen and went into the living room and dropped down on the sofa. What

the hell was wrong with him? Why did the thought of Wyatt and Tanner, or any other man for that matter, hitting on
Mac make his blood boil? Why was he feeling possessive,
territorial, to the point that he wanted to hit something at
the thought of another man touching what he considered
as his?

His.

Until now he had never considered any woman his and
was suddenly forced to accept what he could no longer
deny. At first he had almost convinced himself that his intense attraction to her would eventually wear off. But each
and every time he saw her at a family function, whether he
was within ten or twenty feet of her, less or more, he was
totally aware of her even when he hadn't wanted to be.

He sucked in a deep breath as that admission crashed
through his mind with the impact of a tidal wave. He then
chronicled the last five years in his mind, including the
night he first set eyes on her. That memory had him getting
up and crossing the room to the mahogany cabinet that held
his favorite DVDs. He immediately pulled out the one he
wanted; the one he had purchased the night of the Brothers'
Auction.

Syneda had been the mastermind behind the auction to
raise money for charity and had encouraged the attendees
to buy the video of the event since the proceeds would go
to charity as well. No one had had to twist his arm to get
a copy; especially since Mackenzie had been the center
of attention near the end of the affair.

He would never forget the moment he had walked out
on stage and become the man to bid on. All he could do
was hope and pray the bidding went quickly and that he
didn't fall into the hands of Angela Meadows. What he
hadn't counted on was looking out over the audience
and locking eyes with the most beautiful woman he had
ever seen, a woman so striking she had taken his breath
away.

He had stood there and basically stared at her and she

had tilted her head and stared back. Any curious onlookers would have thought he was staring nonchalantly at some fixture in the back of the room. But both he and Mackenzie had known that had not been the case.

I had singled her out.

Just like the Madaris men before him had singled out the woman who would be their mate for life. A part of him had known it at the time, had understood what was taking place, and had recognized it for what it was. But he had staunchly refused to accept it. He had told himself a million times such a thing wasn't possible, no matter how often over the years he'd heard the Madaris men say that it was possible and in a way expected. Justin had accepted Lorren as his fate; Dex had married Caitlin within two weeks of meeting her; Clayton—who'd been a die-hard bachelor at the time—had fallen hard for Syneda, and Jake, who'd sworn never to marry again, had been zapped of his senses the moment Diamond had set foot on the Whispering Pines Ranch.

But even knowing all that, he had been determined not to succumb to any emotions and had fought the very thought, despite the depth of his attraction to Mackenzie. It didn't matter how often he thought about her and how much she had invaded his dreams. He had pretty much convinced himself she had not gotten embedded under his skin. Until now.

He removed the DVD from its case and slid it inside the player and then clicked on the television. Moments later the night of the auction filled the screen. Grabbing the remote, he fast-forwarded the CD almost to the end, to the part where Mackenzie had emerged from the throng of attendees after making the winning bid on Ashton.

He had been sitting at the table of the woman who'd cast the winning bid for him, but his eyes, like those of every male in the room, had been on Mackenzie. And later that night after joining him, Blade, and Slade for drinks, he saw that she was a beautiful woman who was comfortable and confident with everybody. She accepted compliments graciously and didn't act as if she expected them, like a lot of women he knew. That same night he had also sensed a passion in her, a passion that he'd known instinctively, if he were ever to embrace it, would all but overwhelm him. That was one more reason he'd decided to keep his distance and protect himself from the primitive hunger she was capable of stirring within him. But distancing himself from her hadn't solved the problem because whenever he did see her, he'd craved her, would imagine what it would be like to be the one to uncap her passion.

What it would be like to taste it.

Luke continued to watch the video and when the camera took a close-up of Mackenzie, he froze that particular frame and stared at it as emotions he had fought for nearly five years washed through him. This was the woman he hadn't been able to get out of his mind since leaving her home nearly three weeks ago. This was the woman who had made him feel things he had never felt before. The woman who, from the first time they had made love, had touched a part of him no other woman had been capable of touching. He had made her his that first time, although he hadn't wanted to claim it, had tried denying it, and had even walked away from it.

But he could do so no longer. He could no longer deny what his heart was forcing him to accept. He loved her.

The truth sent a heated rush through him that saturated his skin, every part of him. For a man who assumed the rodeo was his entire life, he was being hit with another revelation, one that consumed his very soul. He'd fooled himself into thinking all he wanted to share with her was a taste of passion. But that night five years ago, he thought, shifting his gaze back to the TV screen displaying Mackenzie's image, he had met his destiny.

And now that he knew the truth, he would do whatever it took to convince her of it. Not being a part of her life, not letting her be a part of his, was no longer an option.

For the first time in his life, something other than the rodeo was motivating him. Winning his title back was no longer his top priority Winning the love of Mackenzie was.

Chapter 23

Mackenzie glanced around the crowded patio. Where were the Madaris women when you needed them? She then glanced at the three men standing in front of her. Oh, goodness, now make it four. When had that one arrived? Their ardent attention was literally holding her hostage. It was as if she were holding court and they were intended suitors.

As soon as she had arrived, coming straight to Whispering Pines from the airport, she had been set upon by Wyatt Bannister, one of Blade's close friends. She had to admit the man was as handsome as they came, but he wasn't Luke. Then there was Tanner Jamison, another of Blade's friends. Neither Wyatt nor Tanner had left her side. The other two were Dean Allen and Malcolm Gamble, close friends of QT's from the D.C. area.

She appreciated their attention but enough was enough. This was the first time something like this had happened to her at a Madaris family function. Most of the men knew her as Ashton's cousin, which was enough to make them keep their distance. But these men seemed determined to monopolize her attention and there wasn't a female in the Madaris family who'd picked up on her predicament and come to her rescue.

"So, Mackenzie, how do you like living in Oklahoma?"

She looked over and met Dean's smiling eyes. He, too, was handsome and, like QT, a recent graduate of Howard University Medical School. And she knew that Congressman Harold Allen was his father. "Oklahoma is my home so I enjoy living there."

And so the conversations continued. She was grateful that the men were all really nice But already she missed Luke's presence. Although during most Madaris family gatherings the two of them had kept their distance, she'd known he was around. It wasn't unusual to look over in his direction once, twice, or possibly three times, and their gazes would connect.

Tanner was now talking, telling about the oil rigs he managed out in the Gulf, and she had to admit that what he was saying was interesting. Suddenly he stopped speaking in mid-sentence as something behind her caught his attention.

She was tempted to turn around to see what or who it was when she felt a rush of heated sensations course through her, and her heart began pounding. And then she knew. Her body knew even if she hadn't yet laid eyes on him. Luke was here. But why? How?

She hauled in a deep breath and quickly decided she needed to keep the conversation going while she had time to regain her equilibrium, force back the desire that had begun churning through her. His presence alone, the knowledge that they were now breathing the same air, was madness enough.

"So, Tanner, you were there offshore mere moments before Hurricane Dolly hit?" she asked, as she felt her heart beating faster. That had to mean he was headed in her direction.

Tanner, suddenly looking a bit uncomfortable, reluctantly brought his gaze back to her and the smile he gave her seemed guarded, wary. "Ah, yes, I was there and . . ."

Tanner continued talking but she could tell he was behaving somewhat awkwardly because of Luke's approach. Okay, she could understand Luke changing his mind and deciding to attend QT's party, but why was he heading toward her when he'd never sought her out before? And it couldn't be because they'd shared a bed, since they had agreed it was just a short-term affair that had meant nothing . . . at least not to him.

And then she felt his presence and knew he was there, standing directly behind her. All the men's eyes were on him but she refused to turn around.

"Luke, this is a pleasant surprise," Wyatt was saying with a little disappointment edging his voice. "I thought Blade said you weren't coming."

"I changed my mind."

His voice had a sensuous roughness to it that seemed to grate across her skin, made goose bumps form on her arm. "I thought I'd come to protect something that's very valuable to me," he added.

And then she felt him step closer to her, so close she could feel the heat off his chest touch her back. And when he placed his arms around her waist to bring their bodies even closer, she almost melted right then and there.

She swallowed, wondering what he was doing and why. He was all but making a public statement, a bold proclamation, that the two of them were more than just family friends.

"Hey, sweetheart," he leaned and whispered close to her ear, though at the same time making sure his voice carried for the benefit of the other men.

Instead of turning around she glanced over her shoulder and looked up. The eyes that locked with hers made her stomach quiver, and when he tilted his lips into one sinfully sexy smile, she almost lost her senses.

"So that's the way it is," Tanner was saying.

Luke broke eye contact with her and looked at Tanner. His smile transformed into a frown. "Yes, that's the way it is."

As if what he'd done needed no further explanation, the four men nodded and walked off. Anger eased up Mackenzie's spine. As far as she was concerned, Luke owed her an explanation for this little stunt he'd just pulled. "What's going on, Luke? What was that all about? And what you are doing here? You said you weren't coming."

He moved to turn her around so that they were facing each other. His smile was back and it had widened to show his hidden dimple. "Boy, aren't you full of questions? Aren't you glad to see me?"

She frowned. "That's beside the point. I want to know why you insinuated to those guys that you and I have something going on."

"Because we do."

Her frown deepened. "No we don't. If I remember correctly, the day you left my place our affair ended."

For a moment he didn't say anything and then he took her hand in his and said, "Come on, we need to have a private talk."

And before she could say anything, he was leading her off the patio and down a walkway toward Diamond's flower garden.

Sir Drake Warren shot Ashton a curious look. "I thought Luke wasn't coming."

Ashton couldn't help but smile. "I'm sure a number of people thought the same thing."

"But you didn't?"

Ashton nodded. "I figured he'd show up."

When the couple was no longer in sight, Sir Drake asked, "Can I assume he's finally ready to accept the inevitable?"

Ashton laughed. "Yes, I think you can safely assume that."

"Well, it seems that Luke decided to show up," Syneda whispered to Mama Laverne when she handed the older woman the glass of lemonade she'd requested. "But then you really aren't surprised, are you?" she asked, lifting a questioning brow as she met the older woman's gaze.

Mama Laverne couldn't help but smile, and to Syneda's way of thinking, it was a shrewd smile. "That's what happens when you're in love."

"And you think he's in love?" Syneda asked.

"Don't you?"

Syneda couldn't help but smile too. "Yes, but it took him a long time to figure it out."

The older woman nodded slowly. "Almost five years. Our family gatherings were becoming quite interesting, as he would sweat trying not to make it so obvious that he was watching her when he figured none of us would notice."

"But you noticed."

"Yes, just like I noticed how things were with you and Clayton. All those disagreements didn't fool me any."

Syneda couldn't help but grin as she dropped into the chair beside Mama Laverne. "So what's next?"

Mama Laverne chuckled. "It depends on Mackenzie. I don't think she's going to make things easy for him, which is a good thing. He probably did such a good job convincing her that being in the rodeo was his life, he's going to have a hard time persuading her that it's not the case anymore and that she has been elevated to the number one spot."

Syneda nodded. "Do you think he can do it?"

Mama Laverne smiled slightly. "I hope and pray that he can."

Luke led Mackenzie to a bench that overlooked a small pond. It wasn't as far away from the partygoers as he'd have liked but at least it afforded them some privacy.

He could tell by the look on a number of his family members' faces when he'd walked in that they were surprised to see him, but then he'd had an uneasy feeling that some had actually been expecting him. Such was the case with Blade and Slade. Blade had gone further and given him a haughty salute. He would deal with Blade later, but now he had to take care of some very important business with Mac. He could tell she had not liked the way he had handled the situation with her group of admirers.

"How are you doing, Mac?"

She actually glared at him. "Let me get this straight," she said in a tone that verified she was upset. "You haven't seen or talked to me in three, close to four, weeks and you just waltz in here with a Neanderthal attitude and want to know how I'm doing?"

Luke wondered if this was a "damned if you do" and "damned if you don't" question since he really didn't know just where she was going with it. So he said, "Well, yes, that's what I'd like to know."

"Why? You made it clear to me that you didn't do long-term relationships and what we were sharing was a short-term meaningless affair and—"

"I never said it was meaningless," he defended.

She inhaled deeply. "Okay, a short-term affair, which would end when you left my place. I didn't expect a call from you, and I didn't get one. I didn't expect you to return for a visit, which you didn't do. So now we're attending the same party. Why are you acting like you and I are still an item?"

From the question she'd just asked and the glaring look on her face, Luke knew he had his work cut out for him. "Can't a guy change his mind?"

She lifted a brow. "About what?"

"About how he wants his relationship with a woman to pan out. What if I told you that I want a long-term affair with you now? That I even want more than that?"

"Then I would wonder, why the change of heart all of a sudden? Do you know what I think?"

Not really, but he figured it was best if he heard it. "No, what do you think?"

"I think you saw those guys talking to me and just wanted to be territorial. We've been at your family functions together before and guys have talked to me and—"

"No they didn't."

She rolled her eyes. "Yes they did."

"The ones who did talk to you, Mac, were family members. Men I trusted who weren't a threat. I wasn't even worried about Blade hitting on you. But I know when to draw the line."

"You don't have a line to draw," she snapped. "At least

not when it concerns me, Luke. You don't love me or anything like that and I—"

"You're wrong. I do love you."

She rolled her eyes. "And I'm supposed to believe that?"

"I don't see why not." He crossed his arms over his chest. "In fact, I'm a little baffled as to why you don't believe me."

"Because if you had loved me, you wouldn't have left Oklahoma in the first place, at least not the way you did, like you were in a rush to leave because hell was dogging your heels. You love the rodeo life and you made sure I understood that. You might love the thought of possessing me, but I'm not a piece of property that you can walk in here and claim, embarrassing me in front of everyone."

"I didn't mean to embarrass you, Mac. I just thought that—"

"That what? You could announce to everyone loud and clear that we've slept together? All those other times you kept your distance from me, and now today you walked in and approached me like a lover."

"But we are lovers, Mac."

"We *were* lovers. There is a difference."

He inhaled deeply. "And what's wrong with me wanting my family to know how I feel about you?"

"And you think that little performance told them that? Think again, Luke." Then without saying anything else, she got up and walked off. He muttered a curse when he saw her continue strolling back toward the house.

"Yeah, think again, Luke."

Luke whipped his head around and met his cousin Clayton's dark eyes. Luke frowned to realize that his conversation with Mac had been overheard. "How long have you been standing there, Clayton?"

Clayton shrugged. "Long enough, and no, I didn't deliberately eavesdrop; I was over here in the shadows waiting for my wife. Syneda and I had arranged a meeting to . . ." Then he quickly said, "Never mind what we were planning to do. I want to know what you were thinking in expressing your feelings that way to a woman?"

"I was being honest."

"Yes, I'm sure you were, but you could have been less direct and more romantic. Take it from one who knows. Women love romance."

Luke looked over in the direction where Mackenzie had gone. She was talking with one of his great-aunts. "I just wanted her to know how much I love her."

"Then I suggest that you tell her again, and this time how about using a softer approach?" Clayton shook his head. "I promised myself a few years ago I would never stick my nose into anyone else's love life, although I think I did a damn good job with Justin's and Dex's. I hate to see you blow things with Mac. You need to tell her again how you feel and work hard at proving it. She was right when she said your life has always been the rodeo. Why should she believe that's changed?"

"Because it has."

"Then prove it. And I don't mean give up being a rodeo star, because I don't think that's what you need or have to do. Nor do I think that's what you should do. But you're going to have to convince her that you can have it all and that having her in your life will be the greatest gift of all."

"You okay, Mac?"

Mackenzie smiled when she saw Netherland Sinclair, Ashton's wife. "Yes, I'm fine, Nettie." Mac then glanced around. "Where are the boys?"

"They're with my parents. Mom and Dad are visiting for the weekend and wanted to take them to the park."

Mackenzie had always liked Nettie and would never forget how, in front of over three hundred people, Ashton had declared his love for her.

"I saw Luke arrive," Nettie said, smiling. "I also saw how he got kind of territorial."

Mackenzie rolled her eyes "Kind of territorial? Just

look around. None of the guys—including your brothers—will even look my way."

Nettie chuckled. "I noticed. I think Luke has effectively made his point."

Mackenzie frowned. "But he had no right to do that."

"Didn't he?"

Mackenzie inhaled deeply. "It's not what you think."

Nettie laughed. "Thinking too much almost got me in trouble when I thought the same thing about Ashton. You probably see him as a career man who's already chosen the path he wants, that it's the most important thing in his life, and that there's no way this man can love me since there isn't any room. He just wants to possess me, make me his, and there's a difference between possession and love."

Mackenzie blinked, surprised. "Yes, that's what I'm thinking."

"But in a way you're wrong, Mac. Loving is possessing. It's also about protecting. And being territorial comes with it sometimes."

"And you think he was right in what he did?" Mackenzie asked.

Nettie smiled. "I think at the time Luke might have done something he thought was right, something that he normally doesn't do."

"Which is?" Mackenzie asked.

"Openly declare his feelings for a woman. I've been coming to these Madaris functions for a number of years, even long before Ashton and I got together, and I've never known Luke to invite any woman to attend with him or to show any real interest in one. I think today he did something a lot of his family members didn't expect."

"What?"

"Wore his heart on his sleeve."

Later that night while lying in bed in the guest cottage Jake and Diamond had given her to use, Mackenzie couldn't help but think about what Nettie had said. She'd also heard something similar from Syneda and Felicia before the party had ended. Luke Madaris, they had taken the time to point out, had never, ever in his life displayed any sign of possessiveness toward any woman. As far as they were concerned, that could only mean one thing.

But for some reason she wasn't feeling it. What she was feeling was a one-sided love affair. She knew her heart belonged to Luke, had known it for a long time, and would even go so far as to say she'd probably fallen in love with him that night at the Brothers' Auction. But even when she considered that there was a chance what Nettie, Syneda, and Felicia said might be true and Luke did care for her, she would remember the talk she and Luke had had that day at the ranch and how he'd made it as plain as the nose on her face that he was already married to the rodeo, and that nothing or no one would ever change that.

Her thoughts then shifted to how the party had turned out. She always admired how the Madarises supported one another. And then there were those they considered friends and she felt honored to fall within that category. She couldn't help but smile when the sheik, Rasheed Valdemon, had made an appearance. The women, mostly friends of QT who'd never seen the sheik before, had begun drooling. She understood. The man was simply gorgeous. And then as if that weren't bad enough, pandemonium had erupted when movie actor Sterling Hamilton arrived.

All the guys had kept their distance from her but Luke hadn't done so. Although he hadn't taken any liberties by touching her in such a familiar way again, he hadn't left her side, which still had his family talking, she was sure. Luke's aunt Alfie had even commented that they made a nice couple.

It took her a moment to realize there was a knock on her door. Getting out of bed, she slipped into her bathrobe. Whispering Pines had a number of guest cottages, and whenever there was a family function, guests stayed overnight.

Diamond had insisted that she stay in a guest cottage instead of driving back to town to stay at a hotel. The cot-

tages were beautifully decorated and provided an ample
amount of privacy. Mama Laverne had declared that everyone who stayed overnight had to attend church service
with her tomorrow, which Mackenzie had no problem
doing.

In bare feet Mackenzie made it to the door and looked
out the peephole. It was Luke. The moonlight hit him at
an angle that showed his white western shirt and the Stetson he wore on his head. Inhaling deeply, she slowly
opened the door. "Luke? What are you doing here?"

A smile touched his lips. "I'm on my way to the airport and wanted to give you these." He handed her a bouquet of flowers in a beautiful vase and she recognized
them immediately. They were from Diamond's personal
flower garden.

"And before you ask, the answer is yes, I did get her
permission. She even gave me a vase to put them in."

Mackenzie couldn't help but smile. And then remembering what he'd said, she asked, "You're leaving?"

"Yes. I need to be in Wyoming tomorrow. The flowers
are my way of saying I'm sorry. I didn't mean to upset you
today, and I hope you'll accept them with my apology."

"Thanks. They're beautiful," she said, looking down at
the mixture of fresh cut flowers.

"No, you're beautiful, and I want you to know that I
meant everything I said earlier today and I'm going to
start proving it to you."

She glanced up and saw the conviction in his eyes. He
wanted to kiss her before leaving and she wanted him to
kiss her as well. Without saying anything she took a couple of steps back and he entered the cottage and closed the
door behind him. He removed his hat and the light from
the floor lamp hit his face. She studied each and every
chiseled plane. He was such a handsome man that it almost took her breath away. And the way he looked standing there in a pair of jeans and a white shirt made him
appear as western as any man could get and as sexy as sin.

She placed the vase of flowers on the table, and because

she knew that after what she'd said today, he wouldn't take any more liberties, she took a step forward. "Thanks for the flowers, Luke, and have a safe trip to Wyoming."

Her voice had dropped and automatically her gaze went to his lips. She knew what she wanted and tilted her head up at the same moment he bent his down. Their lips met, and within an instant, he was devouring her mouth. It didn't take her but a second to respond by devouring his as well. And when she felt him lock his arms around her waist, she melted into him, needing the feel of his warm, hard body pressed close to hers.

Moments later he lifted his mouth mere inches from her moist lips and whispered, "We need to talk, Mac. I have a few days off next weekend. Will it be okay for me to come to Oklahoma to see you?"

She drew in a breath, knowing Luke had never made any time for a woman while preparing for rodeo performances, and was surprised by his request. "Yes."

He smiled and then bent his head to kiss her again.

Chapter 24

"Okay, Mac, you've gotten flowers three times this week so what's going on?" Sam asked as she and Peyton lounged in the doorway.

Mackenzie couldn't help but smile. She *had* gotten flowers three times this week. The first had been calla lilies; the second had been tropical flowers; and just a few minutes ago the florist had delivered a dozen beautiful red roses. Different flowers but the cards had had the same message.

> *I love you, Mac,*
> *Luke*

Each time she'd read it she had felt a tingling sensation run all through her. "I told you that Luke's coming for a visit this weekend," she said, and knew she couldn't contain the happiness or the excitement in her voice.

"Okay, that explains the smile," Peyton said, grinning. "But what's the reason for all the flowers?"

She inhaled deeply as an even bigger smile touched her lips. "Just because."

She knew the reason was a lot more than that but she wasn't ready to share anything in depth about her and Luke's relationship just yet. She was still rocking and reeling at the possibility that he *did* love her. The thought of something so wonderful made her giddy. He had also called her twice during the week and just the sound of his voice had been so uplifting.

"All right, if you want to keep secrets about Mr. Hunk, then fine. Maybe you can bring us up to date on Whitedyer and Coroni and whether the police are closer to finding out who's responsible for messing up your office and poisoning those cattle."

Mackenzie frowned. The entire issue was still a sore point with her. When it came to Whitedyer and Coroni, she wasn't sure who had been the victor. At present both sides seemed satisfied with the turn of events. She had spoken to Detective Adams yesterday and he'd informed her that the authorities were still on top of things and had discovered that the tire tracks that had been near the corral matched the ones found near her demolished brick mailbox. But so far they had no proof that would link Whitedyer to any of the harassing incidents involving her. They were, however, checking out the possibility that as a cover, Perkins may have deliberately set up Whitedyer to appear as the party responsible.

"Nothing really, other than the linking of those two sets of tire tracks. There haven't been any strong leads to connect Whitedyer to any of those incidents, but Detective Adams has promised not to give up. He still thinks there's something being overlooked."

Later that evening after eating a microwaved potpie and going over ranch business with Theo, Mackenzie took a shower and then changed into a pair of short PJs that had been a gift from Peyton for Christmas. Luke was supposed to arrive in the morning, and she was trying not to dwell on it too much, despite the anticipation she felt.

He had said they were going to talk, and she agreed that that was something they needed to do. But he hadn't been playing fair by sending the flowers. Okay, the ones he'd given to her on Saturday night at Whispering Pines were appreciated. The others that followed, as well as the cards that accompanied them, were meant to break down her defenses and get her thinking. And they had.

What if she had been elevated to the number one spot in his life? What if he loved her as much as she loved him? The thought of that made a warm feeling envelop her. She had darkened the house and was curled up in bed with a book when she heard a knock on her door. She wondered if Theo was coming to tell her something was wrong. Ever since the cattle had been poisoned, Jake had arranged for his men to guard the ranch twenty-four/seven.

She eased out of bed and slipped into her robe. Turning on the porch light, she looked out the peephole and her breath caught. Standing beyond her door was one mind-numbing, ultrasexy male. She couldn't stop her body from responding to him or keep the heart she'd long ago declared as *his* from pounding furiously in her chest.

He was leaning against her porch rail wearing a pair of jeans and a light-colored shirt. And as if he was aware that she was looking at him through the peephole, he tilted back his Stetson and gave her one heart-stopping smile.

"Oh, mercy," she whispered through moist lips and had to struggle hard to remind herself he was there because he wanted them to talk. But then another part of her remembered the card he'd sent with each floral bouquet. What the words on those cards had said.

Taking a deep breath, she unlocked the door and opened it. When her eyes met his, she fought the feeling of her limbs melting, and tried to ignore the sensations flowing through every part of her. She then forced herself to speak. "Luke. I wasn't expecting you until tomorrow."

If he had been looking for one defining moment to confirm what his heart had already validated, then this would be it, Luke thought, as he stared at Mackenzie. She stood there, more than just a vision of loveliness. She was the epitome of any man's dream, the personification of beauty at its purest and the embodiment of his future. Every single thing about her exemplified what a man could possibly want in a woman.

And she was his.

He would convince her of that only after making her believe how much he loved her and how much he wanted her in his life. "I finished all my practice sessions early and thought I'd head straight here."

There was no need to tell her that after leaving Wyoming he'd had taken two connecting flights, as well as driven another hundred miles by rental car, to reach her. He felt bone-tired but he would do so again, and again, if it meant looking into her face like he was doing now. "I hope you don't mind my early arrival."

"No, I don't mind," she said, taking a step back and flashing him what was meant to be a smile. After entering her home and closing the door behind him, Luke had to restrain himself from reaching out and grabbing her. The awkward silence that enveloped the room had stopped him. Besides, he knew they needed to talk.

"You're ready for bed. Are you up to talking now? If not, we can—"

"No," she said quickly. "We can talk." She crossed the room to sit down on the sofa and then looked over at him.

Inhaling deeply, he moved to sit in the chair, noticing the flowers he had sent her that week. All three bouquets seemed to brighten the room and provided a nice floral fragrance. But nothing, he thought, letting his gaze drift across the room to where Mackenzie was sitting on the sofa with her legs curled beneath her, brightened a room more than she did. She looked totally breathtaking sitting there in her pink robe, and he was entranced by every little detail about her. From the pear-shaped birthmark on the back of her left hand that he could see, to the little pencil-point mole located at the base of her inner thigh that he couldn't see, but remembered very well. He had definitely developed a taste for the finer things in life. In other words, he had definitely developed a taste for her.

When he saw her watching him expectantly, he knew

it was time to have his say. And he hoped she would be-lieve him. "I'd heard some years ago that a Madaris man would know the woman for him when he saw her. That night I saw you at the Brothers' Auction, I felt uneasy. Syneda had schooled us all week about what we were sup-posed to do. Walk out on stage and capture the attention of every woman there."

A smile touched the corners of his lips. "I walked out on stage, met your gaze, and became the one captured in-stead," he said. "I knew what my plans in life were and that I had yet to achieve a number of them, so I dismissed the possibility that you were the one. I was attracted to you and that was far as I would allow my mind to go."

He paused a moment then added, "Even after we'd made love that first time, I kept fighting the thought, the very idea that you were beginning to mean something to me."

"When did you start thinking differently?" she asked.

He smiled. That was easy enough to remember. "After leaving here that day heading out for L.A. I couldn't stop thinking about you, dreaming of you, missing you, and wanting you. And then Blade pissed me off by insinuat-ing that Wyatt and Tanner would be hitting on you at QT's party. That set me off big-time, made me see red, and I couldn't help but wonder why. Then I couldn't deny my feelings any longer and had to admit to myself that you meant a lot to me. You meant everything and I couldn't, I wouldn't, risk losing you to another man for failing to ac-knowledge how I truly felt."

He breathed in deeply before getting out of the chair and walking across the room to her. She scooted over and made room for him on the couch as he sat down. "I can understand, considering what I told you that day, why you don't want to believe me," he said. "I'd done a pretty good job of convincing you that there could never be anything between us and that there was no way I could ever love you or any woman."

He took her hand in his. "But the truth of the matter is that I do love you, Mac."

A smile touched the corners of his lips. A dimple appeared right center. "I won't lie and say I didn't fight the feelings all the way, because I did. I didn't want to love you. I didn't want to love any woman. I just wanted to be a rodeo star. A wife, kids, home, picket fence, and all that stuff could come later. I was determined to compete with Blade for the oldest Madaris bachelor position. But things weren't destined to be that way for me. Now I do want a wife and more than once I've imagined you pregnant with my baby. After I regain the title I'd like to come back here and open a rodeo school and give other youths who have dreams and aspirations of one day performing in the rodeo the opportunity that Jake and Blaylock gave me by teaching me at an early age how to handle a horse and steer."

His lips curved and then he said, "You said it was all about possession for me, and in a way you're absolutely right. I can't imagine you with anyone but me. I couldn't tolerate you with anyone but me. I want you and I love you. And I will do anything and everything it takes to make you mine."

Mackenzie looked into Luke's eyes and felt an emotion flowing between them that she had never felt before. And then, without a shadow of doubt, in her heart she knew. Immense joy filled that same heart as, fighting tears, she whispered, "I'm already yours, Luke, and I've been yours since the first night I saw you. I knew then that you were unlike any other man I've known. But like you, I fought the very idea that it was more than a physical attraction between us. That night when you looked at me, I knew you were seeing the real me, the one very few people see or take time to get to know. It was as if you were staring deep into my very soul."

She looked down at their joined hands. "I fought my feelings for you, too, but when you came here to recuperate, I had to face them all over again."

She looked up at him and a smile touched the corners of her mouth as she said, "It was then that I admitted to myself what I'd denied over the past five years. That I loved you. And when we made love, I knew within my heart then but was willing to settle for just those stolen moments."

Luke raised her hands to his lips and kissed the knuckles before saying, "I'm not willing to settle for a few stolen moments. I want it all. You. The rodeo. Everything. And I believe I can have everything. It will be a challenge but I can't and won't give you up, Mac. I want to marry you, be with you forever. Father your babies. Make a home for us. Here. Or Houston. It doesn't matter as long we're together."

At that moment it took great effort for Mackenzie to breathe. Was he saying what she thought he was? Her heart soared at the very thought. For clarification, she asked, "What are you saying, Luke?"

He looked deep into her eyes. "I'm asking you to believe in me. To believe in us. And to plan a future together by saying that you will be mine for life."

He eased off the sofa and onto the floor before her on a bended knee and asked, "Will you marry me, Mac, and do that?"

Mackenzie fought the tears that threatened. Her hold on his hand tightened as she stared into the depths of his dark eyes. She drew in a shaky breath and then said, "Yes, I will marry you, Luke."

And then she felt him sliding something onto her finger and glanced down. Her breath caught when she saw the beautiful diamond ring he had placed on her hand.

"I brought this with me, hoping you believe the words from my heart, Mac. By consenting to be my wife, you have made me a very happy man."

Mackenzie couldn't stop the tears. She wanted to say that, in turn, he had made her a very happy woman, but the words wouldn't come. Instead, she leaned down toward his lips the moment he tilted his head up toward hers. Their mouths connected and she felt the contact all the way to her toes. They were sealing his proposal, their agreement to become one in heart, body, and soul.

And then with their mouths still joined, he eased to his

feet and pulled her up off the sofa with him, molding their bodies together as their tongues mated hungrily.

She gasped when he swept her off her feet into his arms. "Luke, put me down! Have you forgotten your injuries? You're going to hurt yourself."

He smiled down at her, taking in the fullness of the lips he had just thoroughly kissed. "My injuries are fine and I'm about to do what I've wanted to do for a long time. Carry you to the bedroom."

And he did just that, moving through the house at a slow pace until he reached her bedroom, then crossing the room and placing her on the bed. He stood back and stared at her, feeling a fullness in his heart. What he'd told her earlier was true. He could imagine her stomach swollen with his child. A child that would grow up bathed in their love.

"Strip for me, Mac," he said, his focus trained directly on her.

She smiled. "If I strip for you will you do the same for me?"

He chuckled. "Gladly."

"All right then, cowboy. Get ready to take your boots off."

Easing up on the bed, she proceeded to remove her robe to reveal the silk short PJs underneath. She tortured him somewhat when she slowly began unbuttoning her top, revealing just a little portion at a time of creamy skin.

"You're enjoying this, aren't you?" he asked when she finally tossed aside her top, showing perfectly shaped twin mounds.

"I'm just giving you what you asked for," she said, shifting her body to remove her shorts. It took only a moment and she smiled when she had accomplished the task, leaving her completely naked. She glanced over at him. "Now it's your turn." She found a comfortable spot on the bed to watch, lying flat on her stomach and resting her chin on her elbows.

He chuckled, bending down to remove his boots and placing them aside. "I don't intend to waste plenty of time like you did," he said, straightening and then nearly tearing his shirt from his body, sending buttons flying.

She laughed. "I guess you have another one of those shirts."

"Yeah, in the rental car outside." And then he went to his belt buckle and slid if off before easing the jeans zipper down. He smiled over at her. "I've been thinking of you a lot since QT's party. You don't know how much I want you, Mac."

She heard an intensity in his voice that sent heat flooding through her, weakening her limbs. "And I want you, too, Luke. So come here."

He had taken off his last stitch of clothing when she'd made that demand and he walked naked over to her and pulled her into his arms, kissing her like a man determined to make her his.

His to love, protect, and cherish.

She was his future, a future he was no longer hesitant to face. "I love you," he whispered as he tumbled her onto her back and followed her down into the soft covers. Those were three words he hadn't thought he would ever say to any woman, but he was saying them to her. And he intended to worship the body that was hers . . . and now his.

Starting at the base of her throat, he took his time as his mouth moved all over her, reacquainting his tongue with the smoothness of her skin, the texture and taste. Driven by the love he felt in his heart, he gave unwavering attention to the twin mounds of her breasts, taking the nipples in his mouth, cherishing them, loving them with his tongue and creating a level and a degree of heat within her that had her unable to stay still.

"Like that?" he asked softly as his mouth began moving lower.

"Yes, but only because I love you."

Her words sparked the flame inside him even higher, and when he settled between her legs and placed his mouth on the swollen and wet area between her thighs he heard her let out a deep moan.

He held her thighs to keep her from moving as he loved her this way, using his tongue to drive her to mindless pleasure. And when he felt her body shudder, a whirlpool of sensations flooded through him and he knew he had to join his body with hers. Now.

He shifted positions and eased his body over hers, settling between her spread legs, leaning down and kissing her at the same time he entered her body in one, deep powerful thrust.

"Luke!"

The moment he was inside, fully embedded within her, he felt her feminine muscles clamp him tight. Let go and then clamp him again. And that's when he lost what little control he still had. He wanted her with a hunger that overwhelmed him and it showed in the way he began mating with her, thrusting in and out of her body, tilting her hips at an angle to take even more of him, as she fluidly moved her body to receive each and every stroke.

And then an explosion hit and he felt his entire body shattering at the same time her nails dug deep into his back and she screamed out his name.

His name.

And when he thrust hard one last time the world surrounding them ceased to exist. It was as if they were suddenly plucked from this place and transported to another, where they were dipped in a sea of earth-shattering ecstasy, searing passion, and fulfilled desire.

At that moment nothing else mattered. Nothing beyond them existed. Intense pleasure was theirs for the taking and they grabbed hold of it and didn't let go.

The following morning Mackenzie forced her eyes open, feeling blissfully content and sexually drained. Luke had told her how much he loved her and then he had showed her the extent of that love when he had made love to her.

She lifted her hand and gazed at the sparkling diamond ring he had placed on her finger last night. It was a beautiful representation of his love. Their love. She felt intense happiness all the way to her bones and could only sigh in pleasure.

She heard the shower going and remembered Luke inviting her to join him there. But at the time she could barely breathe, much less imagine moving her body to do anything other than lie there in bed for a while, trying to regain her strength. It always amazed her how much stamina luscious Luke had. Once unleashed, it was unlimited. And all concentrated on her. And more specifically, the pleasure points between her thighs.

She was about to ease out of bed when the phone rang. She scooted toward the edge of the bed and then leaned toward the nightstand and picked it up. "Yes?"

"Ms. Standfield, this is Detective Adams. I received a call from Alex Maxwell yesterday with more information that he'd uncovered during his investigation. He flew in this morning and I think the three of us should meet as soon as possible to discuss these new findings."

Mackenzie raised a brow, wondering what information Alex had uncovered. "Okay. Is there a particular place you want us to meet?"

"It's Saturday morning, but we need somewhere private that's close to the heart of town. Can we meet at your office?"

"My office will be fine. I'll meet you there in about an hour."

Chapter 25

Less than an hour later Mackenzie was walking down the hall to her office with Luke by her side. Although she'd tried to encourage him to stay home and relax, he had insisted on coming with her.

"What additional information do you think Alex was able to uncover, Mac?"

She glanced over at Luke. He was looking at her intently and that look alone made flutters go off in her stomach so that she had to take a deep steadying breath before answering. When it came to masculine sexiness, the man was a world-class deliverer. After his shower he had changed into a pair of jeans and a blue chambray shirt along with his signature silver-buckled belt and leather boots. He looked rugged, all cowboy, handsome. "I'm not sure but I'm hoping he's found out why Whitedyer was willing to pay so much for Mr. Coroni's land, and also who was behind those incidents."

Once in her office Mackenzie opened the blinds but not before Luke pulled her into his arms for a kiss. The spontaneous kiss sent heat throbbing through all parts of her. "This isn't how I envisioned we would spend our Saturday," he said, against moist lips.

She nodded. "I know, but just think, after this meeting we'll have the rest of today and all day tomorrow." He wasn't scheduled to leave until Monday morning.

"Yes, and I guess at some point we need to contact the

family to tell them our good news," Luke said, smiling. "For some reason I really don't think they'll be surprised."

He was about to pull her back into his arms for another kiss when he heard a knock at the front door of the building. "That's probably Alex, Adams, or both." He turned toward the door and then changed his mind for a second and returned to her. "It won't kill them to wait for a few minutes," he said, before pulling her into his arms again.

Moments later Mackenzie turned from her office window to find Luke had escorted three men into her office instead of two. She recognized Alex and Detective Adams but didn't know the third man. It was Alex who made introductions.

"Mac, this is Larry Griffin and he works for the local FBI office here. I thought it would be best if he were included since he's been my contact in retrieving a lot of the information I've acquired."

Mackenzie nodded as she crossed the room to shake hands with the three men, giving Alex both a handshake and a hug. "I made coffee for everyone," she said, indicating the coffeepot sitting on a side table.

After pouring a cup, Griffin, who'd literally been staring nonstop at Mackenzie since the moment he'd walked into her office, leaned back against a wall and sipped his coffee. Noting the man's interest, Alex, who recalled just how territorial Luke was last weekend, decided to waylay any hope Griffin was harboring by saying, "Mac, I suppose that ring you're wearing means you're now officially taken," Alex said, holding up Mac's hand to check out her diamond ring.

"Yes, she is," Luke said proudly. He smiled over at her before returning his gaze to Alex. "Very much so."

Mackenzie watched as Alex gazed down at her hand. "Nice rock. Congratulations, you two. Has a date been set?"

Luke chuckled. "No, just happened last night. We haven't told the family yet."

Alex nodded, smiling. "Then they won't hear it from

me. But I'm sure you both know they have been expecting it." He then said to Adams and Griffin, "Luke and I are related since I'm married to his cousin."

After everyone had gotten a cup of coffee and was seated around Mackenzie's desk, Alex began talking. "It bothered me that Whitedyer would pay all that money for a piece of land, so I began doing a little more investigating," he said, leaning back in his chair. "It was then that I discovered that another company Whitedyer does a lot of business with, Cunningham Electronics, is housed in Tulsa. Have you ever heard of them?" he asked Mackenzie.

She shook her head. "No. Should I have?"

Alex shook his head. "Not really, I just wasn't sure if the name ever came up in your conversations with Farley. I found it interesting that a few years ago one of Cunningham's top executives, Aaron Gerhard, went missing."

"Missing?" Luke asked, frowning.

"Yes," Griffin responded. "It was believed by some that after he'd embezzled a large sum of money from Cunningham, Gerhard left the country. Those close to him claimed he was innocent and there was no way he would have left the country without taking his wife and child. But everything we had to go on, including a plane ticket in his name, indicated that's exactly what he'd done."

"But now you believe otherwise?" Mackenzie asked, trying to follow the man's train of thought.

"Yes. Personally, I never believed the embezzlement story. It was too pat. Granted, a large sum of money was tracked to a Swiss bank, but even that was too easy to trace. It seemed that someone had gone out of their way to make our job rather uncomplicated for us."

Griffin chuckled. "That was our first clue that something wasn't right, but we didn't have concrete proof of anything."

Alex then took up the tale. "From my investigation it seemed Cunningham and Whitedyer had had some backroom dealings with each other a few years ago. And last year a rumor began circulating that the two corporations

were thinking about merging. That is one of the reasons
the local officials were behind Whitedyer's getting Coroni's
land. The promise of jobs was a sure boost to the local
economy."

"And they could definitely make it happen now that
they've acquired more land for expansion," Luke said.

"Yes," Alex responded. "But that wouldn't justify or
explain the reason they were willing to pay so much for
Mr. Coroni's land, and why that particular tract when
other property owners in the area who were willing to sell
to them were getting turned down. That brings us back to
the question of what made Mr. Coroni's land so damn de-
sirable."

Mackenzie's gaze shifted between the three men. She
saw the intense look in Alex's eyes and knew he was on to
something, so she decided to ask him the burning question. "Why do you think they wanted the land so badly,
Alex?"

Alex leaned forward in his chair. His expression was
serious as he said, "I'm going to let Griffin answer that
question because apparently there's been an ongoing investigation right under our noses."

Mackenzie switched her gaze to Larry Griffin, whose
expression was just as somber as Alex's. "We have reason
to believe that Aaron Gerhard's body is buried somewhere on that land," he said.

"You believe the man was murdered?"

It was Luke who asked the question. He was sitting on
the edge of Mackenzie's desk while the other three men
sat in the wingchairs. He glanced over his shoulder at
Mackenzie, saw the look of shocked horror on her face.
He studied her for a moment longer before returning his
attention to Griffin when the man resumed speaking.

"I figured that's what happened to Gerhard a while
ago, but without a body there was nothing we could do to
proceed in that direction. Marshall Cunningham Sr. had
known connections to organized crime, but we could never

find any link for the son, Cunningham Jr., who is presently the head honcho. But the more we looked for Gerhard, the more we figured his disappearance was another Jimmy Hoffa case in the making. It's our understanding that at the time Gerhard disappeared, Cunningham Electronics was working on something big, and very illegal."

"But what makes you think Gerhard *didn't* embezzle money and leave the country?" Mackenzie asked.

The three men exchanged glances and then Griffin said, "Because the night before he supposedly fled the country with a few millions of Cunningham's funds, Gerhard had met with one of our men and had agreed to be one of our informers after we'd become suspicious about Cunningham Electronics' activities. Unknown to us, they already had considered him a weak link and had set up his demise."

"But if you knew that much then why couldn't you make arrests after Gerhard disappeared?" Luke asked.

Griffin responded, "To do so would have blown our entire case and we would not have accomplished anything; especially since we didn't have any proof to back up our assumptions. Cunningham had done an excellent job of making it appear that Gerhard was still alive somewhere outside the country and on the run."

He shook his head and said, "They went to the trouble of finding a double, someone they could pass off from time to time as Gerhard, but his wife knew the pictures she got occasionally were fakes and so did we. Unfortunately, when Gerhard went missing we did not know about Whitedyer's connection to Cunningham. That information was recently discovered when news of a possible merger was released," Griffin was saying. "Gerhard did tell us another company was involved at the time in whatever was going on, but he never identified the company. I'm leaning toward believing it was Whitedyer."

Mackenzie frowned. A few things didn't make much sense and the attorney in her propelled her to ask, "Okay, let's say your theory has merit. How will Whitedyer gain

anything when construction begins? Once the bulldozers
come in and start turning over soil, they run the risk of—"

"There won't be any construction going on in certain
areas of that land," Adams interjected. "I'd bet any amount
of money on it. After reading over the FBI cold-case file,
as well as the current information Alex has accumulated,
I'm willing to bet Whitedyer was only interested in getting
that land to make sure nobody else did. Oh, I believe they
will do something with it, to satisfy the city's requirement
for eminent domain, but they intend to keep certain parts
intact."

Mackenzie drew in a deep breath. But still . . .

She glanced at the three men. They had thought this
through. Clearly they had discussed the case in detail.
"But if what the three of you are thinking is true, then it
seems you're back to square one. You can't make a company dig in an area they don't want to."

"Yes," Alex agreed. "Unless there is just cause. First
we will need to identify what area of the land Whitedyer
wants to avoid and then get court orders to proceed with
limited excavation. Before that's granted, a judge might
require us to have lab researchers test soil samples for hu-
man remains, but I'm willing to bet it can be done."

He smiled and added, "And if the judge is someone who
happens to be on Cunningham's or Whitedyer's payroll
then we'll go to the governor. I happen to know that he's a
good friend of Jake's, and if he's presented with probable
cause, he'll give us the okay we need to move forward."

"There's only one thing in all of this that doesn't add
up, though," Griffin said as he looked over in Mackenzie's direction. "The harassment against you, Ms. Standfield. If anything, it would have behooved Whitedyer not
to ruffle any feathers, and especially not to do anything
that would draw negative attention. For some reason I
don't think they would have risked it."

"And," Detective Adams decided to add, "after talking
to Farley I could tell the man was actually looking forward to facing off with you in the courtroom. In his mind

he had imagined it as beauty-versus-the-beast, so I can't see him deliberately doing anything to scare you off."

Luke raised a brow and glanced around at the three men's faces. "If not Whitedyer, then who?"

Adams shook his head and he looked a bit frustrated as he said, "That's the only part of this puzzle we haven't been able to figure out yet."

"We need to plan an engagement party, Lucas."

Luke grimaced as he glanced up at Mackenzie who was sitting on his lap while he talked to his mother on the telephone. "You don't have to go to any trouble, Mom."

"No trouble at all. I'm just happy for you and Mackenzie. I can't wait to tell everyone. Now put Mackenzie back on the line."

Luke quickly handed Mackenzie the phone. He'd planned to suggest to Mac that they fly off to Vegas one weekend to marry, but after talking to his mother he knew that wouldn't be happening. His family would want a wedding. They would no doubt expect one.

His hold tightened on Mackenzie as she leaned back in his arms while continuing to talk to his mother. He figured his mother was only the first in a line of Madaris women she'd be conversing with over the next few days. Regarding their wedding, he didn't care how the deed was done as long as it happened in a timely manner. He did not want a long engagement.

Something his mother said made Mac laugh and the sound of her laughter wrapped around his heart. She was happy, he could tell. He was beyond happy. He was exhilarated. The only damper was knowing that when he left her Monday, it would be another two weeks before he would see her again. The Reno rodeo was two weeks from this very weekend and he needed the time to prepare. She understood and said that she would be there in the stands with his family to cheer him on.

"Yes, ma'am. Of course I won't let Luke talk me into flying off to Vegas."

Mackenzie's words reclaimed his attention and he couldn't help but smile to hear that his mother had anticipated his thoughts. He had a feeling that while he was using the next two weeks to get in shape for his competition in Reno, the women in his family would start planning an engagement party and then the wedding.

He thought about the meeting at her office. The issue of who had set out to harass Mac still bothered him. Although no further incidents had occurred, he still wanted the persons responsible found and dealt with. And he wouldn't be completely satisfied until that happened.

Later that night while she was still entwined in Luke's arms after making love, Mackenzie's heart rate had not slowed and sensations had yet to cease flowing through her. However, she found the willpower to shift her focus from the man sleeping beside her to the meeting that was held earlier that day in her office.

What had started out as a case she'd taken on merely to help an elderly man retain rights to his land had now turned out to be a possible murder investigation, if Larry Griffin, Detective Adams, and Alex's theories were right. And then they were still suspicious of Lamar Perkins's role in what had gone down with Mr. Coroni. Detective Adams had confirmed that nothing had changed and they were still keeping an eye out for new developments there. And what role had Farley's assistant played in any of this since she was secretly sleeping with Farley and Perkins? And from what Miller had said, the affairs with both men were still going on. Coroni had received his money so what motive did the woman have to continue her betrayal?

Mackenzie suddenly sucked in a deep breath when she felt Luke's hand begin making circles on her stomach, right below her navel. The way his fingers were lightly touching her skin had pressure forming in the area between her thighs, an area he had claimed a lot over the past twenty-four hours.

She tilted her head back and her gaze collided with a

set of dark, intense eyes. He drew her body closer to his as he continued to stroke her tummy. "You're awake," he said in a low, husky tone. The sound of his voice alone could arouse her from head to toe. She had grown accustomed to the sensuality the two of them seemed to generate.

"So are you," she said as her lips curved into a smile.

"Yes, but you're bothered by something. I can feel it," he said.

Mackenzie kept her gaze locked with Luke's and thought, yes, he probably could since they were so attuned to each other. So much in sync. "I was thinking about our meeting earlier," she said. "A murder is a lot different than a fight for land rights. Different and a lot more serious. You're talking about the taking of another person's life. If what Griffin said is true and Cunningham and Whitedyer were into illegal activities a few years ago and Gerhard found out, I can't help but wonder just how far they would go now to keep things a secret."

Luke shifted, pulling her closer in his arms while keeping their bodies entwined. "Some people are capable of doing just about anything. They're just that greedy for power and money. I have a feeling that Alex, along with Adams and Griffin, will get to the bottom of it. But until they do, I intend to continue doing everything in my power to protect you and keep you safe."

Mackenzie raised a brow. "Protect me? Keep me safe?"

"Yes. Hadn't you noticed the extra men working for Jake around here?"

She nodded. "Yes, he placed them here to keep an eye on his cattle."

He smiled. "Some of them are here for that reason. But I talked to Jake and made sure a number of them had expanded duties. They were to make sure you were safe and to make sure that whoever was up to no good with your mailbox, office, and Uncle Jake's cattle didn't decide to turn their antics personal and start messing with you."

Mackenzie swallowed, deeply touched. "And you were

concerned about them doing that?" The look she saw in
the depths of his eyes revealed more than possessiveness.
There was an insurmountable degree of love that she
could actually feel. He reached out and took hold of the
hand that wore his ring.

"Yes. I couldn't eliminate the threat, but I could do
whatever was in my power to protect you, which I did
while giving Detective Adams time to pursue his investigation. In the meantime, Jake's men were watching the
place, protecting you in my absence," he said.

Mackenzie doubted that she could love him any more
than she did at that very moment. Even before acknowl-
edging his love for her to himself or to her, he arranged
for a way to keep her safe from any possible danger.

The dark eyes holding hers didn't waver and she continued to feel the love. And moments later when he bent
his head and lowered his mouth toward hers, she released
a breathless sign. He was giving her not only a full taste
of his passion but he was also giving her a strong dose of
love. Together they were an overwhelming combination.
Her last coherent thought was that she wanted this; she
needed this, and had been waiting for this probably since
the night of the Brothers' Auction.

And when his tongue swept through her mouth, touching and invading every place it could, her entire being
was submerged in heat of the most intense kind. He deepened the kiss and she felt his hunger, forceful, elemental.
She saw a future where she would love him beyond measure. His strength surrounded her, wrapped her in pure
sensual delight, and she knew that she was destined to
love him forever.

Chapter 26

By the next day everyone in the Madaris family had heard the news of Luke and Mackenzie's engagement and had called to congratulate the couple.

The couple called Ashton after talking with Luke's mother on Saturday and he'd said that he would be honored to walk Mackenzie down the aisle. Although Luke wanted the wedding to take place before the end of the year, he agreed with Mac on a June wedding. That would give him time to research the rodeo school he wanted to start in a year.

Mackenzie had called Sam and Peyton and they couldn't wait until Monday to see her engagement ring. Both had driven out to the ranch on Sunday evening to see the huge rock on her hand and to give her congratulatory hugs. Mackenzie knew her two best friends were happy for her and both agreed to be in her wedding.

Already plans had been made for Mackenzie to come to Houston the following weekend. The engagement party was set for the week following Luke's rodeo in Reno. Mackenzie looked forward to the event, which would be the occasion when she and Luke officially set in motion their plans and dreams of sharing their lives together.

It hadn't been easy for Luke to leave Monday morning. After making love to her one last time, he had gotten dressed and wouldn't even let her get out of bed to walk him to the door. He'd said he wanted to remember that satiated glow about her until he saw her again.

With so many memories of the weekend still fresh in her mind, it was hard on Monday for Mackenzie to concentrate at work and she had even thought of taking half a day off when her secretary buzzed her to let her know that Mr. Coroni was there and wanted to meet with her.

Mackenzie couldn't help but wonder about his unexpected visit since she hadn't seen or heard from the man since he'd accepted Whitedyer's final offer of four million dollars. She still thought Mr. Coroni, probably against Perkins's wishes, had done the right thing when he'd agreed to at least pay the foundation's legal fees out of the proceeds. That proved to her that the old man did have a conscience. "Please send him in, Priscilla."

She was somewhat taken back and moved around her desk when he slowly walked in as if every step were painful. He was a broad-shouldered man but it seemed since she last saw him a few weeks ago he had lost weight, and she couldn't help but wonder if he'd been ill again.

"Mr. Coroni," she said, crossing the room to meet him. "Are you all right?" she asked, offering him a chair.

A pained look crossed his features. "I will be after my visit with you. There's something that I need you to do."

She perched her hips against the edge of her desk. "And what's that, Mr. Coroni?"

"Draw me up a will."

Mackenzie tried keeping the surprise from showing in her expression. "Don't you have one already, sir?"

"Yes, but I want it changed."

She couldn't help but wonder why he was coming to her and not using his personal attorney, Lamar Perkins. But the professional in her knew it wasn't any of her business. Detective Adams had said he would plant a few seeds in Mr. Coroni's mind and she could only assume he had done precisely that. "All right, Mr. Coroni, I can help you with that. It's just a matter of completing some legal papers."

"Thank you."

Less than an hour later, Mackenzie was nearly finished with the paperwork. "Now for the final item, Mr. Coroni, I will need you to name a beneficiary."

"Actually, there will be a number of them," the older man said, drawing in a shallow breath, as if breathing in deeply was becoming difficult for him.

He stood and pulled a piece of paper from his jacket and handed it to her. Mackenzie scanned the paper and then looked back up at him. The list did not contain any one individual's name but reflected several charities—the Cancer Society, the Diabetes Foundation, the Boys Club of America, and the University of Oklahoma. "And you're sure this is what you want?" she felt the need to inquire.

"Yes. I also made large contributions to those same charities yesterday. I felt good in doing that and I could tell they appreciated the donation." He paused and then asked, "How long will it take for my will to be finalized?"

"Within a few days."

"Good." A strained smile touched his lips. "Taking that money from Whitedyer made me lose the respect of a lot of friends who believed in me. I lost it because of greed." He paused and then said, "I learned a very important lesson because of it."

Mackenzie drew in a tight breath and felt compelled to say, "Your decision to hold out for more money wasn't wrong, Mr. Coroni. But what was wrong was the way it was done and deceiving your friends and supporters in the process. You deliberately misled them."

He nodded. "I know," he said, pressing his hands together in his lap. "And I regret doing that. Someone tried convincing me that it wouldn't matter, that big businesses have been messing with the little guy for years and that I had a right to take as much from them as I could get and that I shouldn't care. But I do care. Not about them but about everyone else."

Mackenzie didn't say anything for a moment and then,

"Please clarify something for me, Mr. Coroni. When Whitedyer first approached you directly, were they interested
in all of your land?"

The old man shook his head. "No, only a certain portion of it. They wanted to buy my property on the west
side of where I live, the twenty acres near the lake. It
was only when I refused to sell that they went after all
of it."

She nodded. "So what will you do now?" she asked.
She knew in essence the man no longer had a home, and
from the sound of it, he had few remaining friends. He'd
found out the hard way that money didn't always bring
you happiness.

"I'm thinking about moving to Florida to live in one of
those senior citizen communities. I figured I have maybe
another year or two left and I want to live my life in
peace. I won't be telling a lot of people where I'm going
so I would appreciate it if you ever get any mail from me
with my address that you keep it to yourself."

"I will," Mackenzie assured him.

He bowed his head for a second and when he lifted it
and met her gaze he had a grateful expression on his face.
He looked at her pointedly and said, "I want you to know
that I had nothing to do with your recent misfortunes and
was not even aware of them until Detective Adams paid
me a visit."

She nodded. "But do you know who did?" she couldn't
help asking.

He shook his head sadly and the eyes looking back at
her were filled with honest concern. "No, I don't. There
was no reason to harass you that way. We figured that in
time Whitedyer would give us what we wanted."

Thanks to Alex, Mackenzie knew the "we" and the
"us" who had been involved. His attorney, Larry Perkins,
was the one to advise him. She allowed time for his words
to sink in and for some reason she believed him. He might
have agreed to go along with the plan to get as much
money out of Whitedyer as he could, but she couldn't be-

lieve that he would go along with anything as serious as deliberate harassment of her; especially to that degree. What would have been the point? Like he'd said, there hadn't been a reason for doing so. Whitedyer had played right into their hands, and now knowing what she did about a body possibly being buried somewhere on his land she understood why they would have done so.

Mr. Coroni slowly pulled himself out the chair to stand. "Do you need for me to come back here at the end of the week?" he asked in a somewhat weak-sounding tone.

"No, I can save you a trip and drop by your house for your signature. I'll have Priscilla call you when all the papers are ready."

"Thanks." Then strengthening his voice somewhat, he said, "I appreciate all you've done and I regret misleading you as well. Another reason I would never have been involved in any negative campaign against you is because you've been nothing but kind to me, Ms. Standfield, and I will always appreciate it." He then turned and slowly walked out of her office.

Before leaving for the day Mackenzie placed a conference call to Alex and Detective Adams, to keep them abreast of the new developments, including letting them know of Whitedyer's initial interest in the land on the west side of Coroni's property. Neither Alex nor Detective Adams were surprised about Mr. Coroni's visit. According to information Alex had gotten earlier that day, courtesy of FBI Agent Griffin, recent bank records indicated both Larry Perkins and Camille Yeager had deposited large amounts of money into their accounts. Probably not as much as the two had anticipated, which most likely was the reason Coroni was leaving town and requesting that his destination be kept confidential. Chances were Perkins and Yeager were hitting the old man up for more money; money he had decided to give to charity instead.

Alex thanked her for pinpointing the area of land that held Whitedyer's main interest and informed them that the FBI planned to obtain court orders to proceed with excavation.

"I still wish there was a way for Perkins and Yeager to be exposed. Regardless of how we look at it, ethically they were both in the wrong. Yeager, I understand, is still working for Whitedyer," Mac said.

"But I figure not for long," Miller chimed in to say. "With the money she was able to get from Coroni she has no reason to remain employed with Whitedyer. But as for letting Whitedyer know what she was up to, it will come out once the FBI solves the case. It wouldn't surprise me if they pull everyone in for questioning, even Perkins and Yeager. How do we know they don't know anything about Gerhard's disappearance? I doubt very seriously that they do, but it would be nice to see them sweat."

He chuckled and then added, "And it will do my heart good to see Farley's face when he finds out Camille Yeager used him. He's not going to like that worth a damn."

Mackenzie knew what he said was true. Farley was not going to be a happy camper when he found out.

Chapter 27

"And you're sure that everything meets with your approval?"

Mackenzie smiled first at Sarah Madaris, Luke's mother, before turning to all the other women in the room. She'd often wondered how it would feel to belong to such a large family and now she knew. How on earth she could answer her future mother-in-law's question and not get emotional? From the moment she had been picked up at the Houston airport on Friday evening until now, she had been showered with more kindness than anyone had a right to receive.

"Yes," she said in a voice she knew was close to breaking. "I'm positive. I appreciate everything that all of you have done. I didn't expect it." She then glanced over at Skye and held her gaze for a moment. Since Skye was the newest member of the Madaris family, Mackenzie knew that she understood.

"Okay, enough sappy moments," Syneda said, standing. "It's time to eat." She then headed for the table that was loaded down with all kinds of delectable foods.

That caused everyone to laugh as they, too, got to their feet. Nettie had offered the use of a private room in her restaurant for their get-together, and Mackenzie couldn't help but smile to herself since it was here in Sisters that she had first set eyes on Luke.

Skye walked over and gave her a hug. "I am truly happy for you, Mac. You and Luke make a beautiful couple and are so deserving of each other. And your ring is simply gorgeous."

Mackenzie couldn't help but smile at the compliments. "Thanks and I appreciate your agreeing to be one of my bridesmaids."

Skye chuckled. "I'm glad you asked. You're having one huge wedding."

Mackenzie nodded when she thought of all the plans that had been made. When she arrived in Houston she had assumed it was just to make plans for the engagement party, only to discover the Madaris women had other ideas. They figured since they had her captive in their presence, they would get ideas on what she wanted for the June wedding as well.

"Yes, and I can't wait to tell Luke about all the plans," she said excitedly.

"When will you get to see him again?" Skye asked, her expression showing she could feel Mackenzie's enthusiasm.

"Next weekend in Reno. He's competing then to regain his title." Mackenzie felt butterflies in her stomach just thinking about when she would be seeing him. It had been almost a week since she had seen or talked to him. She knew he was busy concentrating on the upcoming competition and she was fine with that. From talking to Jake earlier that day she knew a number of Madaris family members would be there to cheer Luke on and that seats in the arena had already been reserved.

"I can tell by the look on your face that you can't wait to see him," Skye said, smiling.

Mackenzie returned the smile. "Am I that transparent?"

Skye chuckled. "Only because you look like a woman totally in love."

"That's because I am," was Mackenzie's response.

"You're what?" Laverne Madaris said, reaching Mackenzie's side and leaning heavily on her cane.

Mackenzie smiled and met the older woman's intense stare. "I'm totally in love with your great-grandson."

Laverne chuckled. "Tell me something I don't know. If you recall, Skye, I told you last year at the family reunion that Mackenzie was the woman for Luke."

Skye chuckled. "Yes, you sure did."

Surprise leaped into Mackenzie's dark eyes. "How had you figured that?" she couldn't help asking the older woman.

Laverne chuckled. "I might be up in age but when it comes to my grands and great-grands, I can see very well. Luke had a thing for you. You had a thing for him. I'm glad to see the two of you got together. Now I can turn my attention elsewhere."

Mackenzie didn't want to even imagine in whose direction the woman would be looking next.

"Why do I get the feeling that you've been avoiding me, Luke?"

Luke sighed deeply. In his peripheral vision he saw Nadine Turner. Impulse told him not to acknowledge her presence and just ignore her, but he was too much of a gentleman to do so. He glanced up, pushed his Stetson back on his head, and leaned against the gate. "Nadine. I thought we had an understanding that we *would* in fact avoid each other whenever we could."

Somehow the woman managed to look surprised. "Aw, come on, Luke, stop pretending that you don't want me when I know you do."

He could only shake his head. "Sorry, you're wrong. I don't want you."

A pout appeared at the corner of her lips. "You did at one time."

"Anything between us was strictly physical." Luke was annoyed that he had to spell things out to her once again, and he couldn't help wondering why she refused to believe him. He wondered what happened to her new boyfriend Cam had told him about.

"Well, since I know you're not into long-term affairs, I have no problem with sharing nothing more than a physical relationship with you again."

"I have a problem with it and I'm sure my fiancée would have a problem with it as well."

He saw her stiffen as the meaning of his words registered. "Fiancée?" she all but stammered.

"Yes."

"Who is she?" she asked in a contemptuous sneer.

"You don't know her."

"How dare you lie to me! You said you'd never marry."

Luke inhaled deeply. The woman, as usual, was getting on his last nerve. If nothing else she had the ability to bring out total weariness in a man. "I changed my mind," he said simply.

From the fire that flashed in her eyes he could tell his answer hadn't been good enough for her. "No! I'm the one you should marry. Me and no one else," she all but snarled. "And you will regret the day that you cheated on me for her." She then turned and angrily walked off.

Luke could only stand there, stare and shake his head, not believing the conversation he and Nadine had just had. Her behavior was getting even more irrational and he had put up with it long enough. Something had to be done about this obsession of hers. Her father, Preston Turner, was a likable guy, although he had allowed his daughter to grow up to be a selfish, self-centered woman.

More than once Luke had considered approaching the older man about Nadine's behavior, but he had not done so in hopes that Nadine would finally see reason. Since it seemed that wouldn't be happening he definitely needed to have a conversation with Preston when he saw him again.

Satisfaction gripped Mackenzie after hanging up her phone Monday morning. She had barely been in her office an hour before she'd received a call from Alex letting her know the courts had approved the FBI's request to excavate a portion of the land Whitedyer had purchased from Mr. Coroni. Papers would be delivered to Farley that morning.

Mackenzie would give anything to be a fly on the wall when Farley received the papers.

"Mr. Farley, there are a couple of gentlemen here to see you."

Farley lifted his gaze from the documents spread on his desk. He had gotten behind in a lot of paperwork while handling that issue with the Coroni land. Although costly, the settlement had come too easily. He had been looking forward to squaring off in the courtroom with Mackenzie Standfield. There had been something about her he hadn't liked from the first. She had been too sure of herself, too confident. That type of woman was a total turnoff for him. Most women had brains or beauty, Standfield had both, and more than anything he had wanted to break her.

"Mr. Farley."

He frowned. "And just who are these men?" he asked, getting annoyed. Camille hadn't reported to work for the past couple of days and calls to her home hadn't gotten a response. He wondered what the hell was going on with her. Whatever it was, she definitely owed him an explanation since the woman pitching in for her was doing a lousy job as far as he was concerned.

"One of the men is Detective Adams and the other is Larry Griffin from the FBI."

"What!" He immediately rubbed the back of his neck in an effort to ease the tension he suddenly felt knotted there.

"I said that—"

"I heard what you said. Send them in." He immediately stood and went around his desk. His heart hammered against his rib cage, but he forced the anxiety to pass and remained calm. Why would the FBI be here? Everything was going as planned, although they'd paid out more for Coroni's land than they had intended. The

old man had turned into a money-sucking vulture before
their eyes. But still, Coroni was happy, the city of Oklahoma was happy, and they were happy, so why was Adams
showing up now and with the FBI in tow? Farley didn't like
it one damn bit.

Before any more thoughts could occur his office door
opened and Adams and another man walked in. He could
tell from the smirk he saw on Adams's face as well as the
man's cocky walk that whatever reason they were there
was not good news.

"Detective Adams," he said with more than slight irritation in his voice after introductions to Larry Griffin
were made. "Although I sympathize with Ms. Standfield's misfortunes, I must again reiterate that Whitedyer
had nothing to do with it. And really, was it that serious
that you had to involve the FBI?"

"That's not why we're here, Mr. Farley, although your
claim of innocence is wearing thin in light of new developments."

Farley frowned. "What new developments?"

Adams took a step back so Griffin could step forward.
"You might want to contact your boss," Larry Griffin
said, smiling, as he handed Farley a sealed document.
"This is a court order to excavate a certain section of the
land Whitedyer recently purchased from Roger Coroni."

The color almost drained from Farley's face. "And for
what reason?" he asked in a subdued tone, trying to project a dispassionate expression.

"We have reason to believe the body of a man we've
been looking for is buried there."

Farley shook his head and tried to stay in control. "And
just whose body is supposed to be buried there? Had we
known anything about that we would not have pursued the
purchase of the land so diligently from Coroni and—"

"Can it, Farley," Adams said, rolling his eyes. "Save
the drama for the courtroom; I'm sure you'll have the opportunity to give the performance you've been lusting for.
And to answer your question, we have reason to believe

that the body of former Cunningham employee Aaron Gerhard is somewhere on that land." He then glanced around. "And where is Ms. Yeager today? We need to ask her some questions."

Farley leaned back against his desk to stare at Miller. His expression was no longer unruffled. "Why would you want to discuss anything with her?"

"To make sure that she doesn't know anything about Gerhard's disappearance, since it appears she's kept constant contact with Mr. Coroni's personal attorney, Lamar Perkins, during the entire Coroni-Whitedyer negotiations."

Farley shook his head. "Sorry, but you have your information wrong," he said, smiling, with certainty in his voice.

"Sorry, but I'm afraid our information is right. It's our understanding that she and Perkins are close, personal friends." A smile touched Griffin's lips. "But then, she was your close, personal friend as well, wasn't she? Now where is Ms. Yeager?"

Farley looked down at the document he held in his hand before lifting his gaze back to Adams and Griffin. "I don't know where she is at the moment."

"We'll find her," Griffin said with the same certainty in his voice as Farley had had earlier. "And by the way, excavation starts Wednesday."

"I'll file a petition to have it stopped before it begins," Farley threatened.

Griffin chuckled. "Yes, you can try to do that but the order was given the stamp of approval by the governor himself. Good day, Farley."

The agent, along with Adams, then turned and walked out of the office.

Late Thursday evening Mackenzie received a call from Alex. "It's all over, Mac. I just got a call from Griffin who said that the remains of Aaron Gerhard were found on Coroni's land."

Mackenzie shook her head, saddened by the news. Although she knew it brought needed closure for Gerhard's family, she regretted how the man's life had ended. "So what's next?" she asked.

"Everything will hit the papers and television tomorrow and the FBI will reveal everything, including Whitedyer's eagerness to purchase the land from Coroni to keep the murder covered up. It's my guess that someone with power over at Cunningham decided to get rid of Gerhard when he discovered the two companies had joined forces and were selling illegal electronic supplies to some terrorist group holed up in an area near Pakistan. Everyone was brought in for questioning, even Coroni, Perkins, and Yeager, to make sure they didn't know why Whitedyer wanted the land so badly. So chances are Mr. Coroni won't be leaving town for a while, at least until there's absolute certainty that he wasn't aware of the real reason Whitedyer wanted his land."

Alex chuckled. "And your city leaders are embarrassed to say the least. In essence, Whitedyer cunningly used them to make sure they got that land from Coroni. And from what Griffin said, things got pretty interesting when Camille Yeager had to face both her lovers. Farley was livid when he found out just how far Yeager's betrayal went."

Mackenzie shook her head. It seemed everyone's penchant for greed had backfired. The people who had really lost were those who'd truly believed that job opportunities would come with Whitedyer's purchase of the Coroni land. "Thanks for keeping me informed, Alex."

"Hey, no problem. Because of what went down with you, I began to investigate further and it was only then that the FBI were able to link the two companies. And Griffin wanted me to let you know that both sides, Coroni and Whitedyer, are still maintaining that they had nothing to do with those incidents involving you."

Mackenzie rolled her eyes. "Well, considering everything, I'm sure you understand that I'm not quick to believe them. I don't know which side is responsible but we do know those things did in fact happen so someone was behind them."

Later that night when she prepared for bed Mackenzie tried putting everything dealing with Whitedyer and Coroni out of her mind and shifted her concentration to Luke. She was excited about seeing him this weekend and like a number of his relatives she would be arriving in Reno early Saturday to see him compete in the rodeo that night. There was no doubt in her mind that he would be victorious in getting his title back, and then the two of them would have even more reason to celebrate.

"Hey, man, wake up. I just got a call. The boss is pretty damn upset and wants to meet with us in the morning. From the way it sounds, it's time for us to take things further."

"How much further?"

"Let's just say that by the time it's all over, Ms. Standfield is going to regret the day that she got on the boss's bad side."

Alex couldn't sleep and that didn't bode well. He hated not finishing a puzzle because of missing pieces and he felt there was something in the Whitedyer case that was still out there. Something he was clearly overlooking. What?

He eased from the bed, careful not to wake Christy. He smiled thinking she definitely needed her sleep. Making his way to his office, he eased down in the chair behind his desk and turned on his computer. He was determined to find the missing link. No one wanted to claim responsibility for the mischievous incidents involving Mackenzie, not even when Whitedyer had tried shifting the blame from themselves to Cunningham Electronics to avoid a murder conviction.

An hour or so later, Alex still hadn't been able to figure anything out, but he refused to give up. He shut down the computer determined to check out a few more things tomorrow. That missing puzzle piece was still out there and he intended to find it.

Chapter 28

Mackenzie glanced around the arena, trying not to recall what had happened the last time she'd been at a rodeo to watch Luke compete. It was the last night of the Professional rodeo Championship and just like that night in Oklahoma, the stadium was packed. The only difference was that she wasn't the only person in attendance tonight rooting for Luke. Some of his family members were on hand to cheer him to victory. Everyone knew that this competition, to regain his title, was an important one to Luke.

She had talked to him earlier on her cell phone when she had arrived in Reno that morning, and he had tried talking her into coming down to the arena to give him a good-luck kiss. She had laughingly refused, reminding him of what had happened the last time she'd done that. So she had yet to see him and would do so for the first time when he flew out of the chute.

"It's been years since I've been to a rodeo," the woman sitting beside her leaned over closer to say.

Mackenzie smiled over at Tori Warren. Tori and Sir Drake had arrived in Reno on the same flight as she, and like the rest of the Madarises and their friends, had managed to get rooms at the same hotel. In fact their hotel room was right next door to hers.

"I can feel the excitement," she responded. "Luke should be coming out in the next segment."

"Let me know when he does so I can put my hands

over my eyes," Syneda, who was sitting a couple of seats down, leaned forward and said to her with a smile.

Mackenzie couldn't help but laugh, knowing how Syneda felt. But she had a feeling that her fearless husband-to-be would be just fine. During their phone conversation he had assured her that he was ready and felt confident in his abilities for tonight.

"The next bull rider up is Luke Madaris," the announcer blasted out over the speakers. "This will be Luke's first competition since tangling with a loose bull in Oklahoma and we're glad Luke is back with us and ready to try and regain his title for this event. Let's give him a big round of applause."

From the sound that radiated from the stadium it was easy to see that Luke had become a favorite among the seasoned riders and fans. The arena nearly shook from the noise, and excitement had spread when everyone began applauding and throwing out cheers. Mackenzie pulled in a deep breath, overtaken by a rush of adrenaline driven by all the excitement. She couldn't help but be proud of Luke and what he'd accomplished.

Once the noise had finally died down the announcer then added, "And to even the score, the bull Luke will be riding tonight is Scar Face, that same bull that tried doing Luke in a couple of months ago in Oklahoma City. Scar Face is the one bull Luke hasn't been able to tame but he intends to change things tonight. And as most of you know there is no love lost between Luke and Scar Face."

Mackenzie swallowed deeply as her rush of adrenaline changed direction and panic nearly engulfed her. She couldn't help but recall what a mean-looking and ferocious bull Scar Face was and how upon rushing out of the gate that night he had immediately gone after Luke.

She held her breath while watching Luke ease his legs over the huge brindle's back. Moments later Luke gave a nod indicating that he was ready. No sooner had that nod been given than the gate swung open wide and bull and rider flew out.

Scar Face was in rare form, but so was Luke. Mackenzie saw the smile on his face and she realized that even with all the danger involved in what he was doing, Luke was actually enjoying himself. That was evident in the way his face would light up each and every time the bull lurched and tried with all its might to buck Luke from his back. It was as if the raging bull had gone mad, but Luke held on as if he anticipated the bull's every bucking move. It was clearly a defining moment for man versus beast.

The crowd's roar exploded in Mackenzie's ears. She nervously sat on the edge of her seat wondering how long it would last. How long could Luke hang on? And as if her question had been heard, the buzzer sounded, and when it was safe to do so, Luke jumped clear of the angry bull.

While the announcer was belting out Luke's score over the speakers, proclaiming there was no way he hadn't broken the current record-holder's score. Instead of waiting for the judges to post his score, Luke glanced up in the stands in her direction, to the area where he knew she would be sitting.

Their eyes met and a huge smile touched his lips. It took her a second to realize he was racing across the arena toward her.

"What on earth is Luke doing?" she heard Blade ask.

"Not hard to figure out," was Slade's amused response.

Before she could catch her next breath, Luke had jumped over the rail, sprinted up a couple of seats, and landed right in front of her. "Now for that kiss, sweetheart."

He pulled her into his arms and at that moment she forgot everything. Including the fact that everyone in the packed stadium was watching. Watching and hollering their approval.

When Luke finally released her mouth, leaving her in a somewhat dazed state, he smiled again before sprinting back the way he'd come and then disappearing behind the chutes.

"Wow! That was some kiss," Tori said, smiling over at

her. And from the looks on the faces of the other women in the Madaris family, who were staring at her, Mac had a feeling they agreed.

But then she inwardly concurred that it had been some kiss as well.

Alex looked up from the computer when Christy walked into the room. Less than an hour ago, he had left her in bed naked after they'd shared hours and hours of love-making. Even now he could recall how before leaving the room he had glanced back to see how the glow from the lamp flowed over her, highlighting her features, especially the redness of her hair. She was and would always be the most beautiful of women to him.

Their eyes held as she slowly crossed the room to him and he eased away from his desk to accommodate her when she gracefully curled her body into his lap and wrapped her arms around his neck.

He automatically lowered his head.

His lips brushed hers. Once. Twice. And then he parted her lips with his tongue to go deeper and inwardly reminded himself there was no hurry. The baby was still sleeping and, hopefully, would sleep through the night. This was the time he enjoyed with his wife. Mommy and Daddy time. And Christy had a way of making it so special.

Moments later, he pulled back. "I think," he murmured in a husky voice close to her moist lips, "that you've become an addiction."

She smiled as her arms closed tighter around his neck. "For you. Always. I won't deny I *want* to get in your blood."

He shifted position in order to ease her closer. "Trust me, sweetheart, you're already there."

His gaze left her face to glance at his computer. "Now, if I could already be there with this thing involving Mac."

"You still think you're overlooking something?"

"Yes."

She slowly nodded. "All right then. Tell me about it. It might help to have another ear."

"Okay." He then told her everything, the incident involving the mailbox, the ransacking of Mac's office, and the poisoning of Jake's cows. He also told her how the Coroni and Whitedyer situation had panned out with the finding of the body on land now owned by Whitedyer.

"And you're saying that Whitedyer and Coroni are claiming they're innocent of doing those things to Mac?"

"Yes, and when you think about it, neither had a motive to do so. Farley wanted to go up against Mac in the courtroom so he had no reason to scare her off, and then Coroni's group would not have done anything to scare her off because they needed her to finalize the settlements they were aiming to get."

Christy nodded. "In that case, there has to be another person involved, one not connected to either of those two."

She tilted her head and studied Alex's features and smiled. "But you've considered that already, haven't you?"

He returned her smiled. "Yes. But who would want to harass her? I checked out her old boyfriend, the one both Detective Adams and Ashton told me about. His name is Lawrence Dixon. I found it odd that almost five years after their breakup he was still calling her, especially considering how hé dumped her to marry a woman from a wealthy family."

He didn't say anything for a moment and then added, "But he appears to be clean, although his mobile phone records—which I was able to obtain a copy of last week—indicate he did call Mac on occasion. The last time was six months ago."

Christy frowned. "Why would he bother calling Mac?"

"According to Detective Adams, when he went back and questioned Mac about it, she said Dixon only called when he wanted to gloat about a case he'd won and wouldn't say anything about his wife. Their conversations were always brief and impersonal."

"Umm, but . . ."

Alex lifted a brow. "But what?"

"But what if his wife didn't know that and found out

about the calls he'd made to Mac? A jealous woman is known to do some pretty crazy things."

Alex nodded. "I thought of that as well. But the Dixons were vacationing out of the country at the time of those incidents and—"

He stopped talking and suddenly frowned. "Wait a minute. That might be it. The one thing that I didn't consider."

"What?"

"A jealous woman." He drew in a deep breath. "We may have been looking at this all wrong."

With the confused look that appeared on Christy's face, he went on to explain. "During this whole time we've assumed that the person behind those mischievous attacks on Mac was trying to get her attention. What if the target wasn't really Mac but Luke, because of all the interest he's been showing Mac lately?"

Christy's eyes widened as she eased out of Alex's lap and turned to him. "Luke?"

"Yes. Think about it for a second. You recall what Luke told us about that woman last year, the one who was beginning to get so possessive of him? I was even there with Clayton one day when Luke inquired what could be done if she continued to get out of hand."

Christy nodded. "I remember, but that was last year."

"Yes, but it's worth checking out anyway. Her father owns a huge ranch on the outskirts of Oklahoma City so she was close by. The ranch has a large number of employees and it wouldn't be hard for her to get one or two of them to do her dirty work." He picked up the phone.

"Who are you calling?"

"Ashton. He's attending the rodeo tonight. I'm going to tell him what I think and suggest that he present that possibility to Luke after the rodeo to see what he thinks."

Mackenzie strolled into the corridor that led from the ladies' room as she headed back toward the stairs to her seat. Luke had won all of the events he had competed in so far and would be facing last year's winner in the finals to achieve his goal of regaining his title.

"Excuse me, Ms. Standfield."

Mackenzie turned toward the man who had stepped out of the shadows. Another cowboy dressed in a bull-rider's garb. Mackenzie glanced up at him. "Yes?"

"Luke wants to see you. He's over near the north chute and asked that I bring you to him."

Mackenzie frowned. When she and Luke had talked earlier today, she had adamantly told him she would not be coming to the chute area. He needed his full concentration on regaining that title. He had taken her by surprise when he had sprinted across the arena to steal a kiss from her, but with the season title on the line the last thing he needed to think about was a little hanky-panky.

She placed her hand on her hips, throwing her hair over her shoulder and chuckled lightly, saying, "Sorry. Please go back and tell Luke that he knows our agreement and I'll join him after the rodeo and not one minute sooner."

Surprise flitted across the man's face, and then Mackenzie's blood suddenly chilled at the cold look that appeared in his eyes. She quickly moved to step around him but he caught hold of her wrist in a tight grip. "I hate to tell you but you're coming with me anyway, and I wouldn't make a sound of protest if I were you," he said in a low voice. "I won't hesitate to use this if I have to."

Mackenzie glanced down and saw the small gun he held in his hand. She then looked back up into his face and held his gaze. Stark fear ran up her spine. "I don't understand. Who are you and what do you want?"

"Your questions will be answered soon enough. Let's go."

She felt her heart thud deep in her chest. "To where?"

"You'll know when we get there. And remember, don't give anything away. I'll use this thing if I have to."

* * *

Ashton's phone was answered on the first ring. "Alex?"

"Yes, it's me," was Alex's response. He could hear a lot of noise in the background. "Enjoying the rodeo?"

"Yes. Luke made the finals," Ashton said, trying to talk over the noise. "The last event of the night is when he tries out for the championship. There's no doubt in my mind he'll take home this season's title. What's up?"

As quickly as he could over all the noise in the background, Alex told Ashton his latest theory.

There was a pause and then Ashton said, "Umm, that is a possibility, although I can't see a woman doing all those things alone. She would have had help."

"I'm thinking the same thing. Talk to Luke after the rodeo and see what he thinks. Until then, keep an eye on Mac."

Ashton glanced down to where Mac had been sitting. Her seat was empty. "Hold on, Alex." He leaned over and called down to Tori, "Where's Mac?"

"She went to the ladies' room." Frowning, Tori said, "Come to think of it, she's been gone a while. I'll go check on her," she said, getting out of her seat.

"Mac went to the ladies' room," Ashton said to Alex. "Tori is going to check on her."

Tori was turning the corner toward the ladies' room when she saw Mackenzie with some man who was leading her away. And it seemed as if he had a firm grip on her arm.

The former CIA agent in Tori immediately sensed danger. She knew she had to get word to her husband about what was going on and quickly pulled out her cell phone and punched in their secret emergency code, hoping Drake got her text message. She needed to follow and keep Mac and that man in plain sight and take action when the opportunity presented itself.

Ashton stopped talking in mid-sentence to Alex when Sir Drake got his attention. Drake had stood up and there was a fierce expression on his face. "What's wrong?" Ashton asked, immediately on alert.

"Tori just sent an emergency message. She needs help."

"Alex, something is wrong," Ashton then said quickly as he stood also. "I'll call you when I find out what it is." He hurriedly hung up the phone.

Ashton reached out and touched the shoulder of Trevor Grant, another friend of theirs. "Let's go." No explanation was given. Those words were all that were needed for Trevor to get on his feet.

"Is something wrong?" Blade leaned over to ask when he saw the three men heading for the exit. Ashton was glad that the other Madarises were focused on the rodeo events in the arena while waiting for Luke to take part in the final competition.

"Not sure. But we'll know in a little while. In the meantime if anyone asks, just tell them we went to talk to Luke about something."

Luke stood talking to a few of the other bull riders behind the bucking chutes. Tonight had gone just the way he had wanted. So far he had done exceptionally well, and in the final competition, regaining the title he'd lost last year was within his reach.

He had to smile when he remembered how he had sprinted across the arena floor and vaulted over a fence to get into the stands to give a surprised Mac an unexpected but satisfying kiss. He still tasted her on his lips and could hardly wait until the rodeo was over and they'd be alone. Hell, he was even contemplating skipping the victory party that was held the last night of each PRCA championship.

"Luke," a familiar voice said behind him, and he automatically stiffened before turning around.

He frowned and excused himself from the other men to walk over to Nadine. He had talked to her father earlier and had given the old man fair warning. If his daughter continued to harass him, he wouldn't hesitate to take legal action. It was time for him to make that clear to Nadine as well.

"Nadine, I don't know why you're here but I talked to your father and—"

She laughed. "You think I care what you've told my father? If you do then think again, Luke. But I see that thinking is something you don't do well, otherwise, you would have paid attention to my warnings and left her alone."

A cold chill suddenly spread up Luke's spine. "What are you talking about?"

"You and that woman, the one you want to convince me that you're going to marry. The same one you insulted me by kissing that night in Oklahoma months ago. That's why I got back at you and used Scar Face to do it."

Luke was taken aback by her admission, and anger all but exploded within him. "You're the one who opened the gate to let the bull out that night?"

A smug smile touched her lips. "That's right. And then when you moved in with her at her ranch, that really pissed me off, so I hired someone to knock down her mailbox and mess up her office. And when you still didn't heed my warnings about her, I went further."

"By poisoning her cattle," Luke finished for her.

He breathed in, wondering what Nadine was accomplishing by admitting all she'd done. Did she honestly think that even if he wasn't in love with Mac, he would consider a relationship with her after all she'd just told him?

As if reading his mind, she said, "We will be together because I'm getting her out the picture once and for all."

Luke's heart nearly stopped beating. "What did you say?"

Her lips curled into a sneer. "You heard me. I ordered my men to snatch Ms. Standfield and they've already phoned me to say they have. Her fate lies in your hands, Luke. She won't get hurt if you give me what I want."

He was seeing red. "And just what is that supposed to be?"

She smiled so sweetly it almost made him sick to his stomach. "Marriage. I want us to fly to Vegas and marry tonight. Forget about winning the title back. You're going to have to prove to me that I'm more important to you than that."

Tori, who'd been following at a discreet distance, figured she had to do something when the man, still holding firmly on to Mac, was about to exit the arena for the parking lot. She had to plan things carefully since there was no doubt in her mind that he had some sort of weapon, possibly a gun. But she needed to get close and she needed to do it *now*.

Coming up with an idea, she emerged from the shadows and called out. "Hey, Mackenzie, you're not leaving before Luke's final event, are you?"

The man whipped around with a surprised look on his face. He frowned, tightening his jaw, and it was then that Tori saw the small pistol. Now it was pointed at her. "Bad timing for you so I think you better join us," he said, smiling coldly at her. "Now get over here."

Tori refrained from smiling back. Although he didn't know it, he had just given her the opportunity she wanted. In the end, she would all but make him eat that gun.

"Why? What's going on?" she asked in a frightened tone of voice, as if she didn't have a clue.

"You're going with us and then the boss will decide what she wants to do with you. We've already been given orders about what to do with Ms. Standfield," he coldly informed her.

Tori came to a stop in front of him and quickly assessed the situation. He had Mackenzie close to his side but not too close. Tori made rapid eye contact with Mackenzie, enough to alert her that something was about to happen. "And you think it's going to be easy handling both of us?" Tori asked in a cocky tone.

To any other person, the smile that materialized on the man's face at that moment would have made their skin crawl. "It will be a piece of cake," he responded in a confident tone.

"Then maybe you should eat it."

Before he could blink, Tori's body went into action, and with a quick, high karate kick of her right leg, she knocked the gun from his grip before, with a succession of karate chops to the man's midsection and lower abdomen, he crumpled to his knees. But not before staring at her with a shocked expression on his face.

"Now for you to eat it." Angrily, she quickly picked up the gun, intending to shove it down his throat, when a voice behind her stopped her.

"Tori!"

She whirled around and smiled when she saw her husband, Trevor, and Ashton.

"We're here now," Sir Drake said to his wife, taking the gun from out of her hands before she could do further damage to someone who'd been stupid enough to threaten her. He glanced over at the man, who was actually shaking on his knees. "I think you've done enough."

She would have agreed if the man hadn't managed at that moment to mumble the word "bitch."

Tori smiled sweetly at Drake. "Evidently not." Before Drake could stop her, she whirled again and gave the man one hard karate kick to the side of his face that sent him sprawling to the cement floor.

Mackenzie rushed over to them and grabbed hold of Ashton's arm. "There's another man outside, waiting in a truck. And we've got to get to Luke," she said in a frantic tone. "Some woman is going to try and make him withdraw from the final competition in order to save me."

Luke could only stand there and stare at Nadine, totally convinced that she had gone off the deep end. "Where is Mac?"

"Don't worry, she won't be bothering us any longer," she said confidently.

Luke could only stare at her. "You're crazy if you think I'd marry you."

A fierce frown disfigured Nadine's face and a pout touched her lips. "You will marry me or you will be sorry."

Luke took a step toward her, angrier than ever. He would shake Mac's whereabouts out of her if he had to.

"Luke, you're up in ten minutes," the timekeeper called out to say.

Luke didn't even turn around. Competing in that final event was the last thing on his mind now. Nothing was more important to him than finding out what this crazy woman had done to Mac. "Where is she, Nadine?" he said through gritted teeth, barely able to keep his anger in check. "Tell me where she is now."

"It's too late. You can't help her."

He reached out and jerked Nadine to him, almost snatching her off her feet. "Dammit, where is she?"

"I'm here, Luke."

Keeping a tight grip on Nadine, he turned and saw Mackenzie quickly walking toward him with Sir Drake, Tori, Ashton, and Trevor in tow. Nadine saw Mac and nearly went berserk. Relief flooded his insides and he released Nadine.

"How did you get away! Barry was supposed to take you somewhere and make sure you never bother me and Luke again!" Nadine all but shouted.

Ignoring what she'd said, Luke rushed off toward Mac, who threw herself into his arms. He hugged her tight.

Nadine pulled a pocketknife from her boot and prepared to attack Luke. Again Tori was quick with her feet and Nadine crumpled to the floor.

"You might want to call security for her as well," Tori said to Drake, Ashton, and Trevor.

"Luke, you have five minutes," the timekeeper called out.

Luke ignored the man as he continued to hold Mac in his arms. He hadn't been so frightened in his life. Nadine was a madwoman and the thought that she had arranged for something bad to happen to Mac had him quaking inside.

Mackenzie pulled out of his arms. "You have to go, Luke, for the—"

"There's no way I'll be able to compete again tonight. I almost lost you, and nothing, this rodeo, the damn title, means more to me than you."

Mackenzie fought back tears. "And nothing means more to me than you. I'm safe, Luke. Don't let her win by losing your chance to regain the title. Tonight is your night. You've worked hard and you deserve that title. When it's over we'll keep to our plan to celebrate in our own special way."

"You're up next, Madaris!" The timekeeper's voice boomed out.

Luke stood there and stared at Mackenzie before pulling her into his arms and kissing her. When he released her, he said, "Tonight isn't my night, Mac, it's *our* night."

He then glanced over at Ashton. "What about her?" he asked, motioning toward Nadine.

"Security is holding her two cohorts," Ashton responded. "The police have been called and are on the way. They will probably want to talk to you after you compete tonight. They'll need to piece everything together from the beginning."

Luke nodded. "That's fine. I suggest someone page her father, Preston Turner. He's around here somewhere."

"Last call, Madaris!" the timekeeper shouted.

Luke kissed Mackenzie once again before sprinting off to where the chute crew stood waiting.

Several hours later Mackenzie stirred in Luke's arms, and when she opened her eyes it was to find his gaze warmly caressing hers. She inwardly acknowledged for the hundredth time that night just how much she loved him. Shivers ran through her body each and every time she thought of how, for the sake of her safety, he'd been willing to walk away from reclaiming the title.

But fortunately, he hadn't had to do that. Nadine Turner and the two men she had hired to cause havoc to get

Luke's attention, and, when that hadn't worked, to get rid of Mackenzie, were now behind bars. No doubt Nadine's father wouldn't waste time getting his daughter the best attorneys, but what she really needed was psychiatric help.

Mackenzie shifted her gaze to look past Luke's shoulder and glance out the window. Day was just beginning to break. Suddenly she was filled with memories of the time spent in Luke's arms once they had left the party that was to celebrate Luke's winning the season title once again. They had refused to let what had happened with Nadine put a damper on things, and had made their appearance at the party. Later they had gone to his hotel room where they had had their own private victory party.

"The entire day belongs to us, Mac."

At his husky words she glanced back at him and smiled before saying, "No, the rest of our lives belongs to us."

His arms reached for her and she went to him willingly, and then he kissed her, stoking the embers into a flame and together they shared a taste of passion once again.

Epilogue

June

It seems that everyone turned out for what many thought was the event of the year—rodeo superstar Luke Madaris's marriage to Oklahoma attorney Mackenzie Standfield. The wedding took place on the grounds of Luke's uncle Jake's ranch, Whispering Pines.

It was a huge affair with guests coming all the way from the Middle East, and everyone was more than happy for the newly wedded couple, who were presently making their rounds greeting their many guests.

Mama Laverne Madaris, who was sitting on a bench with one of her great-grandsons standing beside her, wiped tears from her eyes as she gazed upon the couple.

"You need a hanky, Mama Laverne?"

She glanced up at Blade, her great-grandson who thought he was above getting married. "No, but you can make me happy by settling down with *one* woman, preferably a wife."

He looked aghast. "Why would I want to do something like that? I don't want a wife."

She rolled her eyes before taking her cane and tapping him on the leg, and not too gently, with it. "Ouch," he said.

"Listen up. I'm living long enough just to make sure it happens with you, Blade."

He chuckled. "Then I guess that means you'll be around for a long time."

"But you have to admit Luke is a lucky man. Mac's a beautiful bride," Mama Laverne went on to say.

"Yes, she's beautiful," Blade agreed. He was talking about Mac, but his gaze had shifted to one of her bridesmaids. The one she called Sam. The one who wore her sexuality like it was some mind-drugging scent. In other words, she was a looker, stunningly so with an exotic look. They had met briefly last night and for a reason that he was still trying to figure out, it was instant dislike. At least on her part. The look she'd given him had nearly chilled him to the bone. He couldn't help wondering what her problem was.

"Somewhere out there is a woman just made for you," Mama Laverne said, interrupting his thoughts.

Blade smiled. "Possibly, but I'm in no hurry to meet her. You might want to warn her of that. In the meantime I'll just go about enjoying life to the fullest."

His gaze shifted from the woman named Sam back to his grandmother. "Don't you get tired of trying to marry us off?"

"No."

His gaze shifted back to Sam. She was an unnerving and disturbingly very sexy woman. "Sorry to hear that," he said to Mama Laverne, shifting his gaze to her glass of punch. "Do you want a refill?"

"Yes, I'd appreciate it." She watched him walk off and shook her head. Whether the boy knew it or not, his days as a bachelor were numbered.

Jake Madaris lifted a brow as he watched Rasheed Valdemon approach him with an intense look on his face. "Is something wrong, Rasheed?"

His friend shook his head. "I just got a call from my future brother-in-law, Sheik Jamal Ai Yasir. His sister, the woman I am to marry, graduated from Harvard a few weeks ago and was to return to Tehran to start planning our wedding. Jamal's call was to let me know she's missing."

Jake lowered the wine glass from his lips. "Missing?"

"Yes, missing." Rasheed inhaled a deep breath and

then told him in a very irritated tone, "It seems she's decided she's not ready to return home just yet. She likes it here in the States and wants to have fun before settling down and marrying an *old* man."

Jake couldn't help but laugh. At Rasheed's frown he quickly sobered up "Sorry, Rasheed. What are you going to do?"

"Find my future bride, and when I do, she's going to regret the day she decided to deliberately get lost. Please give my regrets to the bride and groom, but I must leave."

Jake nodded. "I will and I'm sure they'll understand."

Rasheed turned to walk off and Jake couldn't help but smile. He had a feeling Rasheed was going to be teaching his future wife a thing or two when he found her.

The sun going down over the lake was the perfect setting for the last of Luke and Mac's wedding pictures. Luke was grateful since it seemed the photographer had taken a million of them already. But no photograph would be able to capture Mac's beauty the moment she had walked down the aisle to him on Ashton's arm. She had taken his breath away just like she had the first time he'd seen her that night at the Brothers' Auction. And today, as she had walked toward him, a vision of beauty in her wedding gown, both love and desire had pounded in his chest with every step she'd taken.

"Ready to go take off our clothes, Luke?" Mac asked.

Luke smiled. "Sweetheart, I've been ready."

She rolled her eyes. "What I meant is that since we've finished taking all the pictures and mingled with our guests, we can change into our traveling clothes."

Compliments of Sheikh Rasheed Valdemon, they would be spending two weeks in Dubai, a city that was located along the beautiful Persian Gulf. In recent years Dubai had emerged as one of the world's largest business hubs and was considered a vacation paradise.

Luke pulled his wife into his arms. "I knew exactly what you meant. I guess we're just going to have to wait until we get on the plane to get naughty. Start our own Mile High Club."

Mac could only smile at what he was suggesting. "I thought it was nice of Jake to have his private jet fly us over there and then come back to get us."

"I thought so, too," Luke said. "In fact everyone has been nice. If I didn't know better, I'd think they were glad to see us get married."

"I think they were."

"Excuse me, Mr. and Mrs. Madaris. I can't resist asking if we can get one more photo? This one of the two of you kissing with the sunset in the background," the photographer approached them and asked. "I think it would make a beautiful picture."

"We'd love to," Luke said.

And then Luke pulled his wife into his arms in a passionate embrace and whispered, "I could never resist kissing you."

"And I never could resist being kissed by you," she countered, before reaching up and pulling his mouth down to hers.

Carnival Cruise Line

New York Times and *USA Today* bestselling author BRENDA JACKSON lives in the city where she was born, Jacksonville, Florida. She is a graduate of William M. Raines High School, and has a bachelor of science degree in business administration from Jacksonville University.

Brenda is a retiree who worked thirty-seven years in management for a major insurance company. She is also a member of Romance Writers of America and Delta Sigma Theta Sorority, Inc. Brenda married her childhood sweetheart, Gerald, forty-seven years ago and they have two sons. She has more than 125 novels in print and many of her books have been adapted to movies. She is currently at work on her next novel.

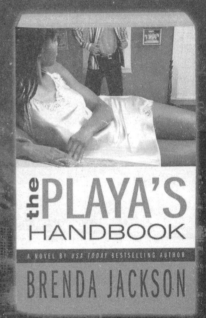